THE FI

IMPOSSIBLE ODDS

Edited by Editing4Indies

❀ Created with Vellum

Books by Jill Ramsower

The Five Families Series

Forever Lies

Never Truth

Blood Always

Where Loyalties Lie

Impossible Odds

Absolute Silence

Perfect Enemies

The Byrne Brothers Series

Silent Vows

Secret Sin (Novella)

Corrupted Union

Ruthless Salvation

Vicious Seduction

The Savage Pride Duet

Savage Pride

Silent Prejudice

The Of Myth & Man Series

Curse & Craving

Venom & Vice

Blood & Breath

Siege & Seduction

IMPOSSIBLE ODDS

JILL RAMSOWER

ONE
Giada

A SMOLDERING REMNANT OF CIGARETTE SMOKE LINGERED IN THE air. That the place didn't smell like the bottom of an ashtray in a dive bar was remarkable. Even with the multitude of smoky clouds wafting up over the slot machines and gaming tables, the air was relatively breathable. I could only imagine how dense the air must have been before the invention of air purification equipment.

Between the smoke, sensory overload, and mobs of raucous tourists pledging to create memories worthy of the Vegas namesake, the place should have been repulsive. Yet I loved every damn thing about it. The bright colors and flashing lights. The excess and indulgence. Luxury and opulence. The intense emotions that saturated the air and electrified my skin, making my heart skip and flutter in my chest. It was all magnified to a point of bursting by the throngs of people who flocked to this den of debauchery from all over the world. Rich people, poor people, people of every ethnicity and culture all crammed together and given license to act out their wildest fantasies. To drop social constructs and expectations and let their freak flags fly.

It was magnificent.

The only complaint I ever had about my time in Vegas was finding my way around the damn casinos. I had no doubt they were specifically designed to disorient and trap their hapless victims within. I hated having to find my way back to the table where I'd left my cousin and sisters. It was always a harrowing journey. If the cleaning staff weren't so diligent, I'd have left a bread crumb trail for myself.

This time, I'd been wandering aimlessly for close to fifteen minutes through the Wheel of Fortune and Monopoly slot machines when I spotted my girls in the distance just past a bank of sparsely occupied gaming tables. I started in their direction but was sidetracked when my eyes were drawn to a man standing at one of the tables, seemingly uninvolved in whatever game was being played. From where he stood, I could see his angular profile as he stared with laser focus at the table where my girls huddled together. They were laughing and watching their own game, oblivious to the attention they had garnered.

I smirked, knowing the Genovese women were an eye-catching group. I could hardly blame the guy. Everywhere we went, we turned heads. Between our good genes and the money to emphasize all our best features, we were striking even on a bad day. Dolled up for the Vegas nightlife? We were unstoppable.

It might have sounded conceited, but it was the truth. I

saw nothing wrong with owning my strengths, whether it be my outgoing personality, my effortless style, or my good looks. Society wouldn't knock a girl for advertising her PhD in astrophysics, so why couldn't I be proud of my thick auburn hair and eyes so green they'd been called hypnotic?

I was confident in my body, so sue me.

Chest out and chin lifted, I slowly advanced on the man ogling my sisters and cousin. Though I couldn't see his entire face, I could tell he was also gifted in the looks department. That was putting it modestly. He was ridiculously gorgeous. The kind of gorgeous that made you forget your train of thought midsentence. Stole your breath and made you wonder if you were hallucinating. Men that beautiful were usually restricted to magazine covers and movie screens.

His profile boasted a straight nose and a strong jaw covered in a smattering of hair the same sandy color as the long locks combed back behind his ears. Judging by his sun-kissed hair and golden skin, he spent plenty of time in the sun, but his tailored suit spoke of boardrooms and pent-houses rather than surfboards and beaches. Curious. I wondered which stereotype more aptly suited him—the businessman or the beach bum. If the intensity of his stare was any testament to his countenance, carefree surfer was no longer an option.

My sisters and cousin melted from existence as his magnetic aura lured me into his orbit. I eased up to the craps table next to where he leaned, propped gently on his elbows with an unlit cigar dangling from his fingers. He was a vision of power and privilege, packaged in expensive Italian silk, his posture dripping indifferent boredom.

Following his line of sight, I stared at the girls for a moment, taking them in as an outsider might. "I hope you don't have your sights set on the brunette in red. She got engaged just a few days ago." I let the words drift toward him while keeping my gaze fixed ahead.

He showed no signs of distress over being caught staring. He didn't even take his eyes from their target. "The one in silver doesn't look legal." The faintest hint of an accent feathered his words, the cadence a caress against my bare skin.

"That's because she's not." Valentina wouldn't be eighteen for another five months, but she had a fake ID and curves that got her into most bars without issue.

The man rolled his cigar between his thumb and fingers next to his lighter and a stack of chips. "That might not bother some men."

"I suppose if you like the blushing virgin who has no idea what she's doing." Val wasn't exactly the blushing type, but he didn't know that. My words were meant more as a challenge to him rather than a reflection of my sister's dating habits.

His gaze finally slid my way, giving me my first view of his eyes, gray like polished steel and equally as sharp. His deep-set eyes had a slight uptick that gave him a regal intensity. The dichotomy of such harsh beauty was captivating. Unnerving.

"Age isn't always an accurate indicator of experience or maturity," he replied. Those reflective eyes were penetrative and severe as if they'd peered into my soul and found me lacking.

If he wanted to judge me, he'd have to get in line.

I continued our parry, unaffected. "Nor is maturity a guarantee of a good time, but it improves your odds significantly. And isn't that what everyone wants when they come to Vegas? To come out a winner?"

"Undoubtedly, but everyone's definition of winning is different. Some of us may have our sights set on simply walking away emptyhanded—no better or worse than we arrived."

"You strike me as the type of man who would have his sights set on far more than breaking even."

"Yet I've already gotten what I came for tonight. Anything more would only complicate things, and I hate complications." He turned fully toward me, leaning on his elbow in a deceptively casual pose. The startling severity of his gaze pushed against me abrasively, a blatant challenge at odds with the air of indifference he attempted to broadcast in every other way. His emotionless features were smooth and unbothered, forming a mask of apathy that would have been believable if it hadn't been for those silver, shiver-inducing eyes. They were raging storms, brilliant thunderclouds rife with lightning and electric wrath. A chink in his armor that gave away just how much more was brewing beneath the surface.

He was captivating and breathtakingly beautiful, not to mention arrogant and detached.

He was also out of luck because this girl didn't beg for any man's attention.

I cocked my head and shrugged. "Too bad. Emptyhanded it is, then." My red-stained lips drew back in a Cheshire grin as I eased away from the table and walked toward my girls without glancing back at the mysterious man.

My hips swayed with each step, the penetrating weight of his stare making me feel naked as I crossed the casino floor. Other girls might have felt awkward or embarrassed, but I preened like a peacock flaring its feathers for maximum visibility. My strides remained unhurried and even as I basked in an adrenaline high just as potent as any drug could provide.

It wasn't his attention that energized me.

The source of my intoxicating rush was far more concrete. I derived my excitement from the small silver lighter clasped in my right hand—the one I'd swiped from the table ledge and was now depositing into my black velvet clutch purse.

How long would it take for the man to notice his lighter was gone? Would he suspect me as a thief or assume he'd left the trinket somewhere else earlier in the day? The threat of discovery and impending uncertainty made my veins course with liquid energy. The high was so addicting, I'd been hooked from the first time I'd stolen back when I was a teen.

The handsome stranger was far from my first victim.

The urge to pocket other people's possessions didn't hit me all that frequently, but when it did, the need was overwhelming. The items were usually inconsequential trinkets—nothing of any real value—but they were always personal to the owner. Something representative of who they were. Something they would notice was missing but wouldn't be apt to call the police over.

I'd always thought my twisted proclivities meant something inside me was broken. My saintly mother was the perfect Catholic, active in the church and a staunch enforcer of its ideals. My two younger sisters rarely stepped out of line. Camilla was fresh out of college and advancing in her career, and Valentina was a straight-A student with Ivy League schools clamoring to recruit her.

I never made it past high school.

What was the point? My family's money meant I never had to work, so why waste my life behind a desk? I didn't want an average, boring existence, but I also hadn't figured out what that meant. I wasn't bohemian enough to want to backpack across Europe. I didn't have a particular desire to risk my life for short-term thrills such as bungee jumping or skydiving. So where did that leave me?

I'll tell you. It left me feeling like something was wrong with me until about five months ago when I learned my father was a high-ranking member of the mafia. The puzzle pieces of my life suddenly rearranged and made a coherent picture. I wasn't a freak.

Being a criminal—a deviant, even—was in my blood.

Not surprisingly, I craved more than two-point-five kids and a membership to the Y. I was made for a different life than most normal people. I just wasn't sure what exactly that meant yet. Fortunately, I had all the time in the world to figure it out, and in the meantime, I had my sticky fingers to entertain me.

When I learned about my father's real job, I'd considered coming clean and telling him about my dirty little habit but decided against it. Shame wasn't the reason I kept my lips sealed. Who were my parents to judge my crimes when their own actions were undoubtedly far more nefarious than my own? At least, that was true for my father. My mother's greatest sin was likely limited to turning a blind eye to whatever my father was involved in. They had no grounds to be upset, but I was unwilling to tell anyone because the key component of my chosen vice was secrecy. Where was the thrill if others knew what I was doing? Every theft was a treasured memory, and I lorded over each with great relish.

Nobody was perfect.

Maybe that was why I felt at home in Vegas.

Sin City, home of the morally corrupt and misguided.

I visited every chance I could get, so when my best friend and cousin, Alessia, announced that she'd gotten engaged on her birthday, I decided a celebratory girls' trip was in order. Plus, it was Halloween, and I'd never done Halloween in Vegas.

It had more than lived up to my expectations.

Alessia hadn't been easy to convince since our last girls' trip had only been a couple of months prior, but she always gave in to me in the end. It was why we worked so well together. My younger sisters, Camilla and Valentina, were far easier to convince. In a matter of days, we had our bags packed and were off for a weekend of female bonding.

The first girls' trip we'd taken had included the four of us plus Alessia's two sisters, Maria and Sofia. This go-round, Maria was pregnant and had deemed Vegas pointless if she couldn't drink. I didn't blame her. Vegas wasn't the same without a steady flow of alcohol thinning your bloodstream. Sofia had just returned from her honeymoon and wasn't up for another trip. Despite our smaller numbers, we'd had an amazing weekend and were winding down on our final night, watching high rollers at the craps tables and playing the occasional hand of blackjack.

"Hey, ladies! Have any luck while I was gone?" I rejoined my girls with a genuine, beaming smile.

"We were until Camilla had Alessia split her hand, then double down, and she lost most of her stash," Val informed me.

"You make it sound like it was my fault she lost the money," Cam shot back at her.

"I told you to never split sixes."

"You couldn't have known for sure what would happen. That's why it's called gambling. There's always a chance we could have won."

"If you ever want to beat the house, you have to stack the odds in your favor. If you're going to play, play to win." Val was showing signs of becoming a real badass woman. We didn't hang out often because of our six-year age difference, but I would have to remedy that.

"How do you know all that?" Alessia asked.

Val's lips curved into a smug grin. "I studied the game before we came. Last time, I had no clue what I was doing, and I wasn't going to make that mistake again." Something told me Val might make a formidable enemy, and I was suddenly glad we were family.

Cam raised a brow. "Some of us aren't always looking for a safe bet. Some of us like to take a chance."

"So says the banking expert who dots every I and crosses every T," I muttered. I couldn't imagine she'd ever taken a chance on anything risky in her entire life, aside from a brief period during high school when she threw around a healthy dose of attitude. Since then, she'd been a model daughter and somewhat hard for me to relate to.

Alessia was also a perfectionist, but that didn't seem so off-putting from someone who wasn't my sister. I didn't have to hear my mother rub in my face how perfect Alessia was at every opportunity.

"All right, ladies. Let's not end our trip fussing at each other. A couple of hundred dollars isn't going to break the bank. Our dinner reservation is in twenty minutes, so let's head to the restaurant. It'll probably take that long to find the damn place from here." Al was the peacemaker, regardless of what group she was among. That quality, more than anything, was why we'd been so close for so long. She indulged my every whim, and I was happy to let her. Our dynamic was also good for her. If it weren't for me and my initiative, she'd never have had any fun at all.

With my loving guidance and reassurance, she was now engaged to a capo in the mafia—a turn of events I never would have imagined possible for my naïve, idealistic cousin. I was thrilled she'd found such happiness and had been brave enough to embrace our family's way of life. There was a time I thought she might cut and run from it all, but she didn't. She stuck around and was more entrenched in the life than ever.

It was amazing the difference six months had made. All three of my cousins were engaged or married. I could only hope the situation wasn't infectious as I had no desire to commit myself to a man at this stage in my life. I hungered for far more temporary, thrilling encounters.

Mr. Stormy Eyes would have been fun, but that ship sailed when I stole his lighter. Now, I was only interested in putting distance between us. We'd head back to New York in the morning, and I would be in the clear, never to see the man again.

TWO
Primo

When I was a child, only about six years old, my mother drove us from our home in Hermosillo all the way to Mexico City on a pilgrimage to see the blessed Lady of Guadalupe, otherwise known as the Virgin Mary. My mother had talked about the iconic Mexican statue for years but was only able to make the trip when her employer, a wealthy Mexican businessman, gave her two weeks off while he took his family on an extended vacation abroad.

She explained that the statue was far more than art. Countless miracles were owed to prayers uttered at the holy site. My child's mind heard what my mother said and imbued great powers upon the statue, seeing it as a glorified telephone to God's house. I couldn't wait to see it with my own eyes.

We lived in the servants' quarters on a large estate and had few possessions of our own, but unlike many of the other staff, my mother had done well enough with her money to own a small car. We made the drive in three days. We stayed in shabby motels and ate the food she'd brought with us, except for the occasional splurge on ice cream or a soda along the way.

That trip was one of my best childhood memories. We sang along with songs on the radio and cuddled together in bed each morning before getting back on the road. My mother was my entire world, and spending uninterrupted quality time with her was a unique gift.

By the time we reached Mexico City, I was giddy with excitement to see the sacred statue that inspired our great adventure. The sight of it more than lived up to the hype. She was clad in a modest robe and floral gown, hands out welcoming the indigenous people around her, a halo of golden sunbeams radiating outward from behind her. With a rocky waterfall backdrop and artfully crafted water fountains arcing sprays of water all around her, the scene stirred something within me.

Several years later, I would disavow all that the sacred Lady stood for, but at that moment, I was in awe of her majesty. Her power and grace. I felt like laughing and crying at the same time, my skin humming with the sense of the supernatural around me.

I never experienced another feeling remotely like it in my twenty years since that day. Not until a certain petite brunette with questionable survival instincts decided she wanted to dance with the devil. It wasn't necessarily unusual for a woman to approach me, but they rarely aroused more than my cock. Something about this woman sent an electric current pulsing through my veins. As a child, I would have sworn the sensation was owed to the hand of God. As an adult, I knew simple adrenaline and the unpredictability of body chemistry were to blame.

Something marked the woman as different from all the other pretty faces around her. Something that enabled her to trigger a reaction within me.

She was bold. Brazen. Confident.

It had taken all my faculties to control my response to her, and I hated it. I despised that someone could have that effect on me. I'd fought too long and hard for control of my life to hand over the reins to another person—especially a woman. They had a way of crippling even the strongest of men.

There was only one individual I answered to, and I owed him my life, so I was duty bound to take orders from him. I refused to allow this woman any power over me, no matter how seductive her efforts.

In what could only be a strategic play to maximize the beguiling effect of her green eyes, she wore a rich forest green dress to accentuate the jade and emerald highlights in her irises. The garment hugged her curvy figure, tying on one side like a package begging to be unwrapped. It wasn't particularly revealing, which only made her that much more enticing. She knew the effect she had on men, and every inch of it was calculated.

She wasn't just striking; she was fucking mesmerizing.

And if the sight of her wasn't enough to capture a man's interest, her sharp tongue was the ultimate lure. Men couldn't help but take on a challenge, and she wouldn't be reeled in easily. Winning her would be its own reward if a man was willing to fall into that trap. He may have won his prize, but at what cost? Falling for a woman would only make a man weak and give his enemies a weapon to use against him.

I would never hand myself over so easily.

As if on cue, the crowd at my table erupted in cheers, drawing me back to the present. I'd had a few hundred dollars riding on various bets at the craps table. The roller had hit paying numbers a dozen times in a row and was amassing quite the payout for his fellow players. Not one to push my luck, I took the opportunity to cash out and pocket my winnings.

I wasn't a fan of gambling and preferred to put my money into ventures with guaranteed payouts. But milling around the casino without approaching a table made a man like me stand out, and I preferred to blend in, if at all possible.

Before I could step away from the table, my phone buzzed. No doubt it would be Naz checking in with me for an update. Nazario Vargas, known as El Zar, was my boss and had been a father figure since he took me in at the age of twelve. I was one of the few people allowed to call him by the familiar nickname, Naz. Anyone else who took such liberties ended up losing a finger.

I had expected him to call rather than wait until I reported back to him. His impatience chaffed, but I could do little about it. He trusted me as much as he trusted anyone, which wasn't necessarily saying much. His hovering presence felt like a leash. I hadn't been a child in need of supervision for a long time, but he couldn't seem to accept that. He always expected the worst in people, but they often lived up to his expectations, so I couldn't necessarily fault him. I wasn't perfect, but if he could have relaxed around anyone, it should have been me. Yet he'd only gotten more paranoid as time went on.

I cleared a path away from the bank of gaming tables

toward the edge of the room to get as far from the casino noise as possible.

"Yes, sir," I answered as I walked.

"I just got off the phone with Juan Carlos. He said the Russians attacked and killed five of his men. I'm afraid the transition is not going as I'd hoped. How are things there in Vegas?"

"Everything's gone well. If we need to follow through with our backup plan, it won't be an issue."

He was silent for a long moment, no doubt rubbing his chin the way he did when he was thinking. "I haven't taken on something this big since I overthrew Martín Alvarez years ago. These things are never pretty, no matter how necessary."

Naz was one of two leaders of the Sonora Cartel. Originally, three kingpins ran independent organizations under the alliance of the cartel, but before I came to live with him, Naz overthrew Alvarez and usurped his territory. I'd been told Alvarez came from a wealthy line of Spaniards, and he had thought himself superior to the other bosses. Naz had never talked to me about his motives, and I didn't care. What I did know was that the takeover had been bloody, and Alvarez's men had resisted the transition.

"You control nearly half of Mexico and eighty percent of the drug trade in the US. Are you certain the expansion is necessary?" I had to be careful with my words. Naz did not take kindly to others challenging him, but it wasn't in my nature to go along blindly with a plan when it didn't make sense. It was rarely an issue during the normal course of operations, but his expansion initiative was different. We were opening ourselves up to attack, and I wasn't certain the payoff would be worth it.

The line was silent for several seconds.

"When I want your fucking opinion, I'll ask for it." Every clipped word was a warning.

I clenched my jaw to keep from snapping back at him. As far as I was concerned, my years of loyal service entitled me to an opinion, but he wouldn't see it that way even though he'd practically raised me.

Even if he had allowed me a say in the business, it wouldn't have mattered. Naz had been convinced of his success before the idea of expansion had even fully formed. It didn't help that his brother was feeding him questionable intel—at least, I suspected he was. Regardless, nothing I could say would dissuade him. The only way to challenge him would be to kill him, and I wasn't prepared to take my dissent that far.

I reminded myself how much I owed Naz and breathed through my frustration. "Yes, sir. I understand. How would you like me to proceed?"

"I want you back in Guaymas for my meeting with Morales next week. Then we move forward with the plan."

"I'll fly back first thing in the morning."

The line was silent, but Naz hadn't hung up, so I waited for whatever he still had to say.

"The dangers we'll be facing are exactly why I need your full support, Primo. Tell me I don't have to question your loyalty."

"I owe you everything, Naz. You know I'll always stand beside you."

"Good. I'll see you tomorrow then." This time, the line clicked dead.

Relaxing into one of the leather swivel chairs outside a casino lounge, I dropped my head back and exhaled an exasperated sigh. For one of the most powerful, feared men in

Mexico, I felt just as trapped as any other man at times like these.

What the hell was I bitching about?

I was wealthier than God and had the world at my feet. Dealing with Naz was a small price to pay. I needed to get my priorities in check and stop thinking like a petulant child.

As I brought my gaze back down to my surroundings, I realized I still had my unlit cigar in my hand. A hit of those sweet Cuban leaves was exactly what I needed. I reached in my jacket pocket and found it empty, then patted down my other pockets, unable to locate my lighter.

I recalled taking it out at the table and realized I must have left it there when Naz called. Weaving back through the crowd to the craps table I'd been at, I asked both the dealer and the pit boss if anyone had seen my silver lighter. Nothing.

I was about to chalk up the loss to my shit day when I recalled that sultry red grin the brunette had given me as she walked away.

Emptyhanded it is.

Surely not. Surely, the woman hadn't stolen my lighter. She didn't know me, but it wasn't hard to guess I wasn't a man to be trifled with, and I certainly wasn't a good target for petty theft. As I replayed the scene in my mind, I grew increasingly certain that was exactly what had happened.

My stack of chips had gone untouched, so she wasn't after money. The little viper had snatched my lighter as a statement. A challenge. A game.

I had sworn I wouldn't be drawn in by her charade, but this was different—at least, that was what I told myself. It was a matter of respect. Pride. What kind of man would allow a woman to steal from him? I would have shot one of our soldiers for such a crime. I couldn't allow her actions to go unaddressed.

Naz had just given me instructions, but I could see my plans derailing before me, alongside the vision of a sultry brunette with mischievous snake eyes. I would go back to Guaymas so I didn't piss off Naz, but after our meeting, I was going on the hunt.

That little girl had no idea what she'd done, but she was about to find out.

THREE

Giada

TWO WEEKS AFTER RETURNING FROM VEGAS TO MY BORING LIFE, I'd resorted to dining with my parents in order to get me out of my apartment. It was amazing how normal our lives were, considering my father was the consigliere to one of the most powerful mob bosses in New York. With such an average daily existence, it was no wonder my parents were able to hide my father's mafia involvement from us girls for so long.

To an outsider looking in, my father seemed like any other respectable businessman. He told us he worked with his brother, my uncle Enzo, at the family construction company. He was always busy, and money was never an issue, so I'd never thought to question him. Knowing what I knew now, I wondered how much more my father kept hidden.

What went on behind closed doors? There was clearly more to my father and uncle, but what? I was insanely curious about these men I thought I knew. What had Uncle Enzo done to become boss? Had he killed people? Did he pay off politicians and the police? How did they make their money? Gambling? Drugs?

I'd tried to glean hints about my father's secret life, but he kept a tight lid on that shit. Years of keeping his two worlds separate made him a master of secrecy. Unfortunately for him, the apple didn't fall far from the tree. I was well versed at being sneaky, and I desperately wanted to know about my father's other life because his lawless shortcomings made me feel less like a screwup. My impulsiveness and need to challenge authority weren't aberrations; I'd come by the traits naturally. His criminal activity served as validation.

I was exactly who I was meant to be.

The revelation had been fascinating, and I'd wanted to know everything I could about this new side of my father. I'd been watching. Learning. My dad couldn't hide everything, like respectful nods from associates or a glare from a local restaurant owner when my dad's back was turned.

Between my observations and tidbits of information passed on from Alessia, I was able to piece together quite a bit. Al's fiancé, Luca, didn't tell her everything, but what she did send my way helped me understand the climate around me. In the past couple of weeks, something was making the men around me tense. The creases between my father's brows had become a permanent fixture on his face.

The drama after Enzo's former underboss turned on him had all been resolved, so tensions should have been easing. But I'd found the opposite to be true. My parents asked me more questions than ever about my whereabouts, and I was sure my mom had a bodyguard with her when I met her for lunch the week prior.

Something was going on, but my father would not give me any information. I'd tried early on to ask him questions and was told in no uncertain terms that *family* business would not be discussed. I just had to keep an eye out and see what I could learn on my own.

"How was church?" I asked my mother as I helped her set the table. Mom had wanted me to go to the special weekday mass, but I refused. As a consolation, I came to their place for dinner after the service. It was a pain in the ass to drive all the way out to Staten Island from Manhattan, but what the hell else did I have to do?

"You should have come. The message was perfect for you. Father Jacoby talked about respecting your elders and the importance they play in your life."

"I'm here, aren't I? Isn't that respect?"

"I'm talking about that mouth of yours. It's hard to be respectful when you pop off without even thinking."

"You know better than to expect me to change, Ma. I'm *hopeless*, remember? Your words, not mine." I'd be lying if I said the words she'd slung at me weeks earlier hadn't stung. She'd no doubt argue that it was a figure of speech, but I knew she'd meant them. It was no secret I'd never measure up to my mother's exacting standards.

Maybe if she could accept me for who I was, I would have been open to curbing my more abrasive tendencies. I could be pushy and had put my foot in my mouth more times than I could count. I wouldn't deny it. But my mother hating those qualities made me adamant about not changing a thing. Her conservative nature made me more apt to be brash, and her need to follow the rules made me want to break every one of them. I wasn't sure what made me so contrary, but it had felt imperative when I was growing up to be as unlike my mother as I could manage.

When I was thirteen, she forbade me from wearing a triangle-cut bikini because it was too revealing. After buying one in secret, I'd smuggle it to swim parties and changed suits after my mother dropped me off. If she curled her hair, I ironed mine straight. She insisted I took Catholic confirmation classes, so I made out with my classmate, Patrick Murphy, in the confessional when Father Jacoby left us unattended.

The more she pushed me, the harder I pushed back. A psychologist would have had a field day with our dynamic. Written papers and analyzed the shit out of it. Maybe someday I'd go talk to a shrink and work through those issues, but for now, I was content to be myself and watch my mother squirm.

"That's enough," my father cut in on his way past the kitchen. "I've had a long day, and I'm not interested in hearing you two go at it."

Sometimes I wished Uncle Enzo and Aunt Lottie were my parents. They were so much more relaxed, and Aunt Lottie was loads of fun. She and Mom were best friends, but I couldn't fathom why. Alessia and I had a similar dynamic, with Al being more like my mom and me like Aunt Lottie, but Al wasn't as uptight as my mother. I couldn't imagine Ma would ever be fun to hang around. Hell, even her cooking was dull.

I took in the lemon pepper chicken and Brussels sprouts with a mental groan. I wasn't any kind of chef, but would it kill her to make a casserole occasionally?

"Giada, will you go up and tell Val that dinner's ready?"

"I'm on it." I walked halfway up the stairs before calling out my sister's name at the top of my lungs and grinning at the mental image of my mother cringing. She hated for us girls to raise our voices and would fuss about not living in the ghetto whenever we shouted. It was petty of me to pull her strings like that, but I couldn't help it. Being at their house made me feel like a belligerent teen again, and it only made things worse when she lectured me five minutes after I walked in.

"You and Mom at it again?" Val groaned as she started down the stairs.

"You know how she is. It's not my fault."

"Bullshit. I know exactly how she is, and I know how you are. You love to poke the angry bear. I may not see eye to eye with her, but I don't have a desire to argue and make my life miserable."

"That's easy to say coming from the child who can do no wrong," I grumbled.

"Doing wrong is one thing, but flaunting it in front of their faces is another. Admit it, you get off on the conflict."

My jaw dropped. "I do *not*! I just refuse to kowtow to her every whim."

Val paused her descent to glare at me.

"Whatever," I muttered, pulling out my phone when it buzzed in my back pocket and ignoring my sister's eye roll as she walked past me.

I had a text from an unknown number. **Did you think I wouldn't find you?**

My heartbeats tripped over themselves as I read the message. What the hell was it supposed to mean? Who would send me such a text? It could have been a prank or a wrong number. I debated blocking the number and erasing the text, but my curiosity got the better of me. **Who is this?**

No reply. So strange. Altogether, it wasn't necessarily threatening, so I ordered myself not to freak out. There were an infinite number of possible explanations for the message. Hell, it could be an old high school classmate screwing with me. There was no telling.

I shoved my phone back in my pocket, took in a deep cleansing breath, and forced myself toward the dining room and another tense family dinner.

"Do you think it's my fault I have a shit relationship with my mom?" I asked Alessia the next day at one of our weekly lunches. I'd been thinking about what Val said and decided I'd get my cousin's opinion. She may not have known my darkest secret, but she knew me better than anyone else.

"I'm not sure any one person is at fault. You two are just very different."

"Yeah, but you and I are different and that doesn't stop us from being friends."

"True, but a mother-daughter relationship is much more complicated. Did you two have a fight or something?"

"I was over last night for dinner, and Val accused me of getting off on arguing with Mom. I thought she was being absurd, but the more I examined her claim, the more I wondered why I didn't just give in to Mom a little more. It wouldn't necessarily kill me to bite my tongue." I pushed around the food on my plate until I noticed Alessia had gone silent. When I looked up, I found my cousin gaping at me.

"That's it." She tossed down her fork. "I'm taking you to a doctor. You're clearly delirious."

I narrowed my eyes and crossed my arms over my chest. "Ha-ha. So you *do* think it's my fault, don't you?"

"No, don't put words in my mouth. I know Aunt Mia isn't

exactly nurturing, but I also know you don't make the situation any easier."

"You think I should just bend over and take it when she points out all the ways I don't measure up?"

"G, you brought this up. Don't get defensive with me." Al raised a brow, an unusual warning from my pacifist cousin.

Point taken.

"Okay, I'm sorry. I just don't understand how else I should act around her."

"Honestly, I think you'd see it all differently if you had something else in your life—a job or a passion. Something that brough you joy and occupied your mind so that her petty jabs wouldn't seem so important. Not to say they wouldn't hurt, but if you had other priorities, your relationship with her wouldn't weigh so heavily. I know you say you're good with filling your days going to spas and shopping, but I disagree. You need more."

My first reaction was to be defensive, but I tamped that down and thought about what she was saying. It was good in theory, but the application was far more complicated. "How am I supposed to figure out what I'm passionate about? I've never found anything that captures my interest the way you love working at Triton or the way Sofia loves art. Maybe I don't have any passions." I slumped back in my chair, losing my appetite.

I was lucky enough to have a trust fund that floated my bills and kept me living a life of luxury, but there was truth in what Al had said. I talked a big game about loving my freedom and preferring to go to nail appointments rather than a day job. It wasn't as fulfilling as I would have liked. I needed something more in my life, but I had no clue what would fill that void.

"I think the only way you can figure it out is to try

things. Maybe look into some different volunteer opportunities. There are all kinds of classes out there for every hobby under the sun. Try a few and see what captures your interest."

I sighed heavily. The task sounded daunting, and I couldn't shake the feeling that no amount of crocheting or serving breakfast at a soup kitchen would make me happy. I needed something more. Something edgy. Something Alessia would never understand.

Hell, I wasn't sure I understood it.

"Alright, I'll see what I can do, but no more talk about my mess of a life. Tell me what's new with you. Have you set a date for the wedding yet?"

A beaming smile lit her face. "Not exactly. We're thinking September to give plenty of time to plan, but we haven't nailed down a specific date."

"You going to strongarm Aunt Lottie into letting you be involved in the planning?" Alessia's mom lived for planning events.

Fuck, even she has a passion.

I was going to have to work on that.

"I'm absolutely going to help her plan. No more pushover Alessia. I get one shot at a wedding, and I want to make sure it's exactly the way Luca and I want."

"Good for you! My sweet little cousin has grown so much in the past year."

Al smiled mischievously. "Guess who's turn it is now?"

I shook my head. "We'll see. That doesn't mean I'm giving up on fun, so I'll still be me. And on that note, I think we should go out this weekend for a drink."

"It's supposed to snow tomorrow," she balked.

"Okay, then we go out Saturday." I smiled, unfazed. "We can ask the other girls and see if anyone wants to join."

"Fine, but only if the roads aren't bad. I'm not busting my ass for a girls' night."

"Please, it's only November. How bad could it be?"

Eighteen inches of snow fell in the city that Friday night. All of Manhattan shut down, but street crews had the roads cleared by the next morning, and the rising temperatures had worked magic on the icy sidewalks. By Saturday evening, New York City was back in full swing.

We recruited Sofia and Camilla to round out our trip to the Lotus Club, the hottest new bar overlooking the river. Apparently, we weren't the only ones who needed a night out. After the winter storm had everyone stuck at home the night before, club goers were out in droves.

Aside from a packed nightclub, the weather had also affected our wardrobe—no slinky dresses or strappy heels. Instead, I was rocking skinny jeans, leather booties, and a sweater draped off one shoulder. I felt hella cute and ready to get my dance on.

"Let's get a drink first, then hit the dance floor," I called to the girls over the blaring music.

They all nodded, and we squeezed through the crowd to the bar where two overworked bartenders raced to keep up with the demand. Ten minutes later, we toasted to a night with the girls, and I reveled in the feel of the cool vodka martini warming my stomach.

"You guys have to save me if some guy tries to dance with me," Alessia ordered. "I know it's not technically cheating, but it feels wrong."

"I totally understand," said Sofia. "Hopefully, if we all dance together, we'll be left alone."

I scoffed. "Speak for yourselves! I'd like nothing more than for some hottie to join us on the dance floor. Now drink up and let's get out there."

Al shook her head but downed the rest of her drink. We danced with one another, gyrating with the pulsing beat of the music and laughing hysterically when one of us tried a silly dance move. Soon, we attracted the attention of several men, one who was bold enough to insert himself into our small circle.

He wasn't bad-looking and was a decent dancer, so I moved forward and draped my arms over his shoulders. His warm hands clasped around my waist, and he pulled me close, wearing a devilish smile on his lips. I relaxed in his grip, allowing him to lead our movements.

When the song transitioned to a slower beat, he leaned in close to my ear to tell me his name, but his words never registered. I was too distracted by what I saw over his shoulder across the room.

A man stood perfectly still on a small set of stairs, looming above the crowd. He wore a dark suit without a tie, and his hungry gaze bore down on me, a hunter locked on his prey. The strobing laser lights and distance between us made it hard to see, but my gut flipped and twisted with instant recognition.

The man from the casino. It was him. Or at least, I thought it was.

Before I could be certain, my dance partner pulled back and blocked my view. I lifted onto my tiptoes and strained to see around him, but the other man was gone without a trace.

"You okay?" my dance partner asked with confusion etched in his features.

"I'm fine," I replied distractedly. "Just thought I saw someone I know." I scanned the room, trying to figure out if

I'd actually seen the man or if I'd just imagined it. Could it have been him? What were the chances?

Did you think I wouldn't find you? The cryptic words from my text days before flashed in my mind.

Holy shit.

It couldn't be. I was imagining things after getting that text—letting my imagination run wild. No man would track down a woman across the country just because she'd stolen a simple cigarette lighter.

There wasn't even an engraving on it!

No. It was impossible. My mind was playing tricks on me, and that was the only plausible explanation.

FOUR
Primo

I WASN'T SURE WHAT I HAD EXPECTED WHEN I FOLLOWED GIADA into the club. A confrontation involving tears and a hurried apology? Perhaps smug satisfaction to see an otherwise confident woman tremble with the realization that her actions had consequences. What I did not anticipate was the white-hot anger that engulfed me at seeing her dancing with another man.

She was a petty thief. It shouldn't have bothered me if she was renting herself out by the hour, let alone dancing fully clothed in public. When she walked into the club, I'd known she'd likely dance, although I'd assumed she'd stick with the girls in her group. I sat back arrogantly in the shadows, watching her and relishing her ignorance—a cat toying with his mouse before going in for the kill—until she led her small group onto the dance floor.

Every muscle in my body tensed, rigid and coiled for action. The song blasting over the speakers didn't even finish before a man weaseled his way beside her. That was hard enough to take, but when she reached for his shoulders and allowed him to press their bodies together, fiery rage had me on my feet.

The only thing that kept me from storming across the room and slamming my fist into the man's face was Giada's unguarded reaction when she saw me. She was shocked, as if the world around her ceased to exist the moment our eyes met.

More than that.

She looked as though she were adrift in the ocean, and I was her one chance of survival. Not just longing. Desperation.

Her unexpected response instantly soothed the fires that had my blood boiling. Needing a minute to regroup, I slipped away, staying just out of her sight. She searched the crowded room for me in vain, unable to locate me, but I never took my eyes off her.

She was fucking gorgeous, lips slightly parted and hair tousled. She may not have been wearing a revealing dress, but she was every bit as tempting as she'd been in the casino. I had told myself I wouldn't find her so attractive after knowing she'd stolen from me, even deluded myself into believing she hadn't actually been as beautiful as I'd thought, but it was all lies. She was just as striking as I had remembered and observing her daily life after I tracked her down only added to her intrigue. Rarely did any woman capture my interest.

Yet I couldn't get this one out of my head.

She was fucking up everything.

I shouldn't have been in the club. I had orders, and Naz would be pissed when he learned I'd ignored them. He was stubborn and unbending. I had convinced myself that a small deviation in our plans wouldn't change anything. Once I was back in Mexico, he'd get over my brief detour, and I'd have dealt with the little viper poisoning my bloodstream. It would work out best for everyone in the end. Well … maybe not everyone. Giada would have to accept her consequences whether she liked them or not.

I wasn't even sure what kind of punishment I'd intended to dole out, but fear was a central component. I wanted her to regret messing with me. Regret her siren-like allure that ensnared men. Made them set aside their responsibilities and challenged their loyalties. I wanted her to regret approaching me the same way I did because I hadn't been able to stop thinking about her since.

Once I saw the fear in her eyes and she cowered away from me, the spell would be broken, and I could go on with my life.

Feeling far more in control and determined, I made my way down a hallway toward the restrooms and constructed a plan. The door across from the women's room was locked but easily opened with a tool I kept in my wallet for just such an occasion. Inside was a storage room that would be perfect for my needs.

Once the trap was set, I found a place to wait where I could keep an eye on Giada. When she made her way to the restroom a half hour later, I followed her and stationed myself beside the door. My fingers twitched with the need to touch her. The second she exited the restroom, I wrapped my hand over her mouth and shoved her into the storage room.

She was momentarily too shocked to struggle, fumbling to stay upright and gasping against the palm of my hand. My veins surged with adrenaline. I'd been waiting for this moment for two weeks, tracking Giada down and biding my time for the right moment to strike. Now, I had her in my arms and at my mercy.

The rush of power was intoxicating.

Exhilarating.

Addicting.

The storage room light was set to a motion detector, so harsh fluorescent light flooded the space when the door flung open, making it hard to see since my eyes had adjusted to the dim lighting of the club. The far wall was lined with shelves containing supplies, and mops in buckets along with brooms and vacuums filled the center of the cramped room. That was fine with me. All I needed was a small space away from prying eyes.

As soon as we were inside the room, I slammed the door shut and spun Giada around. Pressing her back against the wall beside the door, I instantly replaced my hand over her mouth. The club was loud, but she could easily be heard by people in the hallway if she screamed.

The second our eyes met, shock and fear melted into recognition and … indignation? Her wide eyes narrowed to harsh slits of emerald rage, and she ceased struggling, her back stiffening and muscles tensing.

Who was this fucking audacious woman?

She had stolen from me, yet she had the gall to glare at me as if I were in the wrong. I wasn't sure if I wanted to knock her down from her high horse or worship at her majestic feet. Just like before, she stirred an inferno of conflicting emotions inside me.

I held her gaze, steady and unyielding. She was brave, I would give her that, but too much courage could be foolhardy. Sometimes it was good to know when to yield. The more she stood against me, the more my primal side wanted to conquer her.

"Somebody's been a very naughty girl," I purred, breathing in her sharp citrus scent. "Did you think you were making a statement by stealing from me? Surely you could tell I'm not a man to toy with, which means you must be very self-assured. If I had to guess, I'd say this wasn't your first foray into stealing from people, but I'd be willing to bet I'm the first who's caught you. The first to confront you with your crimes."

Her eyes flashed and nostrils flared just slightly, giving me my answer.

The corners of my lips lifted into the hint of a caustic smile. "This time, you got a little too brazen. A little too cocky. The problem with stealing from someone you don't know is you could get yourself in terrible trouble. I'm not a man people disrespect."

When Giada lifted her chin defiantly as if she had something to say, I was shamefully eager to hear what that might be. With a warning in my eyes, I slowly lowered my hand away from her mouth.

"It was a silly lighter. If it means so much to you, I can give it back."

"This has nothing to do with the lighter. I told you, it's about respect." *And a fucking insatiable lust,* but I wasn't going to tell her that. If she knew how hard I was for her, it would give her power over me, and that wasn't an option.

"So, you're going to teach me a lesson for taking a five-dollar trinket? This is ridiculous." She spat her words at me in feigned ferocity, but a treacherous quiver to her voice betrayed her underlying fear.

"I've killed men for less."

Her jaw snapped shut, eyes flaring. "My father is the consigliere to Enzo Genovese, the boss of the Lucciano crime family. Do you have any idea what that means? You fuck with me, and you fuck with the Italian mafia." She pressed her lips together in a thin, satisfied smile as if she'd played the ultimate trump card.

Slowly, I lifted my hand and trailed the backs of my fingers from her temple, curving over the soft line of her cheekbone, down to her strong yet feminine jaw, then ghosted over the delicate skin of her neck where I gently placed my hand around her throat. "Of all the men in this club, I am probably the only one who doesn't give a fuck who your father is."

What I didn't tell her was that I already knew. The identity of her family had only added to her mystery. Why would someone with money feel the need to steal trinkets from strangers? Did being raised in a world of crime skew her view on reality, or was it more about the thrill? Did Giada Genovese simply have a craving for a darker, more dangerous side of life?

"Then you're fucking crazy," she hissed.

"I've been called worse."

Giada flailed, making a weak attempt at struggling against me for the first time since entering the storage room. Her face was still rigid with contempt, but her body was giving in to the fear. "My sister and cousins are here with me. They'll start looking for me if they haven't already."

"You know what I think?" I asked in a low rumble with my mouth close to her ear.

Her movements stilled until the only motion in the room was the rhythmic vibrations from the music.

"I think you don't want anyone to find us. I think you take things hoping one day, someone just like me will track you down and make you answer for your crimes."

Her breathing shuddered in the abnormal stillness of our isolated bubble buried deep within the chaotic nightclub. The pounding bass penetrating through the walls pulsed at the same frantic rate as her rioting heart. The contrast between the frenetic energy outside and our cocoon of strained silence magnified the senses. It made time stutter on its continuum as if the universe itself knew the poignancy of this moment. A tilting of the Earth's axis until nothing made sense.

A shift had occurred in those eternal seconds.

Something monumental and catastrophic.

Overwhelming and divine.

The tight lines around Giada's eyes smoothed, and her pupils dilated until the only color remaining was a ring of deep forest green. She took in a long, steadying breath as if gathering her courage, then parted her lips.

"And if you're right?"

The words were a whisper. Barely more than a shaky breath, yet so much more.

They were a reluctant confession.

Surrender.

Giada's gaze was still guarded, but a new wary vulnerability was embedded in her features. I searched deep into her kaleidoscopic gaze to make sure I hadn't misread her, but there was no derision, only desire.

Like a shark scenting blood in the water, my predatory instincts screamed at me to claim my prize. To seize what was being offered with greedy abandon. But even drunk on the prospect of victory, I knew that yielding to my hunger for her would be disastrous.

Deciding to test her resolve and give us one last chance to avoid disaster, I lifted myself away from her, leaving a foot of space between us. She could have shoved me backward onto the buckets, giving herself plenty of time to slip away, but she didn't. The brazen temptress didn't move a muscle.

"Turn around," I ordered firmly, the gravel in my voice betraying the slip in my control.

Giada held my gaze as she debated internally.

I refused to soften my stance or give her any reassurance. I wasn't there to coddle her. If she was brave enough to toy with the devil, she could summon the courage to dance with him as well.

Eventually, her lips pursed with determination, and she spun around to face the wall. "What exactly are we doing here?"

"You're doing as I say and not asking questions." It was the only response I could give her because I had no other answer. I had no fucking idea what we were doing or where it would lead.

She peeked over her shoulder. "What does that mean? I don't want you to hurt me."

"Shouldn't you have considered that before you stole from me?"

Giada started to turn back around.

"*Stop,*" I barked, freezing her in place. "The only thing that may hurt when we're through is your pride. I'm not in the habit of brutalizing women. If you want to leave, then leave, but if you have the strength to accept the consequences of your actions, then turn around and put your hands on the wall."

Her eyes slid briefly to mine before she complied.

Watching her bend to my will, obeying my commands, raised a mighty storm of masculine pride in my chest. I felt invigorated, as if I'd scaled a mountain and stood on its highest peak, towering above the rest of the world.

This lioness of a woman was giving herself to me, and I would take all I could get.

"That's a good girl," I murmured, closing in behind her. My hands drifted to her waist, and my mouth lowered to the smooth skin of her exposed shoulder, but I didn't kiss her. I simply inhaled her tangy, sweet scent and trailed my lips to her neck and up close to her ear. "I told myself to ignore you after our conversation in the casino. To forget every dirty thing I wanted to do to you and stay focused on my job, but when I realized what you'd done, it was too much. I had to find you."

Giada arched with my words, her head angling to give me more access to her neck.

I lowered my hands, winding them around to the front of her jeans and deliberately popped open the top button. "Are you already wet for me? Shall we find out?" I lowered the zipper, then eased my hand inside her pants but left her silk panties between us.

My touch drew a breathy moan from her lips. Her panties were drenched.

"Someone likes a little kink in their play. Does a taste of fear turn you on, Giada? Do you get off on not knowing what I might do next?" I retracted my hand and clasped her pants, yanking them down over her hips, along with her underwear.

She gasped at the sudden movement but never shifted her hands from their place on the wall. "You rejected me that night. I came onto you, but you rejected me."

"Like I told you then, I didn't want to want you." I leaned back to admire her rounded backside, stroking my palm over the supple curve of her ass. "But that didn't stop you, did it? You had to go and fuck with my head, rearranging my priorities." In one swift motion, I pulled back and brought my hand down hard against her firm flesh, the sound reverberating in the confined space. My hand immediately returned to the site of the offense, caressing over her heated skin.

I was curious how Giada would respond to being struck. It was entirely possible someone as strong-willed as she was would be outraged, incensed over being degraded. I should have known better. Giada wasn't like any other woman I'd known.

Her responses were unpredictable.

She didn't cry out or curse me. Struggle or lunge to escape. No. The little temptress released a guttural moan that had my cock swelling painfully against my zipper. She didn't hide her emotions or give a man what she thought he wanted to hear. She was untamed and raw, and I wanted to conquer and claim every bit of that purity.

It made me furious.

A woman was not on my agenda, and a relationship did not fit in my life. I wasn't the type of man to have a girlfriend, let alone settle down and raise a family. My anger bled with my desire, stirring up a tornadic burst of emotion.

I pulled back and unleashed a second strike on her opposite cheek, my breathing becoming rushed and heavy. I was losing control. This woman made me feel unstoppable and utterly powerless at the same damn time.

When my hand dropped down between her thighs, seeking her warm center, what I found leached all sanity from my reeling mind. Giada wasn't just wet; she was dripping arousal. The thick, sticky evidence of her lust coated the inside of her thighs.

It was too much.

Unable to withstand the temptation any longer, I reached my hand around to cup her from the front, finding her opening and surging inside. "Fuck, Giada. You're every fucking fantasy come true." I wrapped my free hand around her chest, drawing her close as I fucked her with my fingers. My palm rubbed against her stiff bundle of nerves while my fingers found the sensitive spot inside her, massaging and coaxing every ounce of pleasure from her.

Giada writhed at my touch. Her head rolled back on my shoulder, and she ground her ass against my raging erection. She was more than responsive. She was a sexual goddess, unbridled and free. As much as I wanted to sink my cock inside her, it would be a grave mistake.

Fingering her was one thing, but coming inside her would seal my fate. I would have become hopelessly addicted, and I couldn't allow that to happen. At least that one tiny shred of my control still held.

Instead, I used the friction between us to ease the ache in my balls, pulled tight against me and begging for release, and focused my attention on seeing Giada come apart.

I didn't have to wait long.

Within minutes, her breaths became shallow pants, and her legs quivered beneath her.

"That's it, little monster. Get my hands filthy with your cum."

She exploded at my words, crying out and arching so sharply, I had to step back to keep us upright. Her body slowly softened as I teased out every tiny contraction until she returned to reality and stiffened with the realization of what she'd done and who she was with.

When she leaned away and supported her own weight, I reached for her panties and jeans and pulled them back up over her hips. Her body was still facing away from me, but she turned to glance at me over her shoulder.

I stepped forward, bumping her gently and forcing her to press her front against the wall. "You can keep the lighter," I whispered into her hair. "I've found something infinitely more appealing. I'll be in touch."

Before she could say a word, I slipped from the room and disappeared into the club.

FIVE

Giada

THE STORAGE ROOM DOOR SLAMMED SHUT BEHIND HIM, LEAVING me standing dazed and alone. Only then did the sharp scent of chemicals register. I glanced around at the cleaning supplies stacked on metal shelves and wondered what the fuck had just happened.

Did I really just get finger fucked by a strange stalker guy in a club? *Holy shit!*

If my cheeks weren't flushed already, they became engulfed in flames—no doubt, I was red as a tomato. Why? Was I embarrassed? Not exactly. I saw no reason a woman couldn't have just as much casual sex as a man. One-night stands weren't my habit, but they'd been known to happen.

What had just transpired was different. This guy wasn't

someone I'd met on Bumble. I'd stolen from him, and he'd tracked me down across the country to confront me. To punish me.

And I'd let him.

I'd had guys spank me or try to act all dominant before, but I rarely bought into it because that play couldn't be faked. Men often liked to think of themselves as assertive, but I'd yet to come across one who wielded the requisite authority and self-assurance to pull it off.

Until now.

Every single aspect of that man's being radiated power. Control.

For once in my life, I wanted to obey. All thoughts of challenge drowned in a vast sea of anticipation. My bare skin pricked with awareness, and when his palm collided with my ass, a stampede of sensation careened through my body.

I think you take things hoping one day, someone just like me will track you down and make you answer for your crimes.

The truth in his assertion rang loudly. Why else did I take things? Yes, the thrill of getting away with my crimes was a part of my enjoyment, but I also possessed a sick curiosity about getting caught. The theft of worthless items wasn't nearly as exciting if the person never knew the object was taken. And with him especially, I had wanted him to know what I'd done. I hadn't expected him to track me down, but I'd wanted him to know it was me. Wanted him to remember me.

What was the point of denying his claims and fighting him when I didn't want to be free of him? I had wanted to know exactly what it felt like to have his full attention.

The thrill was off the charts.

But so was the fear. I hadn't planned to broadcast my father's mafia activities to a stranger, but he literally had me backed into a corner. It was the only weapon at my disposal, but he didn't even flinch at my threat. It was terrifying, but somehow that fear was also exhilarating. I'd been interested in sleeping with him back in Vegas had our initial conversation gone differently. Having him chase me down only made our encounter that much more erotic.

How could lust survive alongside fear? Was I demented? Did other women get turned on when they were scared? Maybe my mother was right, and I did need help.

When our faces were inches apart in that closet, and I could see the intensity in his gaze, it felt transformative to be the focus of that electric energy. The high was greater than I ever could have imagined, and now I wanted more.

He said he'd be in touch, but what did that mean? Was he staying in New York? Was he even from Vegas, or did he live somewhere else? Where would he find me next? Shouldn't I be afraid?

As I buttoned my jeans, questions and emotions assaulted me from all directions. I did my best to set them aside and collect myself. I hadn't been lying when I said my cousin would be looking for me. If I knew Alessia at all, she was close to calling the cops.

When I stepped from the storage room, the world around me shifted and rearranged to form a far less familiar picture. The club was physically just the same, but everything took on a new and exciting sheen. Scrutinizing the faces around me, I searched dark corners for watchful eyes and jumped each time someone bumped against me.

Ten minutes with him and my life was unrecognizable.

My face split in a wide grin.

"Where were you? I've been looking everywhere for you," Alessia chided when she spotted me near the bar.

I briefly debated telling her about my closet romp, but the

words wouldn't come out. "I just stepped outside for a minute. I'm so sorry I didn't tell you first."

"Are you okay?" she asked, her brow suddenly furrowed with concern.

"Yeah, just a little headache. I think I may head home."

"Well, I don't need to stick around without you. I'm just here to be with you and the girls. Let's find them and get out of here."

I wrapped my arms around her in a warm hug. "Thanks, Al. Sorry again to drag you out and then bail."

"You know I'm not big on clubbing anyway. Now, come on." She grabbed my hand and led me to where Sofia and Camilla huddled together at a table.

I scoured the bar for the man as I walked, wondering if he was still there. Was he watching me? The thought had my head reeling. I barely acknowledged the other girls and followed absently as Alessia dragged me to the front entrance and into a waiting car. Her father insisted his daughters use the drivers he provided. It was one of the few ways Uncle Enzo was stricter than my father, who had never gone to that length.

I continued to contemplate a barrage of questions on the way home. How had he found me? Why did he come after me? Was it just because I'd stolen his lighter, or had he wanted me from the beginning?

The escapade in the club had been the most erotic moment of my life, and I didn't even know the man's name. In fact, it was not knowing him that made it so exciting.

No way was that normal.

It was one thing to fantasize about being with a stranger after he'd stalked and nabbed you, but it was different to actually be in that situation. To get wet for that man and crave his touch. I would never call myself broken, but I was clearly abnormal. I should have been terrified, and while I was scared to a degree, I was also insanely turned on.

Our interaction wasn't tender or sweet. It was primal and raw, and I loved every second of it.

Alessia's driver dropped me off at my apartment building. I walked unseeing to the elevator, riding up to my floor in a muddled haze. I only snapped to attention when I neared my door and realized the man probably knew where I lived.

A heated shiver trickled down my spine, and I didn't know if it owed to fear or excitement. Possibly a healthy dose of both.

Opening the door, I glanced around, but the place looked empty. For now, I was alone.

After spending almost a full year renovating my apartment, I loved it. It was a sacrifice to live in a dingy rental during those long months, but it had been worth it. Everything about my place was exactly to my specifications from the layout to the paint colors to the fixtures, and the place was perfect.

After tossing my keys and purse onto the counter, I headed straight to my closet. Up on a top shelf behind a stack of blankets and squirreled away where no one would look was my treasure chest. An ornate wooden box where I kept each trinket I'd ever stolen. I could remember how I'd obtained every one of them, like some kind of fucked-up scrapbook.

I'd seen documentaries about serial killers who kept mementos of their victims and wondered if that was the path I was headed down. I didn't feel like I was insane. I didn't have any particular need to kill anyone, but maybe that was how they started out too. Every time I pondered the issue, I eventually decided to shelf the debate until my proclivities became a real problem.

Until casino man, it had been almost a year since I'd stolen anything. That could have been because the last theft was a particularly unethical incident. My mother often guilted me into volunteering at the church, and one day, she offered my services when the paper-folding machine broke, and they needed someone to help fold the weekly service leaflet. I was put to work with the crotchety old woman who worked in the church office. She'd had the job as long as I could remember, and I couldn't ever recall seeing the woman smile.

I tried to make small talk with her while we worked and was met with cynicism and negativity. She even had the audacity to insinuate I was a harlot because my skirt didn't touch my knees. She riled me up so badly that by the time we finished, I couldn't help but lift the small black wiener dog paperweight from her desk. There was no excuse for what I'd done, and I did feel bad about it afterward, but at the time, it had felt imperative to teach that cow a lesson.

When I opened the treasure box, my eyes skated over the objects, falling on the paperweight, then drifting to the silver lighter. Seeing it brought back the memory of standing next to him at the craps table. I could recall the rush, then feel a secondary wave of euphoria seep into my veins, heightened even further after the scene in the storage closet.

I picked out the lighter, then put the box back on its shelf and placed the lighter in my jewelry box on the dresser. I wanted it to be accessible. Close to me. Having it nearby felt like having a piece of him near me, and that was oddly comforting.

As I closed the lid on the jewelry box, I looked up at my reflection in the mirror above the dresser. Who the hell had I become? I should have been scared out of my mind or upset for bringing this stranger into my life. The last thing I should have been doing was fondling the lighter as though it was some kind of beloved keepsake.

I could have been in serious danger. Just because he hadn't hurt me yet didn't mean he wouldn't. After all, what kind of man hunted down a woman like that? Then again, I kept mementos of my crimes like a deranged serial killer in the making, so who was I to judge?

I didn't know what the hell I'd done, but one thing was for certain.

My life was now far from boring.

SIX
Giada

"WHY DO WE PROMISE GOD WE'LL TRY TO BE GOOD EVERY WEEK, then go out and do whatever we want until next Sunday's Mass?" I breathed the question to Camilla, who sat next to me on our family pew. For as long as I could remember, we had occupied the same pew at the front of the church every Sunday without fail. My sisters and I sat in order of age with Mom the farthest in by Val and Dad on the outside next to me.

Mass usually lasted an hour, but today's homily must have been personal to Father Jacoby because he'd been rambling for nearly thirty minutes. Normally, he gave us a quick fifteen-minute pep talk of a sermon and sent us on our way, but the issue of immigrant rights had apparently lit a fire under him. I'd spent the past half hour lost in my own thoughts.

Camilla eyed me curiously. "It's called Catholicism. Look it up." Someone listening in might have thought Cam was rude, but I was well acquainted with her brand of dry humor.

I snorted a laugh, covering my mouth and glancing warily at my mother, who had thankfully not noticed the commotion. Deciding to push my luck, I leaned in and continued our banter. "I'm familiar. Twelve years of Catholic school was plenty of education on the subject."

"Apparently not if you think this is more than ritual. Maybe you needed to pay attention better in school."

"I paid attention just fine. Just because I wasn't the principal's lapdog didn't mean I wasn't a good student." I used to tease Camilla endlessly about being a Goody Two-shoes because she was always helping in the principal's office.

"Exactly what I mean." Cam turned and glared at me. "You needed to pay better attention."

My forehead scrunched in confusion. "What the hell is that supposed to mean?"

She shook her head. "Just that if you think we're all here for some kumbaya betterment of our souls, you're the only one suffering a delusion. Church is about discipline and order—keeping the masses in line and on a certain path—not spiritual growth and enlightenment. I'm pretty sure Catholic guilt never helped anyone grow."

"Well, that sounds rather jaded if you ask me."

She huffed out a laugh. "Don't I know it."

I peered at my sister out of the corner of my eye, but she kept her gaze fixed on the dais ahead. She'd always been a little odd, at least from my perspective, but I'd never given it much thought. She had her friends growing up, and I'd had mine. Even though we were only a year apart in school, our circles rarely overlapped. Had something gone on during high school that I'd been unaware of, or was my middle sister just being dramatic?

The middle of church was hardly the place to hash it out. I made a mental note to bring it up again later and did a silent cheer when we all stood at the close of the homily.

After church, I had a quick lunch with my parents and excused myself for some retail therapy. I couldn't stop thinking about my mystery casino man, so what better way to distract myself than clothes? Nothing like getting lost in a Nordstrom to take a girl's mind off her worries.

Three hours later and my protesting feet had brought me back home for a rest. I felt somewhat better, but my thoughts never settled. I didn't want to tell anyone what had happened, but as an external processor, I needed to talk through my problems before I went crazy. Things festered and stewed inside me until I said them out loud and could discuss them with another person. I'd often debated whether that quality was a gift or a curse, but I'd never reached a concrete conclusion. It was good to know how I functioned best, but I wasn't crazy about needing to tell people my problems to work through them.

Regardless of the merits, I needed to spill. Digging my phone out of my purse, I sent Alessia a text, setting up a lunch date for the following day. Once the arrangements were made and relief was in sight, my anxiety eased.

Wine helped, too.

Three glasses in, and I was sure I could handle anything.

"You know how back in May you told me all about meeting Luca and how you learned he was in the mafia and you made me promise not to tell anyone?" We'd been at lunch all of five minutes when I hit Alessia with my confession.

Her sandwich stopped its momentum toward her mouth, and her eyes flicked up to mine. "Oh shit, G, what have you gotten yourself into now?"

"Hey! That's not fair. You act like I'm some kind of trouble magnet. I wasn't the one who got kidnapped a few months ago."

"Okay, you're right," she conceded, lifting a hand to calm me down. "Although, you do have a history of far more drama than I do but go on."

I glared, brow raised. "Are you done?"

She motioned for me to continue.

"I need you to keep an open mind. This may sound a little crazy, but it's not as bad as you might initially think. So … back on our last night in Vegas a couple of weeks ago, I met a guy."

"You met a guy? When? We were together the whole time."

"It was quick, just a short conversation on my way back from the restroom before dinner on the last night. I approached him, and we talked briefly. It wasn't worth mentioning when I got back to the table because I'd never see the guy again. Except …"

"Except?" Her eyes rounded.

"The other night at the club, he showed up." I bit my lip, waiting for her to freak out.

"Holy cow, that's crazy! What a coincidence that you'd see him again. Did you two talk?"

"Al, you're not getting it. It wasn't a chance encounter. He somehow found out who I was and tracked me down. We didn't run into each other, he found me." There was no way I was admitting that he'd tracked me down because I'd stolen from him. Leaving that tidbit out made him look that much more dangerous, but it couldn't be helped.

She stopped breathing. "Oh, shit."

"Now, before you freak, try not to get carried away. I don't think he's dangerous. I admit, him finding me was a surprise and maybe a tad stalker-ish, but he's not like some weirdo off the street."

"Not dangerous? Giada, what the actual fuck? How did he find you? Did you give him your name or number?"

My gaze dropped to my plate, my appetite suddenly drying up. "No, I didn't. I'm not sure how he found me. I hadn't actually thought that part through." I'd been so damn caught up with the fact he *had* found me and wondering what might happen next that I'd forgotten to question *how* he'd found me.

"Have you called the police? Do you even know his name to report him? Wait … you're not expecting me to keep this a secret, are you?" She gaped at me as if I'd told her I wanted to shave my head and move to a monastery.

My spine stiffened. "No, *you* wait. Don't you remember—you and Luca and the *mafia*? You came to me with your secret, and I kept my mouth shut. I expect you to do the same."

Her shoulders sagged, and she sighed. "I don't know, G. This seems so much more dangerous. This guy sounds like a stalker. Do you know anything about him?"

"No, but what I do know is I had the most erotic moment of my life at the club with him two nights ago. I don't want to call the cops on him."

"You *fucked* him? In the club?" she whisper-yelled.

I was far from prudish, but answering her questions had

me squirming in my seat. "Not exactly. He fingered me, and it was insanely hot."

"So while we were worried sick looking for you, you were off in … the bathroom?"

"Supply closet."

"The supply closet … getting freaky with your stalker?"

I shrugged. "Basically."

She dropped her head into her hands for a second before meeting my wary gaze again. "G, you don't know this man. Tracking down someone like that isn't normal. He may not have hurt you yet, but that doesn't mean he won't. You need to call the police or tell your dad."

"You know we don't call the police, not with our family, and there's no way I'm telling my dad. Aside from not wanting him to know my business, I truly don't think I'm in danger. You remember when you met Luca? You had a gut feeling he wouldn't hurt you. Even though you were scared, you felt like you could trust him. I know this all sounds fucked up, but this guy could be my Luca." I infused my gaze with pleading, hoping she'd understand.

Worry lines creased her forehead, and she gnawed on her bottom lip. "I just don't want you to get hurt."

"I know, but I need you to trust me on this. Hell, I might never even hear from him again."

"I can't say I would be disappointed," she grumbled.

I grinned. "Thanks, Al. I wanted you to know what was going on, and saying it out loud is helping me sort it all in my head."

"This helped?" She looked at me dubiously.

"It did, actually. Believe it or not, I do have some semblance of self-preservation and had worried about whether I should tell Dad. Now that I've talked it through with you, I'm certain I don't want Dad sending someone out to track him down. This man isn't going to hurt me, at least, not in a bad way." My cheeks heated.

"Oh, Jesus. I do *not* want to know." She shook her head, then her gaze softened as she peered back at me. "You're a little crazy, you know that?"

"I do, but I hope that doesn't change anything between us." It had always worried me that Alessia would see my more unscrupulous side and flinch away in horror.

She only smirked and placed her hand over mine. "Never. You're the yin to my yang. The fact that we're so different is what makes us such a great team."

"Oh, hell. You're gonna make me cry." I wiped at an invisible tear, and we burst into giggles.

"Okay, now that the ugly part's over with," Alessia added, "it's time to tell me what this man candy looks like. I want to know whatever I can about the man who has the unflappable Giada squirming in her seat."

We spent the next half hour going over my mystery man in critical detail, from his devastating good looks to his sinfully talented fingers. By the time I got home, I was so wound up that it took two rounds with my magic wand to satisfy the ache. After a pasta dinner with a glass of wine, I was positively blissed out until a knock sounded on my apartment door.

Panic launched me into action. I jumped off the couch but froze in the middle of my living room, unsure what to do. My first instinct was to go to the door and use the peephole to see who was there, but then I reminded myself that I was in pajama pants and a stained camisole—hardly an alluring wardrobe choice if my mystery man had resurfaced.

If you don't answer soon, whoever is there will leave.

Okay! I fumbled to the door and peeked at my visitor, my heart dancing its way into my throat before being doused in a cool bucket of icy suspicion. I backed away and glared silently. What the hell was going on?

"Open the door, Giada. We can see you moving around in there," Maria called out in exasperation.

I would have ignored her if I didn't think she'd break down my door just to piss me off. I liked my cousin well enough, but she was a little intense.

"What are you doing here?" I asked as I opened the door, positioning myself to bar her entry and trying to play it cool when I discovered she wasn't alone. "Who's this?"

"You remember Filip? He's Matteo's brother. Let us in; we're here to install some cameras."

Filip winked, and I tried not to get distracted.

Matteo was Maria's husband and the boss of one of the Five Families. I didn't know his family well since they hadn't been married long, but he seemed like a decent guy. He put up with Maria, so that was something. If Matteo was a Rottweiler, Filip was the puppy version—cute and playful but clearly a predator in training.

My mind raced with questions. Dad and Uncle Enzo had been tense lately—did whatever was bothering them have Matteo upping security as well? Or more likely, whatever Matteo had told Maria had caused her to crack down on surveillance. Either way, I wasn't letting them leave without answers.

"What's going on? Why would I need cameras at my apartment?" I opened the door and allowed them inside.

"Does it matter? We're going to install them whether you want them or not." She dropped a duffel bag of equipment on the coffee table and started examining the area above my front door.

"You have a stepladder?" Filip asked.

"What? Yeah, there in the hall closet." I turned back to

Maria. "What's going on? I'm not leaving you alone until you tell me what this is all about."

She dropped her head back, then spun around to glare at me. "You want to know what this is about? Fine. I had a little chat with Alessia earlier. She's worried about you, that's it."

My jaw dropped to the floor. "That *rat*. She promised she wouldn't tell anyone."

Maria just rolled her eyes. "She said you'd say that. Look, she didn't tell your dad, and I'm not planning to either even though I know I should. We're just going to install some cameras and keep an eye on things. No harm, no foul, so don't get bent out of shape."

"It's not the cameras I care about. It was my personal business she shared, and she had no right to say anything." Alessia was only trying to protect me, but I couldn't help my anger.

"If it's any consolation"—Filip set down the stepladder and smirked—"I have no clue what kind of trouble you've gotten into, although I'm seriously curious. In fact, if you want someone to keep an eye on her, Maria, I'm happy to help. This couch looks plenty comfy. I can just crash here." His eyes glinted with mischief. He was giving me a hard time, but I was *not* in the mood.

"Absolutely. Not," I ground out, crossing my arms.

Maria huffed out a laugh. "Filip, you get yourself in enough trouble of your own. I don't need you making things worse."

He shrugged impishly. "Suit yourself, but the offer stands."

"I can't believe this," I said to the ceiling. "One camera on the front door, and that's it. Do I need to worry about who'll be watching the video feed? I'm not interested in being anyone's entertainment."

"Matteo has a security team. The feed will be streamed to them, but I'll make sure only the door is in view. I'm also installing a camera in the hallway and one on the elevator. They're wireless, so it shouldn't take long."

"Fine," I grumbled. "But you can tell Al she's on my shit list." I stormed back into my bedroom and slammed the door.

SEVEN

Giada

By Tuesday morning, I was so sick of thinking about the mystery man that I wished he would show up just so I could give him a piece of my mind. He said he'd be in touch, and now it was three days later without a word. Had he changed his mind and left town? I wouldn't have expected a normal guy to necessarily text right away, but the uncertain nature of the situation made me more on edge about hearing from him.

I spent the morning doing yoga to help calm me down. Alessia ran and Maria was kick-ass at martial arts, but I was a little more zen with my exercise. I'd been doing yoga since my teens—one of the few suggestions from my mother that had actually paid off. Not only was it a great workout but I always felt more centered after a sweaty session of hot yoga.

From there, I had lunch with a friend, then went home to clean up before making the drive out to my parents' house for our weekly family dinner. I hadn't wanted to sit around in my apartment thinking, so I arrived at the house early. Mom was still at a church committee meeting, but I found Lucy in the kitchen working on dinner. She was mostly a housekeeper but cooked for Mom occasionally.

"Hey, Lucy! What's on the menu for tonight?" I gave the sweet older woman a hug and peeked into her simmering pot.

"You're here early, mija. What a lovely surprise. You can help me clean up." She grinned impishly. "I made Sopa de albondigas—meatball soup. The hard part's done; it just has to cook now." Lucy was friendly with everyone, but she took a special liking to me. I was pretty sure it was because I was the shortest person in the family and, therefore, the only one who didn't tower over her four-foot-ten frame. She'd only come to work for my parents three years ago, not long after I'd moved out, but she quickly came to feel like part of the family.

"I have nothing better to do, so I'm happy to help." I collected a cutting board full of chopped remnants and swept them into the sink. "I hope you didn't put too many peppers in those meatballs. You know how picky Dad can be about spicey things." Lucy was Hispanic, so it had been tricky to find dishes she made that Dad would eat.

"I don't think so, but sometimes a spicy one sneaks in there. I'll just have to hope he's in a good mood." She winked at me and started scrubbing the dishes in the sink. "You look extra pretty today, mija. Is there anything special going on?" The older woman glanced at me coyly, making me chuckle. She was always asking about my love life, telling me I needed to find a good man and settle down.

"Absolutely nothing, just felt like getting dolled up." There may have been a little purpose in my *Cosmo* hair and makeup. I might not have seen my mystery man by the end of the day, but I liked knowing that if he did appear, he'd get a taste of what he'd been missing.

"Tú mama will be home soon."

I only grunted in return.

"What? Did you two have a fight?" She paused her scrubbing and peered over at me.

"No, just the usual. We make each other a little crazy."

"Ah." She nodded. "That's the way it's supposed to be. It encourages young people to go out and get lives of their own. If we were all content to stay with our parents, we'd never leave. I never had kids of my own, but I know my sister and her daughter fought like cats until her daughter finally moved out. Then once they had their own space, things got better."

"Well, I moved out years ago. It helped a little, but she still can't help telling me what to do."

"She just wants you to be happy."

"I *am* happy. Or at least, I would be if she'd leave me alone."

Lucy rinsed out the empty sink and took off her apron before looking at me sadly. "Are you? Do you truly believe you're happy, mija?"

Suddenly everyone had an opinion about my life. What was the deal?

I dropped onto a counter barstool and sighed. "I don't know, Lucy, but her meddling definitely doesn't help."

"It will get better, trust me. One day soon, you're going to figure out what you want from your life, and everything will change." She smiled warmly and came over to pat my arm.

"From your lips to God's ears."

Lucy yipped and chuckled while crossing herself, making me giggle.

After dinner with my family, I made the hour drive back home to my quiet apartment. I mulled over what Lucy had said and the fact that both she and Alessia suggested I should make some changes. I was somber by the time I got home and ready to lose myself in some mindless television and binge eat my weight in ice cream. However, before I even had a chance to change into comfy clothes, a knock sounded on the front door.

If Maria wants to install more damn cameras, she's got another thing coming.

I charged to the door and flung it open only to find *him* waiting on the other side. My mystery man. He wore a dress shirt, the cuffs folded back, and his hands resting casually in the pockets of his navy slacks. He was ruthlessly handsome, annihilating a woman's senses with his masculine grace. His hair was combed back but not in an overly harsh manner. Just like before, he looked deceptively casual—calm and relaxed in a way a leopard might appear right before it pounced.

His quicksilver eyes watched me with unnerving patience as I took him in. Defined cheekbones, perfect nose, and full lips all came together to form a vision of unnatural beauty. He was spellbinding, and the shock of seeing him stole my breath. Seized my lungs and summoned an inky blackness at the edges of my vision.

"You're here," I breathed. The sound of my voice cleared the fog from my brain, allowing me to recall how annoyed I'd been for the past two days. Regaining my composure, I crossed my arms over my chest and took a calming breath. "I wasn't sure I would hear from you again."

His chin lifted infinitesimally. "I said I'd be in touch."

"That was three days ago. I figured you'd changed your mind."

His lips curved into an icy, feral grin. "Impatient," he tsked as if to himself. "I had work to attend to."

"It's fine. You don't owe me an explanation. I'm just surprised you're here." I waved my hand in the air nonchalantly, but I wasn't fooling anyone.

He stepped forward, one small but purposeful step at a time until he invaded my personal space, forcing me to retreat backward into my apartment. He swung the door shut behind him, his gaze never leaving mine. The blistering heat in his eyes held me captive. Commanded me with delicious coercion like the sweet melody of a snake charmer's flute.

He lowered his face, bringing us within a breath of each other. "I'm here now."

"And that means I'm supposed to drop everything?"

His eyes cut to the side, lips quirking up. "You don't exactly seem busy."

Ugh! Men. That wasn't the point.

I re-crossed my arms. "Maybe you're just not very perceptive."

He grabbed my wrists and wrenched my body against his. "Fuck, that mouth makes me crazy." He slammed his lips down on mine, pressing inside me with unrestrained savagery.

Lust, raw and demanding, dug its claws into me, addling my brain and melting my resolve. I'd been struck by lightning, a bolt of heady pleasure firing straight between my legs and pooling in my belly. His hands dug into my waist, holding me immobile and recklessly affected. A supple piece of clay to be molded by an erotic artist. He was a god of seduction. How did this man wield such power over me?

"Wait ... wait." I panted helplessly, fighting to think

clearly. "I shouldn't be doing this. I don't even know your name." I shook my head, eyes on his chest so I didn't fall victim to his hypnotic stare.

He leaned in, using his tongue to trace the line of my upper lip. "My name is Primo, and I've been waiting for this for three days. No more stalling." Deep, predatory, and unapologetically lustful, his voice purred across my skin.

I was lost. A paper boat drifting on his sinful ocean of promised pleasure. It was only a matter of time before I sank beneath those dark depths. I surrendered any hope of survival. I needed his turbulent waves more than I needed to breathe.

Primo lifted me in his arms, wrapping my legs around his waist, and devoured me in a kiss. He carried me effortlessly to the bedroom, leaving the lights off so the ambient glow of the city was the only illumination.

I worked at the buttons on his shirt as he walked, resting my palms against the hard plains of his chest beneath. His skin was warm and smooth, hair-free and taut over sculpted muscle. The feel of him sent another greedy command whispering darkly through my core.

This man made my body respond as no other man had before him. Just his presence sent a sledgehammer of sensation rocketing through me, rendering me mute and dumb. A mindless creature consumed with only one thing … him.

I wasn't in the habit of giving men that power over me, but with Primo, there was no choice. The pull between us was greater than logic or rational thought. I didn't think I could say no to him if I wanted to.

Everything about it was dangerous. Irresponsible. Maddening.

And so very right.

Primo set me down gently, then wrenched my shirt up

and over my head. I pulled his button-down out of his pants just before he ripped the remaining buttons off and dropped the shirt to the floor without a second thought. We raced to rid ourselves of our clothes, each taking in an eyeful of the other in the dim glow of the bedroom.

When nothing was left between us, he bent down and slowly pulled his leather belt through the loops of his discarded slacks. A fissure of fear skated down my spine, cinching my nipples into rock hard pebbles.

"Give me your hands." His coarse, devastatingly deep voice caused a relay of electricity to light up my nerve endings.

The intoxicating nature of his command made me want to comply, but my questioning nature gave me pause. I hadn't exactly been safe with him in that storage closet in the club, but I felt even more vulnerable isolated here in my apartment. He'd told me he didn't hurt women, but words meant nothing when they came from a stranger, especially one who might be a stalker. Allowing him in my apartment and letting him strip me was as far as my trust would go, and that was more than most women would have given him.

I shook my head. "No. I can't … I'm not ready for that."

He didn't argue, tossing the belt back onto his pile of clothes. "On the bed, clasp your hands together and raise them above your head."

I did as I was told this time, crawling onto the bed and reveling in the feel of his hungry eyes on my backside. I rolled over onto my back, entwining my fingers and lifting my hands above my head before soaking in the vision of him towering over me.

His body was masculine perfection, all hard angles and rigid contours honed for conquering. And his cock, sweet Mother Mary, his cock was a gorgeous specimen of male arousal. Thick and lined with angry veins, his erection pointed heavily toward me as if pulling its master in my direction.

He prowled toward me on the bed, nipping at my flesh and grazing his teeth along my most sensitive areas. "This shouldn't be happening," he murmured. "I told myself not to come here, but you're like a fucking drug. Getting inside you is all I can think about." He pressed back on his knees, then spread my legs wide, holding my gaze for a pregnant moment before dropping his eyes to drink in the sight of me. "I have to get a taste … just one taste," he breathed before diving in to lap at my slit.

I arched against his irresistible mouth. Moaned at the stampede of pleasure coursing out to my farthest extremities. He didn't just taste me; he devoured me. Licked and sucked and teased until nothing remained of my sanity. And just before I slipped into an abyss of pleasure, he pulled away.

"Oh, *God*. Please, I need more," I whimpered.

Primo ignored my plea, coming closer to place two pillows behind my head and neck. Once he had me positioned to his liking, he moved up my body, his knees on either side of me, and his throbbing cock nearing my face. He placed his thumb on my lower lip, slowly swiping along its surface. "I know you use that sharp mouth of yours as a weapon, but let's see how sweet it can be." He leaned in, the scalding tip of his cock bouncing against my bottom lip, commanding entry.

I was only too happy to oblige. To taste his masculine essence and feel the thick ridges of his veins glide against my tongue. I devoured as much of his hard length into my mouth as my position beneath him would allow.

Something was irrepressibly erotic about the vulnerability of my position. Knowing I was helpless beneath him, I sensed the voracious intensity of his restrained hunger. His painfully careful movements, rocking himself inside my mouth without choking or scaring me, spun the delicate fibers of trust. It was empowering. Elating. I felt precious and coveted. Wanton and ravenous.

"Christo, viborita." The words were wrenched from him, shaky and unbidden.

I wanted to see him come apart at my ministrations, but it wasn't to be. He pulled away and grabbed a foil packet from where he'd tossed it on the bed. I watched raptly as Primo tore the wrapper from a condom and rolled the rubber sleeve over his shaft. He then lowered himself, his breathing shuddering as our bodies aligned. His jaw flexed and rippled with restraint, eyes sparking with electric need.

He lowered his lips to my nipple, tugging at the taut peak, then soothing the sting with his tongue and repeating the delicious torture on the other side until I writhed beneath him. While I was lost in the sensation, he surged inside me, catching me unaware and stealing the air from my lungs.

I gasped, and he moaned, our bodies moving in sync as we both arched into one another. A rhythm developed, our bodies moving in perfect harmony as if we were two parts of a whole. The room filled with the sounds of pounding flesh and heaving breaths.

Before I knew it, my body hummed with a chaotic energy threatening to overpower me. It built between my legs, spreading up into my stomach and reaching out to the tips of my fingers. It sizzled and sparked until it caught fire and incinerated within me. My body shattered into millions of tiny pieces, transforming me into sharp points of brilliant white light.

Primo roared his release, rocking into me one final time and dropping down on top of me. I was too ruined to worry about his weight on me. I was lifeless and limp, without a care in the world. Fortunately, he eased to the side seconds later, and I sucked in a deep, rejuvenating breath.

Way to stay strong and demand answers, G. You sure showed him.

What the hell had I just done? I was insanely attracted to Primo, and I didn't want my father to kill him, but I also shouldn't have screwed the man. Not yet, anyway. Not before I had some answers.

"How did you figure out who I was and track me down?"

Primo slowly rolled onto his back beside me. He let the question linger as we both stared at the ceiling. "I confirmed you were staying at that hotel. The rest was simply a matter of money. You can accomplish anything with the right amount of money."

"You know this isn't normal, right? That guys don't normally track down girls like that?"

He turned his head toward me, his eyes catching mine. "*I'm* not normal."

What did that mean? A jittery sense of trepidation pricked down my arms and legs.

"Should I be scared of you?" I asked in a whisper, the words catching in my throat for fear of the answer.

His eyes darkened in shadow. "Absolutely."

EIGHT

Primo

Giada's face grew wary. She was looking for reassurance I couldn't give. I couldn't tell her she was safe with me because she wasn't. Not entirely. I was a danger to her, whether I wanted to be or not.

"What does that mean? I need to know what's going on here." Courage. She possessed such strength and courage. It was good because she would need it.

"I can't give you the answers you're looking for." Frustration ignited a nervous energy inside me. I rose from the bed and went to discard the condom in the bathroom.

Coming here was a fucking mistake, and I'd known it even before I arrived at her building. I'd tried to stay away. I'd told her I'd been working during those three days, but that was a lie. I hadn't contacted her because I'd never be able to have her and let her go. It was best for everyone if we didn't go down that path. But the longer I stayed away, the more insistent the craving. I'd been nearly feral with the need to see her by the time I arrived at her door.

Now that I'd been inside her, there was no turning back.

But what did that mean? I had a job to do and a life that didn't have room for a woman. I needed time to consider my options, but that was one luxury I didn't possess. I would have to return home in a matter of days, and I was growing more convinced that I couldn't leave her behind. Taking her with me would be dangerous and beyond stupid. She might even hate me for it. Yet the compulsion in me insisted it was the only way.

I walked back to the bedroom and dressed. "I need to finish up some business while I'm in town."

"When will you go back home?"

"A few days."

"Will I see you before you leave?" Though her words were straightforward, the vulnerability in her voice drew my attention. I hadn't known her long, but it didn't take a genius to know it wasn't like her to show a softer side. To peel back those protective layers and allow an outsider to see what was beneath. It was a gift of trust, and though it was sorely misplaced, I consumed it greedily.

Stepping over to the bed, I sat on the edge next to where she lay on her side, now draped in a white sheet. "I'll come to you before I go, one way or another." I trailed my knuckles down the smooth slope of her arm, unable to keep from touching her, then picked up her phone from the nightstand. "Open it."

She took the device from my hand and unlocked it, then handed it back. After keying in my phone number, I sent myself a text. "Now you have my number. Text me if you need me. Otherwise, I'll come to you when I can."

"What if I don't want you to leave?"

I stilled. "Don't ask that question with such longing in your voice. You won't be happy with the result."

"Are you sure?"

I met her gaze, mossy green in the dimly lit room. "I've never been more *un*sure of anything in my life."

An hour later, I could still smell Giada on my skin as I walked into the home of my boss's brother. Juan Carlos was twenty years younger than Naz, but no less powerful. If anything, his youth and convincing portrayal of a family man made him even more dangerous because he was easy to underestimate. He was known to most as El Tigre, and his kill tally rivaled my own.

He'd never been my biggest fan, and I daydreamed ways to put him in the ground. Naz figured out early on that it was best if Juan Carlos and I didn't work together often. Unfortunately, my trip to New York made seeing him a necessity. This was the first time I was meeting him at his home.

I wasn't surprised to find it was a small fortress. Juan Carlos liked to make a statement, and though he was supposed to be flying under the radar, he had still acquired an impressive home as his base of operations. The perimeter of the property was lined with a stone wall, and while there was no gated entry, a guard met me at the front of the house.

When guests arrived at the home, they were greeted with a Greco-Roman fountain and two gargantuan stone columns flanking the front entry. The place was easily twenty thousand square feet inside, if not more. I had a good size home of my own but saw no need to possess rooms I'd never use. It was just one of the many ways Juan Carlos and I would never see eye to eye.

"Señor Vargas is in his office, Señor Primo. Please, follow me." The front door guard nodded respectfully and led me back to his boss. As we approached, Vargas's daughter rushed from the office, hands balled at her sides and eyes glassy with unshed tears. She nearly walked straight into us before she pulled up short in surprise.

"Oh, excuse me," the young woman gasped, then ducked her head and scurried past us.

I didn't imagine living with Juan Carlos as a father was a pleasant experience. I may not have had a stellar childhood, but there was a definite possibility hers was worse. It was unfortunate, but not my business.

"Primo, I was expecting you days ago. Where have you been?" Vargas asked when I passed through the threshold of his office.

"I've been looking into a few matters for Naz." As I spoke, I took in the grand executive office lined with mahogany bookshelves and designed to emphasize the importance of its primary occupant. Like the rest of the house, it was ostentatious for my tastes, but it suited Vargas.

"The Russians? I told him I would handle that. With a little more time, I can get them to back off."

"Naz has determined that course of action is no longer an option. I'm here to carry out the backup plan."

"What backup plan?" he bit out, jaw clenched.

I trained my eyes back on Vargas, keeping my features schooled. "If Naz hasn't told you, it's not my place to do so. We only have a couple more weeks until that shipment comes in, and we can't afford to waste any more time. Naz has come up with a new plan to gain access to a port. If you want to know the details, you're free to ask him." I would not come between the brothers any more than I already had. Naz knew that Juan Carlos's dislike for me could lead to him interfering with my efforts, endangering my success. The internal discord in our management was a problem but not my place to fix. Naz needed to keep his brother in check, but instead, he often looked the other way and avoided dealing with his ambitious sibling.

Juan Carlos's face darkened with a crimson rage, a vein visibly bulging on his forehead. "That's fucking bullshit."

"It's a fucking ten-*million*-dollar deal and the start of a new trade relationship. That's not *bullshit.* Potentially hundreds of millions are on the line here, and you don't get to fuck it up by insisting on doing things your way." I usually kept my cool when I dealt with Juan Carlos, but I found myself lacking patience and straining to keep my fists from balling.

"Then why are you here if I'm to be kept in the dark?" he sneered.

"Aside from informing you to cease your efforts with the Russians, I came to give you a heads-up. Two possible scenarios could unfold. One of them, should it transpire, would require your assistance."

He tipped his head back, his lips blossoming into a satisfied grin. "I see. So, you might need my help, but I'm not permitted to know with what."

I raised my hands with a shrug. "It is what it is. I don't make the rules."

In a flash, his sneer was back. "You have my fucking number. Maybe I'll be available when you call." He turned his back on me, returning to his desk chair in a show of dismissal. For one of the most feared men in our business, he could act like an overgrown child.

I couldn't help smirking from the satisfaction of being the source of his tantrum. It was time to leave before matters devolved further. As I turned to exit, something on one of his shelves caught my attention. I froze, examining the delicate features of an object I knew well. A small statue of the Lady of Guadalupe. I walked to the place where she humbly stood, arms outstretched in welcome.

"What are you doing?" Vargas barked, but I was too stunned to reply.

I picked up the figurine, only about four inches tall, and turned it over in my hands, studying every tiny detail. In particular, I stared at the three broken prongs of light radiating from her left side. All the other prongs surrounding her were intact, but those three had been cut in half.

"Did you go to see her?" I asked.

"No, I never made it there," he answered warily, unsure of my intent.

"Seems odd to have a souvenir if you never went."

"That's because it's a souvenir but not from the holy site."

I nodded, eyes never leaving the figurine. "My mother took me when I was young, and we bought a statue just like this while we were there. Two years later, I accidentally knocked it over and broke off three of the rays, just like this one." Finally, I lifted my steely gaze and glared at him.

Vargas's eyes narrowed as if he were suddenly seeing me for the first time. "I can't believe it," he murmured. "I always wondered why my brother took in a rat off the street, but now it makes sense."

"What are you talking about?" My stomach clenched with unease, sensing I would not like what he had to say next.

"You're his son."

"Nazario?"

"No—Alvarez."

"The dead cartel leader? I wasn't his son—I grew up dirt poor, not living in some mansion." I was so confused about how he could possibly jump to such a conclusion.

He shook his head. "But you did, didn't you? You lived in an enormous house, just not on the main floor. Alvarez was with a woman when I killed him. I wondered what he'd been doing there in the servant's quarters, but I figured he was simply talking to the staff. That wasn't it at all, was it? That woman was your mother. I took the statue from her room to remind me of our accomplishments that day."

I racked my brain, trying to remember what I could about those early years of my life. My mother had worked for a rich man, but I was a child and had paid little attention to the man. Everyone called him El Jefe, or boss, inside the house. Later, it had never occurred to question who my mother's boss had been. I lost that life, spending two years on the streets after her death and quickly leaving every vestige of my childhood behind.

What Juan Carlos claimed was possible, but I couldn't wrap my mind around it. Disbelief and denial clouded my vision. I refused to accept that Naz had been responsible for my mother's death. I'd viewed him as my savior for so long. My foster father. How could the one person who gave me hope during my darkest hours be the same man responsible for my greatest grief? It was too much to comprehend.

"You're fair, just like him. Did you ever question why you looked so unlike your mother?"

I shook my head absently. "There's plenty of non-native people living in Mexico. That didn't mean Alvarez was my father."

"No, but it makes sense, and somehow, Naz figured that out. That's why he brought you home with him."

I slammed the figurine back on the shelf as if it had stung

me, then stepped away from the offending object, overcome with emotion. I couldn't breathe. As though the walls were closing in around me, and if I didn't lash out, I'd never survive. I had to get out of there before I did something I would regret.

"I believe we're done here." My words were clipped, strained with my effort to maintain control. I didn't wait for him to respond. I stormed out of the house and tore off in my car at speeds only rivaled by my racing heart.

NINE

Giada

I wasn't sure I'd be able to sleep when Primo left, but between my relief at seeing him again and being sex drunk from the orgasm of a lifetime, I passed out cold within minutes of his departure. I woke the next morning deliciously sore in all the right places. My mouth spread in a feline grin as I recalled the events of the night before in glorious detail.

My mystery man had a name, *and* I had his phone number.

Whatever it was that was growing between us wasn't over. It was just beginning.

Primo may not live near me, but plenty of people managed long-distance relationships. I would get to see him before he went back home, and who knew where things would go from there. The world was suddenly my oyster, full of possibilities.

I rose from my bed with renewed energy and purpose. Normally, it took at least two cups of coffee to summon that kind of enthusiasm first thing in the morning. Yet today felt different. Like a new beginning.

What better way to start an adventure than with yoga? No matter where my life took me, yoga would always be a part of my routine. I threw on my workout clothes and got ready for my day, including brewing a cup of coffee because my need for the dark brew would not be diminished by any amount of natural vivacity.

I was bringing a mug to my lips for that first delectable sip when someone pounded on my front door.

Did security at the front desk not stop anyone from coming up?

I mean, really. It was freaking Grand Central Station around here.

I couldn't imagine Primo had come back already. The only other person who paid me unexpected visits was Alessia, but she didn't tend to break down my door when she knocked. I readied myself for whoever I'd encounter on the other side and opened the door.

Maria stood in the hallway, swathed in a cloak of indignant fury. "Do you have any idea what the *fuck* you've gotten yourself into?" She stormed forward, forcing me aside.

"What the hell are you talking about?" I closed the door behind her and tried to tamp down the surging sense of unease churning in my stomach.

She set down her purse on my kitchen counter and fished out a stack of photographs, handing them to me. "I'm talking about *him*. The man you picked up in Vegas is the sicario Matteo hired to find Sal."

I glanced at the still shots of Primo entering my apartment, taken from the security cameras Maria had installed. "You *know* him?"

"I only saw him briefly when we went to finish Sal. He's a sicario, Giada. Do you know what that means?"

"Like Benicio del Toro in that movie? Aren't they Columbian or something?"

Maria rolled her eyes. "That may have been where the term originated, but it means he's a cartel hitman. He works for the Sonora Cartel, the largest and most ruthless trafficking organization in America."

"Wait. You said Matteo hired him?"

"I'm not sure exactly what their past is, but yes. Matteo knew him somehow and had him help us find Sal down in Vegas. That's how we were finally able to finish him."

Sal had worked as Uncle Enzo's underboss, which I only discovered when I learned about the mafia. They'd been childhood friends, but their connection went far deeper. Sal turned on my uncle, and shit hit the fan until Maria and her now husband, Matteo, went to Vegas to put an end to Sal.

Maria was telling me Primo was a cartel hitman? I wanted to argue there was no way, but that would have been a big fat lie. Primo seemed every bit the criminal, and I had just ignored that minor detail.

"I have no clue how you got in with him"—Maria cut into my thoughts—"but you need to walk away and fast. That man is dangerous."

"Yeah, but isn't that the world we live in? Isn't Matteo dangerous? And what about our fathers? You can't tell me their hands are clean. How is Primo any different?"

Maria snatched the photos from my hand and shoved them back in her purse. "I'm not arguing with you about this. You can take it up with our fathers." She opened her phone and began to dial.

"You can't tell them!" I hissed.

"Fuck that. If you think I'm keeping quiet about this, you're deranged." Her eyes darted away as her call was answered by a masculine voice. "I've got a situation. Can you and Uncle Edoardo meet me in an hour at the house? I appreciate it ... see you then." She lowered the phone and glared at me. "Come on, we're leaving."

"A fucking sicario? Jesus, Giada. Your mother warned me you would end up in trouble, but I didn't think you'd find yourself this deep." My father massaged his forehead and paced along the wall of Uncle Enzo's office.

The force of his words was a punch straight to my gut. I wasn't sure what was worse—the disappointment in my father's voice or having him berate me in front of others. Uncle Enzo, Maria, and Matteo all eyed me in varying degrees of wariness and irritation. I told myself they were all just trying to protect me, but I felt as though I was being attacked, which made me defensive and angry.

"Every one of you is a giant hypocrite, pointing fingers at Primo like he's some monster because he's in organized crime. Are you too high and mighty to see that you're just the same?"

"He's a part of a cartel, Giada," Uncle Enzo cut in before my red-faced father could lash out. "Those men are not like us, despite what you might want to believe. They have no code or honor among them. Their world is cutthroat—kill or be killed. They are savages. I can't speak to this man, in particular, but any association with that world is dangerous. That's why we're concerned. We got word a while back that the cartels were moving in on the East Coast. Recently, they had trouble with the Russians, but we haven't had any direct encounters with them. We knew they would show up eventually, but we've had no cause to act so far. I believe this could be their first move on us."

"And that's precisely why they're so much worse than us," my father spat. "Going after women and children."

"It's not like that," I hurried to explain. "We met in Vegas, and he didn't even know who I was."

Dad huffed, and Maria rolled her eyes, but it was Matteo that spoke up.

"I'm not sure you grasp what the cartels are capable of. No one here is claiming to be innocent. However, our organizations and actions are a far cry from the depravity that has unfolded in Mexico, where the government has lost control over crime lords. Public executions, slaughtering pregnant women, trafficking children and women into the sex trade, even bombing public places. They are the worst kind of terrorists, preying on their own people, and there is no one to stop them down there. They have absolute authority and no conscience whatsoever. We are businessmen, though more ruthless than most, but they are tyrants."

An unsettling chill permeated deep into my bones. Hearing Matteo give a calm, impartial analysis of the cartels put their concerns in a different light. He wasn't an overreacting father or an uncle looking to keep me in line with exaggerated threats. I hardly knew him, so my death would mean little more to him than a funeral and consoling a mildly upset wife. He had no reason to lie. His explanation held a resounding note of truth, and I worried Primo posed far more danger than I'd imagined.

He told me straight out that I should fear him. Maybe I needed to heed that warning. But if he'd wanted to hurt me, he could easily have done that already. Although, Matteo implied that any association with the cartels was dangerous. The threat wasn't just Primo.

I didn't know what to say. It was entirely possible I'd gotten myself in worse trouble than I realized.

Uncle Enzo filled the silence. "We don't know what this man wants or what is going on yet, so until he's left town and things settle, I want guards on the women of this family. We can communicate the threat to the capos and see what more we can learn on the streets."

"What does that mean? Am I going to be on lockdown or something?"

"Not exactly, but I don't want you leaving your apartment unless it's necessary. If you do, we'll need to get someone to escort you. I don't want you out unprotected." Enzo raised an eyebrow in warning.

"I'm not trying to be difficult, I swear, but I can't just stay in my apartment indefinitely. I have a nail appointment tomorrow, and I'll have to get out occasionally just to stay sane."

"Enzo," Matteo interjected, "unless you have someone in mind, I'm happy to volunteer my brother, Filip. I believe he's already met Giada and is familiar with the situation."

Uncle Enzo nodded. "If you can spare him for a while, that would be a great help. Giada, we won't ask anything oppressive of you, but I expect you to work with Maria and Filip while we sort this out. Will that be a problem?"

My heart ached with a crushing disappointment that my sordid affair wasn't to be all that I'd hoped. I felt an inexplicably strong connection with Primo, and I bitterly regretted not getting to explore where that might take us. I told myself it was best to end things if he was truly a part of something so horrific as Matteo described, but it was still hard to process that the man I'd met could be so evil.

"It's not a problem, Uncle Enzo. I'll make sure to be safe." My voice sounded weak and brittle to my ears, and I hated it. I didn't want to be a wounded butterfly in need of saving. Yet that was where I stood, and it was all my fault. Leave it to me to fall for a criminal so dangerous that even my outlaw family didn't approve.

Maria drove me back to the city, but neither of us said a word. I thought about everything we'd discussed in Enzo's office. They believed Primo had targeted me, but they didn't know the truth. I'm the one who had targeted *him*. He had only hunted me down because I stole from him. His involvement in the cartel was merely circumstantial, but I couldn't tell them that. Explaining how I'd stolen the lighter would be even more degrading than watching them all scowl at me for simply knowing Primo.

He may be part of something dangerous, but he wasn't nearly as conniving as they would believe. He had only responded to the situation I had created. Was there a way for me to get that point across without telling them all the sordid details? If there was, the solution escaped me.

I didn't want to be the family fuckup, but it also killed me to think of not seeing him again. Aside from having the most incredible sex of my life, being with Primo made me feel alive. It was as though I'd been stuck in a holding cell all this time, waiting for my fate to be decided. Seeing him was that verdict I'd been waiting for, but instead of setting me free, it looked like I'd be locked up indefinitely.

My thoughts and feelings were a chaotic jumble. I tried to convince myself I hardly knew the man and couldn't possibly miss him, but cutting ties with him felt like losing a part of myself. The part that would help me realize my identity. Help me find my place in the world.

Equal parts heartbreak and anger caused tears to cloud my vision.

Never in a million years would I admit I needed a man to complete me. To make me happy. So why was I falling into that trap now? Yes, I was overwhelmingly attracted to Primo, but I didn't *need* him. I was a strong, independent woman who didn't need any man—especially one who could be dangerous to my family or me. It would be selfish to put the people I loved at risk so I could have a relationship. There were plenty other men out there. I needed to stop acting like a child.

I wiped my eyes, hoping Maria didn't notice, then took out my phone. Scrolling to Primo's name in my contacts, I typed out a message with trembling fingers.

This isn't going to work. Please stay away from me.

I hit send and tried not to panic.

None of my family knew I had his number, and I wasn't going to tell. The fact that I'd ended it was all that mattered. Seeing him in my contacts was the one vestige of him I got to keep for myself. That, and his silver lighter would be all I'd have to remind me of the man who lit my soul on fire.

TEN

Primo

I SPENT THE AFTERNOON CONTEMPLATING WHAT JUAN CARLOS had asserted about my past. It made sense, no matter how hard it was to admit. My father had been right there in the same house as me, and I'd never known. My mother hid it well. Although, I'd been a child and likely wouldn't have picked up on changes in her behavior when he was around.

What had their relationship been like? I was certain it had to have been consensual. She talked about her boss highly, even in private. It made me wonder if he cared about her. He'd been married with a family, so he couldn't acknowledge an affair with one of his staff, but he also didn't send her away. We were always lucky enough to have money for a car and other treats when others who worked at the house couldn't afford such luxuries. As a kid, I never questioned it, but now, I wondered if Alvarez didn't provide for us beyond my mother's wages.

I'd been told my father was a soldier and had died near the time of my birth. A convenient story, yet so unlike my mother. She was a devout Catholic. My conception and the resulting lies must have weighed on her terribly. Perhaps enough to make a pilgrimage across the country to seek forgiveness at the feet of the Lady of Guadalupe.

It was amazing how one bit of new information changed your perspective on everything. My mother's memory was the one thing that remained unblemished. Her lie was never meant to hurt me. She could never have known things would end for her the way they had. She was one of those gentle spirits who couldn't have hurt someone if her life depended on it, and Naz had killed her. She'd been nothing more than collateral damage.

The day she died, I came home from school to find the estate in flames, surrounded by the local police. I raced through the crowd calling for my mother until the cook spotted me and held me firmly in her arms. She'd been at the market when it happened. As far as she could tell, no one in the house had made it out alive.

I wept inconsolably. She tried to comfort me, but life as I knew it was over. I may have only been ten, but I'd heard stories about the corrupt homes that children were sent to when their parents died. I refused to accept that fate. As the tornadic flames whirled and danced, greedily consuming my childhood, I gathered my courage. When only crackling embers and smoke remained, I slipped away from the authorities and started my life on the streets.

For two years, I fought for my survival every day. It

wasn't pretty, especially at first, but I learned quickly and was resourceful. When Naz found me, I was entrenched in an illegal fight club where I brawled with other teens for money. I was savage. Brutal. Making money and earning respect from some of the toughest men in the business.

The day he came to the warehouse, men who I saw as kings began to whisper and sweat. Someone explained how Nazario Vargas, or El Zar as they called him, was the boss of bosses—more powerful than any man I'd known.

He was drawn to me almost immediately, asking me questions and wanting to see me fight. I assumed he was interested in my skill and the chance to bring in young talent and train me to his liking. I believed what I wanted to believe because it was easier than questioning his motives. I wanted to go with him and breathe easily for a change. Life with Naz promised to be far superior to what I'd had on the streets.

Now that I was finally analyzing the truth of what had happened, his motives were opaque at best. Most men at his stage in life didn't adopt kids off the street out of the kindness of their hearts. Was it his way of twisting the blade into my father's back even further? Or was he attempting to ensure I never tried to reclaim my father's throne?

Did it matter either way?

The past couldn't be changed. He'd equipped me to succeed in life and made me a wealthy man at a young age. There was no way to guess where my life would be had my mother not been killed or had Naz not rescued me from the streets. A game of what-ifs was always a losing battle.

I needed to focus on work before my emotions carried me away and I did something I'd regret. It was probably time to check in with Santino and make sure all was well back home. He was my right-hand and one of the only people I trusted with my life. When I had to leave town, he was my eyes and ears back home.

I took out my phone and realized I'd missed a text from Giada an hour earlier. I'd been too wrapped up in my thoughts to remember I'd silenced my phone.

This isn't going to work. Please stay away from me.

The text wasn't entirely unexpected, but my already turbulent emotions magnified my response. My veins coursed with undiluted hostility at whoever had frightened her away. I'd seen the cameras at her place and knew there was a chance her family would figure out who I was. The message had to have resulted from their interference.

Perhaps they didn't know who I was but had interfered anyway. The only person who could have identified me was Matteo De Luca, as far as I knew, and he was a part of a separate mafia family. We had believed the families were highly independent of one another, but they might share more information than we anticipated.

I began to regret leaving the cameras functional, but I'd done it for two reasons. The first being the chance of identification was so slim. The second was a byproduct of my own weakness. The pathetic part of me that had hoped they'd discover me and force sense into her.

I wanted to grab that part of me by the throat and rip out its jugular.

It took several calming breaths before the chaos in my mind settled. I needed to see things logically. Rationally. I needed to take her withdrawal as a sign and move forward with the plan without deviation, leaving Giada in peace. However, the selfish, vile part of me that knew no mercy reared and bucked against its bridle. He wanted Giada, regardless of the consequences. That cancerous voice inside me whispered seductively that I could keep her safe—that she wanted me, regardless of what her family may have told her.

It should have been her choice to make, not theirs.

I teetered on a precipice. A knife's edge between redemption and damnation—walk away and save her or drag her down with me on my hellish descent.

I had no pictures of my mother, so her image had faded in my mind's eye. Sometimes, I intentionally pushed aside thoughts of her so she wouldn't know the wretched things I'd done. But other times—times like these—her presence was too hard to fight off. Her memory reminded me how the underworld I now called my own had been the cause of her untimely death.

I didn't want that for Giada.

But isn't life about free will? The mutinous voice of self-interest hissed inside my head. *Shouldn't it be Giada's choice and not yours or her family's?*

Fuck. It was hard to argue with that logic, which presented a third option to consider. I could go to Giada one last time and see if walking away was truly her choice.

The soulless creature that lived in the darkest parts of me leaped at the opportunity. One more chance to touch her. To taste her.

I told myself it was best to leave it up to her because I didn't want to admit the truth. I was too weak to do the right thing. To walk away and never contact her again.

No matter the warnings, I would seek her out and let her decide both our fates.

The next day, she had a guard with her when she left her apartment. I followed them to a nail salon and observed through the plate glass windows as her escort stationed himself in the front waiting area. I walked around to the back of the building, locating a rear entry and finding a man outside smoking with the salon door propped open. I didn't give him time to make a sound. With practiced speed, I looped my arm around his throat and held him in a chokehold until he passed out. He'd be fine when he woke up, and I'd be long gone.

Slipping inside the salon, I navigated my way to the pedicure stations where Giada sat alone, her feet in a small tub of water and eyes glued to her phone. She was cut off from view of the front entry by a half wall and decorative beads strung from the ceiling. The chair next to her was unoccupied, so I walked over as if I belonged there and took a seat.

"I didn't think you were the type to let others dictate your life."

She gasped and nearly dropped her phone into the tub of water. "You're here." Her eyes were wide with shock, and I detected an undercurrent of relief in her whispered response. Had I imagined it? Or was she truly pleased to see me?

"I told you I'd come before I left town. At the time, that didn't seem to be a problem." My eyes cut over to the front of the salon where her escort waited for her.

"You shouldn't be here," she hissed, growing more agitated. "My family knows who you are, and they'll hurt you if they find you here."

"I'm not worried about them."

"Well, I am. I'm worried about everything. They told me you're a part of a cartel. I don't want me or my family to be in danger."

Exactly as I'd suspected. Her text had nothing to do with her feelings for me and everything to do with the garbage her family had fed her. As if they were saints. Bullshit.

"Have I hurt you in any way?" I demanded.

A crease formed between her brows. "No, but that doesn't mean you aren't a danger to me." Her statement was fraught with uncertainty. I was gaining ground.

"If you truly believed I was dangerous, you never would have let me touch you. I gave you opportunities to walk away, but you didn't. You wanted me just as much as I wanted you. Your family's prejudices shouldn't get in the way of that."

"You warned me away yourself. I can't just ignore that." She shook her head, chewing on her bottom lip.

I pulled back and allowed a curtain of frigid air to fall between us. I should have let her pull away—accepted her retreat and moved on with my original plan—but I couldn't. I had to make one last effort to convince her not to run.

"The woman who approached me in the casino and who came on my fingers in a nightclub closet wouldn't let anyone tell her what she wanted or who she could see. If that's truly who you are, and you're brave enough to trust yourself, you know my number. I'm in town two more days." I stood and started to leave.

The challenge was harsh, but I was a man used to getting my way. And besides, there was more strength in her pinky finger than in her entire family. She just hadn't figured that out yet.

"What does that mean?" Giada asked, grasping my wrist, then releasing me when she realized what she'd done.

"It means I want you to come with me."

"To stay with you? Like a vacation?"

"If that's what you want—stay as long as you like. I'm as unsettled by whatever this is between us as you are, but I know I'm not ready to give you up yet. I won't force you, but

I'll ask that you reconsider. To listen to your instincts and not let someone else dictate your life."

"This is crazy. I hardly know you."

"It is whatever you want to label it, but the choice is yours." I slipped out the back as quietly as I'd entered. All I could do now was wait.

ELEVEN
Giada

I SAT THROUGH THE REST OF MY PEDICURE IN STUNNED SILENCE. Primo wanted me to go with him. To disregard all my family's warnings and risk my life to be with him. I shouldn't even consider it, yet my heart was threatening to burst from my chest, drowning my bloodstream with liquid elation.

I may have barely known him, but he'd seen the worst side of me—my brashness and mischievous tendencies—and he still wanted me. Primo sparked something inside me no other man had. Would it be so terrible to see where that spark took me? I could always change my mind if I went with him and decided he wasn't the man I thought he was.

The prospects filled me with nervous energy until I could hardly sit still. Ignoring the protests of my bewildered nail technician, I slipped from the chair the moment she finished polishing my nails and headed to the front counter to pay.

"You finally done?" Filip had not been thrilled with his assignment. He'd been all too happy to volunteer himself for a slumber party, but shadowing me around town was a different matter. From the minute he arrived at my door that morning, he'd been surly and uncommunicative.

"You think women are just buffed and polished naturally? It takes time and money to look like this." I handed my cash over to the receptionist and thanked her before turning for the door.

"You don't want to hear what I think," Filip grumbled.

I ground to a halt and glared at him. "Oh, I'd love to hear this. What exactly is it that you think about women's appearances?"

A chilling shift overcame Filip, his playboy façade melting away and leaving in its place something unquestionably more ruthless. More intense and complex than I had ever imagined him capable of.

He prowled forward, closing the distance between us. "I think the only red a woman needs on her body is the flush on her skin from a man's capable hand. No clothes. No makeup. No pretenses. Just a blindfold and complete submission. The rest of this bullshit"—he flicked his head toward the salon —"is for you guys, not us."

Well, I'll be damned. Filip's got some bite.

I wasn't sure I could fathom being subservient, but I had to admit, the way he presented it made me wish I could. Young Filip wasn't so different from his brother as I'd thought. He'd initially seemed like a naïve kid compared to the stoic, self-possessed Matteo.

I stood corrected.

Clearing my throat, I asked, "How old are you?"

"Twenty-eight. Now, come on. It's time to get you home. I have other shit to do." He started toward the car, leaving me no choice but to follow.

"You seemed younger," I called after him.

He smirked back at me. "I've been around long enough."

Not long enough to know he should have kept his eyes on me at all times. I liked Filip and was now more than a smidge curious about him, but he'd slipped up on the job. Primo had gotten past their defenses, and now, I had a decision to make.

I went home and tried to think, got frustrated, then actively avoided thinking. Thursday night bled into Friday night, and I still had no answers. My arguments with myself bordered on schizophrenic, and I began to worry about when exactly Primo was leaving. He said I had two days, but that was rather vague. It could mean he was leaving anytime from Friday through Sunday.

If he'd been anyone else, I would have been confident I could take a flight out to meet him regardless of when he left, but Primo was different. I was fairly certain his offer was finite. If I wasn't on that plane with him when he left, there would be no second chances.

Time was slipping away from me, but I was torn. I wanted him, but my family's warnings weren't unfounded. Would I be making a horrible mistake if I went? Would I resent my family forever if I didn't?

By Saturday evening, I was so sick of my own vacillating thoughts that I wished someone would just put a bullet in my brain and put me out of my misery. I'd reached an impasse. The only way I could see moving forward was to flip a coin or something equally as arbitrary. I needed something to tip the scales, and my cousin was the perfect person to help me. She didn't know it, but she was about to make the decision of a lifetime for me.

Saturday evening, I curled up on my sofa with my phone and dialed Alessia.

"Hey, G. What's up?" she answered cheerily.

"You know how you're always telling me I should think about going to school or volunteering or something?"

"Yeah?"

"I've been thinking about it a lot, and I'm really interested in photography."

"Oh, Giada! I think that would be a great field for you."

"Hold up, there's more. The thing is, the stuff that interests me the most is the amazing shots of ocean life—whales and dolphins and coral reefs. I think that could be my calling." I had worked hard to craft a proposed career that suited my needs—it had to be something remotely believable with an element of obvious danger. She already knew I loved the beach, and photography wasn't an unreasonable stretch in the realm of my interests. In actuality, beneath the guise of my metaphor, we were talking about a relationship with Primo, but she would never know that, at least not until it was too late.

"Ummm ... well, it's definitely an exciting career path. It would mean a lot of travel—you can't exactly take pictures of those things here—and wouldn't it be kind of dangerous too? I certainly never expected something like that from you." Her words floundered, but her tone remained positive.

"It encompasses everything that interests me, and I think it could be my one great passion in life. But like you said, there are drawbacks. I know my parents will hate the idea, and there are definite dangers."

"You can't always make them happy. I think if it's your passion, you have to take the risk. Not everyone is able to find something in their lives that they live and breathe for. If you think this could be it for you, I think you should give it a try." As she spoke, her voice grew stronger, reinforced with conviction.

I grinned broadly. "Thanks, Al. I knew I could count on you to understand."

It was misleading to trick her like that, but I needed an unbiased opinion. I realized after hearing her reaction that I'd been leaning toward taking the risk and just needed her unwitting support to reinforce my gut reaction. Yes, being with Primo might be dangerous, but I would always regret not taking that chance. I'd never been the play-it-safe kind of girl, so there was no point in being cautious now.

I ended my conversation with Alessia and pulled up my text thread with Primo.

Me: I want to come with you. I held my breath, my finger hovering over the phone before I finally hit send.

Within seconds, the conversation dots popped up.

Primo: That's more like it.

Primo: Can you get out of your apartment alone?

Me: I think so.

Primo: Meet me at the Applejack diner around the corner from your building in an hour.

Me: See you then.

Nervous energy pulsated beneath my ribs, vibrating out into my extremities and making my head dangerously dizzy. I had one hour to pack my things for a trip of unknown duration to a mystery location with a man I hardly knew.

I had to be insane.

Please, sweet baby Jesus, don't let me live to regret this decision.

I crossed myself and leaped from the couch to pack. I assumed we were going to Mexico, so I grabbed my passport and a slew of beach attire, then threw in some slacks and cardigans just in case. I initially set out enough clothes for a month-long hiatus but put most of it back when I decided I didn't want to show up with sixteen suitcases.

It might have looked presumptive.

I whittled my wardrobe down to the necessities—I could buy whatever else I needed once I was there. It was tight, but I got it all in one suitcase. Before I lugged it out into the living room, I plopped on the bed and contemplated how I could get out without alerting whoever was monitoring my security cameras. I stared at my doorway for several minutes before I gave up.

Fuck it. I'll be gone before they can do anything about it.

I wheeled my suitcase out the front door and into the elevator, eager to get to Primo. When I arrived at the diner, he was standing out front, leaning against a black Mercedes. His eyes sparked with possessive pride, making my heart do its impression of a Cirque du Soleil performer.

As soon as I was within his reach, I held out my hand and uncurled my fingers to reveal his silver lighter. "I believe this is yours."

He ignored my offering, clasping his hand behind my neck and tugging me in to bring our lips together in a passionate kiss. We moved hungrily, kissing and biting and breathing each other in as if starved from our last encounter. The world melted away when I was with him, and it didn't matter if the Pope himself was there on the sidewalk to witness our kiss. I lost myself in Primo's touch, pulling away only when my need for oxygen overruled my maddening desire.

"We need to go," I told him. "They'll know I've left."

He placed one more delicate kiss on my forehead before putting my suitcase in the trunk and helping me into the passenger seat.

I tucked the lighter back into my pocket, relieved he hadn't taken it from me. "Where are we going?"

"To a private airport where I've chartered a plane."

"Am I allowed to know our final destination?"

"Guaymas, Mexico. It's on the northwestern coast across from Baja California. It's beautiful there. Unique. Arid with a desert climate, so there are beaches but not much vegetation. The sunsets are breathtaking. Nothing like New York." He spoke of the area fondly, and I looked forward to seeing it. Mexico was a part of him just like New York was a part of me —seeing the land and its people was just another way to get to know him, and I leaped at the opportunity.

The airport was only a twenty-minute drive in Upper Manhattan. Primo drove with confident ease, maneuvering in and out of traffic as if he were born in the city. I got the sense he was adaptable to his surroundings.

As he drove, I took out my phone and sent a single text to Alessia. **I decided to go for it. Please don't worry about me. I promise I'll be safe and will be in touch soon. Love you much, G.**

Knowing she and my family would panic and try to reach me, I turned off my phone and prayed I'd made the right decision.

TWELVE

Primo

ALTHOUGH GIADA HAD SAID SHE WAS COMING, I WAS STILL somewhat surprised to see her arrive at the diner. It hadn't escaped me that leaving town with a man she'd only just met was exceptionally risky. I wouldn't have faulted her if she had reconsidered her decision, as long as it was her decision and not simply pressure from her family.

Regardless of whatever turmoil she may have dealt with internally, she marched up to me with a determined set to her jaw and cheeks flushed from the cool evening air. I couldn't help but kiss her. Taste that bittersweet undercurrent of fear belying the confidence she professed. There was no such thing as courage without fear, and Giada was unquestionably scared and so very, very brave.

Would that bravery pay off? Not even I had that answer.

Once we were in the car, she shot off a text to someone. There was no way her family could stop us at this point, but I was curious about what she might have told them.

"Did you tell anyone you were coming?"

"No, not exactly. I texted my cousin a somewhat cryptic message. She'll figure it out soon enough. I want to make sure she and my family know I wasn't abducted or anything. I'm sure they'd think the worst if I didn't."

I appreciated her efforts, but they were futile. Nothing she said would convince them of her safety, and that was the way it should be. Our organizations were not allied, and relations were about to take a steep downward slide into hostile territory.

"So," Giada started coyly. "Do you hunt down random women and fly them home with you often?"

I cut my eyes over to her. "No. This is a first."

She was dying to ask more questions, and I wished she wouldn't. It seemed an outgoing personality and insipid curiosity were a package deal, at least in her case. I didn't want to encourage her but caved when the pressure inside the car from her unspoken questions became stifling.

"Just ask whatever it is you want to know."

She said nothing for a long minute as she weighed her words. "I want to know *why*. Why go out of your way to find me just for a lighter?"

That was exactly the type of question I had hoped to avoid. I breathed steadily, taking my time to formulate my response. She probably wouldn't be thrilled to hear that my pursuit of her had hardly been out of my way. Instead, I'd explained in the best way I could. "Why didn't you steal my chips? I had thousands of dollars in high denomination chips sitting next to the lighter, but you never touched them."

"That's easy. I didn't want your money. I just wanted … your attention, I guess."

"There you have your answer. You demanded my attention, and I was too intrigued not to give it. Not many women would be so bold as to spar with me the way you did. At first, I refused to take your bait, but when you raised the stakes, I couldn't resist. I had to learn more about the woman who had dueled with me and managed to get in the final blow."

She glanced down at her hands. "About that. I swear I'm not normally a thief. I mean … not to say I've never done it before, but it's not something I do often. I don't want you to think I'll take anything from you again, now that I know you."

I smirked. "That's good because I don't think I'd be so forgiving a second time."

Giada was quiet until we reached the airport. I'd arranged for staff at the airline to handle the return of my rental car—one of the many perks to flying out of a small, privately-owned airstrip. Giada even had her passport, making our departure that much smoother. I was pleased I didn't have to involve Juan Carlos. He was probably pissed that I hadn't asked for his help. I would have made the call had it come down to that, but I was relieved it hadn't. His maniacal behavior was enough to keep me away, but now I was especially reluctant to see him knowing he'd been the one to kill my mother, even though he hadn't known who she was at the time.

I was leaving Juan Carlos behind me and had Giada in my possession. The only hitch in my current course was Naz. He would be pissed, but he'd get over his anger soon enough. I hoped. After the dust settled, we'd deal with what I'd learned about the past. My emotions hadn't settled on the matter, and I would not broach the subject until I was clear-headed about it. I needed to know how I felt before I demanded answers.

Giada climbed aboard the Cessna jet as if she was accustomed to flying on private jets. I wasn't sure if that was the case or if she was just adept at controlling her reactions. She slipped into one of the soft leather captain's chairs, and I seated myself in the chair facing hers.

"The plane is beautiful," she said, glancing around the cabin, taking in the creamy leather and chestnut wood finishes. The inside only had room for six passengers, making it feel rather confined, but it was crafted in the finest luxury materials to ensure a comfortable ride. "Do you travel often?"

"Frequently, yes, but usually not quite so far from home. I go to Vegas for work frequently."

"I love Vegas." She tried to hold back a grin. "In fact, I look back on my last trip there rather fondly."

I shook my head. "Buckle your seat belt, viborita, before you tumble onto my lap, and I devour you whole."

She took a shuddered breath, then clasped the belt across her lap. "What does that mean? Viborita?"

I held her gaze intently, making her squirm in her seat. "It means little viper. That's what you reminded me of with those hypnotic eyes and your ability to strike when someone least expects it. A hidden danger, never to be underestimated."

Giada stilled. "How is it you see me better than people who have known me my whole life?"

"Sometimes it's hard to see someone we've grown up with as something different than they've always been. I see you without any preconceived notions, just as you are. Nothing more, nothing less."

She swallowed. "And do you like what you see?" She wasn't fishing for compliments. Her question was rife with uncertainty. Despite all her confidence and courage, Giada wrestled with insecurities, just like the rest of us.

"Far more than I should." With that clipped admission, I turned my gaze out the small window as we advanced down the runway.

Neither of us spoke again as we were catapulted into the air, but I sensed her steal furtive glances in my direction. The silence in the cabin acted as a pressurizer, thickening the tension around us. Uncertainty magnified desire and vice versa, the two feeding off one another, charging the air with friction.

As the plane leveled out, I unlatched my belt to put an end to the mounting pressure but didn't make it to my feet before my phone rang. Fucking Naz. The man needed to learn some patience.

I pulled out my phone to see what he needed but was surprised to find it wasn't his number on the display. Matteo De Luca was calling. I inhaled a long, calming breath through my nose before answering.

"De Luca, what a pleasant surprise."

"I seriously doubt that it's pleasant or a surprise. Do you have any fucking idea what you've done?" His voice was layered with cultured violence. A barely restrained warning kept in check by the fraying thread of our past.

"I know you're upset, De Luca, but she's with me of her own free will." I held Giada's vibrant green gaze, enjoying the indignation stiffening her spine.

"It doesn't matter if she bought the plane ticket herself or was coerced at gunpoint. The families will not tolerate meddling in their world, no matter how *innocent* your intent may be." His sneer of the word innocent made it clear he didn't believe my intentions were pure in the slightest.

I respected De Luca—had even owed him a debt up until

recently—and I appreciated that we could talk to one another as equals. He was a competent leader of his family and for a good reason. He was correct about my intent and had every right to be upset. I didn't have a particular desire to make him my enemy, but unfortunately, my hands were tied.

"I'm not sure what I can do to assure you of her safety aside from giving her the phone and letting her tell you herself." I reached out with the phone, handing it to Giada.

"Matteo, this is absurd. I'm absolutely fine." She tilted her chin up, imperious and commanding. "It's too late, we're already in the air. Tell my father and Uncle Enzo to stop worrying … I know exactly what I'm doing … If I need help, I'll be sure to let you know, but it's time for all of you to let me live my life as I see fit. Goodbye, Matteo." She hung up and handed the phone back with her lips pursed haughtily.

I couldn't hear what De Luca had said, but her stubborn determination was evident. She wouldn't let God himself push her around. She would make my life infinitely more difficult, yet I couldn't help myself. Docile, malleable women were great for a quick fuck, but there was no interest there. Giada was different. A natural-born queen and she didn't even know it.

I took the phone and dropped it into a cupholder before crossing the aisle to taste the righteous fury on her lips. However, the plane took a sudden dip, sending me lunging forward. I caught myself on the armrests of her chair, our faces just inches apart, her cinnamon-laced breaths making me even more ravenous. Giada giggled, and I shook my head. Then the plane took another jarring lurch, and the pilot came over the speakers informing us of the high probability for a turbulent flight.

If I didn't want to risk injuring one or both of us, I'd have to pull back the reins on my hunger. I grunted my frustration and eased backward into my seat, refastening my seat belt.

"They say anticipation of pleasure is pleasure in itself." Her voice was a seductive caress, teasing my already frayed nerves.

"*They* have never had this kind of temptation sat before them." My eyes grew hooded, traveling a sensual path down her body. I took in each succulent curve and valley, watching as her pert nipples pressed fiercely against the confines of her bra, and the pulse point at her neck fluttered with exertion. By the time my eyes finished their erotic journey, Giada's lips were parted, and her pupils dilated.

Mission accomplished.

The flight home would be a long one, and it was only fair we suffered together.

THIRTEEN

Giada

PRIMO'S LUST WAS A TACTILE FORCE, GHOSTING FEATHER-LITE touches over my skin and sending sensual vibrations directly to the center of my belly. His desire for me was more of a turn-on than porn could ever hope to be. If I was going to keep from going insane, I would need to distract us both.

"Tell me more about how you know Matteo."

"As you may know, his family runs the waste management industry in the city. The large number of trucks they run requires a substantial amount of auto parts and tires throughout the year, which he acquires through a contract with my boss's company. Two years ago, I accompanied the president of our auto parts organization to a meeting to negotiate a new annual contract. The Chinese Triad somehow found out about our meeting and decided they wanted to make a play for the business. They followed my associate and me to the meet location and caught us off guard—one of my greatest failures and a lesson I took very seriously. They killed the man I was with and had me at a disadvantage when De Luca showed up. It was luck that he arrived early, but he was under no obligation to help me. Many others would have walked away and left me to my fate. Despite having no weapon on him, De Luca entered the fray, and together, we were able to fight them off. I wouldn't have walked away alive that day if it hadn't been for him."

I was stunned to hear the two had such an involved past. What were the chances that I'd pick out and hit on someone Matteo knew while I was in Vegas? Not just someone he knew, but someone who had owed him a life debt. The odds were astronomical. Impossible.

"So, when we needed to find Sal and discovered he was down in Vegas, Matteo went to you for help?"

"Yes, and I was happy to repay him."

"He must respect you a good deal. Finding Sal was a high priority to the men in my family. He wouldn't have trusted just anyone with something so important."

He shrugged. "Since dealing with the Chinese, we developed a mutual respect for one another."

"But apparently not enough respect to convince my family that you're not a danger. It's just absurd." I shook my head.

"They're only looking out for you. I can't blame them for that."

I appreciated that Primo didn't begrudge my family for their prejudice against him, but it still bothered me. I wanted my family to see him as I did. Of course, there was still the small issue of his possible involvement in human trafficking. I desperately wanted to ask him about it, but it was too sensitive a topic for the moment. Maybe once we weren't stuck in the confines of a tiny airplane and had spent a tad more time together, I would feel capable of raising such a delicate subject.

"What about your family?" I asked, redirecting the focus of our conversation. "I'd love to hear more about you."

"There's not much to tell. I never knew my father, and my mother was killed when I was young." His eyes dropped to his hand as it swept away invisible lint from his lap.

I got the sense he was uncomfortable with the subject, which was somewhat surprising considering how stoic he was and that the loss occurred some time ago. "I'm sorry to hear that. My mother and I don't get along great, but losing her would be horrible."

"It was a long time ago. My boss, Nazario, took me in off the streets and practically raised me. He made me finish school and taught me discipline. I owe him my life."

"He sounds like quite the man. I look forward to meeting him," I smiled.

Primo's features hardened. "Don't misunderstand me. Naz is no saint. He can be ruthless, and I'm not sure how he'll react to you. He won't hurt you, but he also may not be thrilled to see I've brought you back. Just be prepared."

Well, that was a little unsettling.

I nodded. "We can't help how our families react. I have no room to judge your boss—you saw how my family has behaved. My father's never even met you, but he was willing to keep me under lock and key to make sure you couldn't get to me."

He glanced out the window, lips thinning as if something I said agitated him. I had no clue what that could have been, but before I could dwell on it, he turned back and redirected the conversation.

"You say I know your family, but not in the way you do. Tell me more about them."

"There are my parents, and I have two sisters—you saw them in Vegas, along with my cousin who was in red. I'm the oldest of us three girls and the black sheep."

He narrowed his eyes. "How could you possibly be the black sheep?"

"Easy, I never follow the rules like I should. My mom is a devout Catholic, and my father is a strict disciplinarian. Whatever I do is never what they think I should be doing. It drives them crazy, even now that I'm grown and out of their house." I wasn't a black sheep in the sense some people might think. My parents were unlikely to disown me, and I was still an active member of the family, but I didn't belong. Like a redheaded stepchild who never quite fit the mold.

Primo studied me, his eyes a gunmetal gray in the dim light of the airplane. "And is that why you're here? A statement of defiance?" His tone was even, not accusing or judgmental, but his stiffened posture led me to believe the possibility upset him.

I didn't rush to reassure him. Instead, I did my best to be open and truthful. "I considered that at first, when I was trying to decide if I would go with you. I didn't want to put myself in a precarious situation just to spite my parents. It's not easy to look at your own motivations honestly and pull that thread until you get to the source of an emotion or desire. Every time I followed the trail, it simply led me back to you. Not my parents or my disenchantment with life. I wanted to be with you because of the way I feel when I'm around you. I know we haven't known each other long, but it's been long enough for me to know I didn't want to walk away."

Oh, God. I wasn't sure if I should have said all that, but there was no undoing it now. It was just like me to open my mouth and for words to come tumbling out before I'd considered their impact. Most men would freak out at the slightest showing of early attachment by a woman. Call her needy and emotional before running out the door. Would Primo fall in that camp?

My shoulders tensed as I waited for him to realize what a mistake he'd made and backpedal out of the situation faster than a cat in water.

His eyes darkened like the sky on a moonless night, velvet shadows hiding all manner of secrets. "You're a fascinating creature, Giada Genovese." The Spanish lilt to his words caressed my skin, making me shiver.

"Is that a good thing?" A smile formed on my lips, a little unsteady and far more shy than I was used to.

"That would depend on who you ask. My cock couldn't be happier, but I'm not sure your family is quite so thrilled."

The word cock coming from his lips tightened the knots already coiling in my belly. Within seconds, the sexual tension in the cabin was back to blistering levels. The only relief came from frequent bouts of jostling turbulence that ratcheted up my anxiety and distracted me from the mindless need threatening my sanity.

The torture only subsided when the plane touched down on the runway, and my mind became consumed with what would happen next. It was dark when we landed, so I couldn't see the landscape well. City lights twinkled in the distance, but I'd have to wait until morning to get a better view of my temporary home.

We taxied to the tiny airport, another private affair where a man waited for us with his car right on the tarmac. He was dressed in a suit, hands clamped together in front of him, and a grim set to his mouth. He was around Primo's age with short dark hair, good looking in a serious sort of way.

"Giada, this is Santino," Primo offered. "He'll be on call anytime you need him if I'm not around."

"It's good to meet you." I extended my hand in greeting.

Santino warily accepted, but his questioning gaze was glued to Primo as if uncertain what was going on. It was understandable. He probably hadn't expected his boss to come home with a woman in tow.

We climbed into the back seat of the Land Rover and were off. Santino updated Primo on local matters that he'd missed while he was away. I mostly tuned out the conversation and watched the passing scenery to distract myself from the sticky nausea filling my belly. I was excited but also anxious about this new adventure. Together, the two emotions did a number on my stomach.

The drive lasted approximately twenty minutes. His estate was gated and manned by a guard who recognized the car and allowed us through without requiring us to stop.

"A gate and a guard?" I asked warily.

"People in our line of work have enemies everywhere. It's best to be safe than sorry."

I nodded and tried not to overthink it. I'd grown up living a mostly standard life without the guns and bodyguards that a mafia lifestyle might stereotypically entail, but we'd essentially been in hiding. Uncle Enzo's and my father's identities had been kept secret to protect us when we were little, so I hadn't had to live with the same safeguards someone in the open might require. Primo's lifestyle was probably far more typical of someone high up in our world.

His house was a traditional Mediterranean-style mansion with a red tile roof, carved stone trim work on stucco, and gorgeous arched windows and doorways. The landscaping I could see was meticulous and even boasted a huge statue in the front drive.

When I stepped from the car, the distant hum of gently rolling waves filled my ears. "Is that the ocean?" I asked excitedly.

"It is. The weather is on the cooler side, but you should still be able to enjoy the beach," Primo said as he removed his suitcase from the back of the car.

His own private beach explained the radiant sun-kissed coloring of his skin. Something was safe about the beach and a man who enjoyed being in the sun. It wasn't logical, but I associated love and happiness with the ocean. A blanket of welcome reassurance wrapped around me, comforting me that I'd made the right decision in coming to this place. It helped ease my tension and settle my stomach.

"Should I take this to the blue room?" Santino asked Primo, removing my suitcase from the trunk.

The front entry was lit with a number of brilliant floodlights, enabling me to see the shadow that crossed behind Primo's eyes.

"That's probably best," he murmured, carrying his own bag to the front door.

It was presumptive of me, but I'd expected to stay with Primo. Their exchange indicated I'd been wrong. Disappointment and uncertainty attempted to darken my mood until I assured myself that the situation was unusual for both of us and not to jump to conclusions. It was probably a good idea for two people so new to each other to have their own space. He was being polite, not pushing me away. I let the subject drop and followed him to the door.

Just inside the thick, carved wood doors, the entry was magical in an old-world sort of way, like stepping through a time warp to an age of wooden stoves and horse-drawn carriages. There were modern touches, but he'd kept the charm of the original structure—arched doorframes and thick wooden beams in the ceilings. Some walls were done in rough stonework with iron sconces in stark relief against the pale hues of the stone and mortar. The furniture suited the home perfectly. It all looked to be either excellently cared for antiques or well-crafted replicas. With the dark brown Saltillo tile floor and an open, spacious layout, the house was a masterpiece.

"It's gorgeous, Primo," I said in awe, still gaping at all the intricate details.

"I'm glad you like it. Let's get you to your room, and you can explore it tomorrow. I know I can't be the only one who's hungry and more than a little tired." He led us to a curved stairwell with an ornate wrought-iron railing, then down a hallway to a bedroom accented in sky blue pillows and curtains.

"This is perfect, thank you." I glanced around, my gaze anxiously finding its way back to him. "Can I see where you'll be staying?"

Primo nodded without a word and led me down the opposite end of the hallway. Inside, the master suite was breathtaking. Not because it was particularly grand, but because of the accordion-style doors that opened the entire wall to the patio overlooking the ocean.

I wandered closer, drawn to the shimmering moonlight dancing across the water. "I can't wait to see everything during the daylight," I murmured, entranced by the surreal beauty.

Primo eased behind me, his warmth enveloping the length of my back. "Hmm," he mused. "Perhaps, but the moonlight casts shadows that capture every dip and curve. There's really nothing like it." He traced his hand over the curve of my shoulder and down my arm, then swept my hair over one shoulder and placed an achingly sweet kiss on my neck.

"Thank you for bringing me here."

The words lingered in the air, and Primo grew inhumanly still before pulling away from me. In place of his warmth was a chilling emptiness.

I turned to face him, confusion knotting my brow.

His gaze avoided me completely. "I'll bring up a tray with dinner. You should get settled in your room." His voice was cold and distant, a far cry from the lusty rumble seconds before.

What was going on? His moods were so turbulent that I was getting whiplash just trying to keep up. I got the sense he wanted me but was conflicted. Why bring me here just to push me away?

"Can I not stay here ... with you?"

Primo's lips thinned. "I think some space would be best. It's like you said—everything looks different in the light of day. This has been a major change for you, and I'm unsure how tomorrow will unfold. When the newness wears off and the dust settles, you might find you prefer to have a room to yourself."

"I'm not sure I understand, but if you think that's best." My voice took on an icy bite of its own, chilled from his suddenly cool demeanor.

Primo only nodded and slipped from the room.

FOURTEEN

Primo

I SENT SANTINO WITH A TRAY OF FOOD UP TO GIADA INSTEAD OF going myself. Maybe it was cowardice, but I needed time to think. I needed breathing room to get my head on straight. I'd been so overwhelmed with the desire to hang on to Giada that I'd glossed over the realities of bringing her back with me. Once I had her there in my house, I was assaulted with doubts.

There was no use questioning whether I'd done the right thing. The point was moot. I'd brought Giada with me, and now the only question was how to move forward. After laying restlessly in bed for hours, I decided on a course of action. I constructed a viable explanation I could feed to Naz in order to gain his compliance and keep him from upsetting Giada.

I rallied enough confidence in my plan to finally calm my nerves and allow sleep to take me. The first rays of morning light drew me awake, anxious to get through the tricky conversation ahead. I spent two punishing hours in the gym that morning, seeking some clarity of mind. Whenever my self-discipline wavered, exercise helped realign my priorities and energized me to stay focused. By the time I showered and joined Giada in the kitchen for breakfast, I was far more confident in my current course of action.

Her hair was heaped in a messy bun on top of her head, and she wore a gauzy long-sleeve shirt rolled up to the elbows with loose linen pants. The look was relaxed and natural, an effortless beauty that was breathtaking. It was no wonder I'd risked my life descending into chaos in order to keep her near me.

"I see you've met Alma," I said as I joined the two women. Giada gazed up at me warmly from where she sat at the bar, and Alma quickly got busy at the sink, ending her conversation with Giada.

"I have, and she's hooked me up with a lovely breakfast. Would you like some eggs?" Giada had a plate full of scrambled eggs, fruit, and papas, which she held up in offering.

"Thanks, but I'll get my own plate. I'm sure Alma's prepared one."

"Of course, Señor," Alma chimed in. "I was just keeping it warm for you." She brought over a heaping plate of food, and I joined Giada at the bar.

"Did you sleep well?" It annoyed me to ask the question. She should have been in my bed, getting little to no sleep. After I talked to Naz, I would rectify that immediately.

"I did, and seeing the ocean this morning was an amazing

way to wake up. If I could figure out what I did with my phone, it would be the perfect morning."

I shoveled in mouthful of eggs, chewing to avoid comment.

Santino stepped in from the porch, drawing our attention to him. "I just got word from the gate that Señor Vargas is here."

Well, fuck.

In an instant, my entire plan went up in flames. I had hoped to go to Naz's house and discuss things with him in private. It was crucial that I introduce the subject properly before he set eyes on her. Before he saw the way she looked at me. And I couldn't allow her to hear my explanation if my plan was to succeed. The situation was quickly devolving to a total cluster fuck.

"Thank you, Santino." My words were clipped. "Giada, I need you to go upstairs until I come for you."

"What? Why?" She looked at me with confusion, and though she wasn't trying to be difficult, my frustration boiled over.

I slammed my hand down on the granite. "*Just go!*"

My burst of temper caused her to flinch, but I didn't have time for her questions. She slipped from the bar chair but only made it a few steps when a voice froze her in her tracks.

"What's all the fuss?"

The message must have been slow arriving from the gate because Naz was already here.

He strolled into the room dressed in a pale linen suit, professional grin in place. He didn't look particularly intimidating to the casual observer. His salt-and-pepper hair was neatly trimmed, and he was always impeccably dressed. At five-foot-eight, he was several inches shorter than me and stayed lean with daily swims in his lap pool. He could have been anyone's grandfather or favorite uncle, judging purely by looks. The only hint at the violence lurking beneath the surface was the unnerving quality of his eyes. So dark, those twin orbs looked as though they were crafted from shards of gleaming obsidian and could be equally as sharp when he cut you with a scathing gaze.

"Primo, welcome home. I see you've brought a guest with you."

I crossed to the doorway, shaking his hand with a confident, firm grip. In my world, you never allowed anyone to detect even the faintest weakness, even your allies. No matter how upset I was on the inside, I would never let it show. "You're welcome to join us for breakfast. I'm sure Alma can throw a plate together."

"No, no. I've already eaten. I was headed into town and decided I'd check in and see how your trip went." He eyed Giada like a child assessing a plate of vegetables. "I can see things didn't go as expected. I'm surprised I'm only learning of this now." He turned back to me, the gleam in his eye a lashing across my cheek. He was livid, but he'd never let that show until we were alone. I didn't always agree with Naz's decisions, but he was the consummate businessman. Private matters were never handled in the company of strangers.

"Naz, this is Giada Genovese, daughter of Edoardo Genovese." I motioned to Giada, who looked at me warily before crossing to where we stood.

"It's a pleasure to meet you, Señor Vargas," she said warmly, extending her hand and exhibiting exemplary manners. I was sure they were well ingrained, but I wished she hadn't.

Naz accepted her offering with feral grace. "Well, this is a surprise. And I must say, you seem to be handling all of this rather well."

I watched helplessly as Naz laid his trap. Giada flushed and smiled, totally unaware that the ground was about to fall out from beneath her.

"It was all rather sudden, but sometimes that's how these things work." She wrapped her delicate fingers around my forearm, whether for reassurance or as a statement of belonging, I wasn't sure. Either way, the movement turned Naz's smile into an icy grin.

His eyes cut to me. "Was it sudden, Primo? Is that why you've brought me the wrong girl? Was there a problem while you were in the city?" The melodic tone of his voice gave his accusatory words a maniacal edge.

Giada looked up at me in confusion, then back at Naz, her hands slowly falling away from me.

"She's Enzo's niece," I explained coolly. "She will serve the same purpose."

"Purpose?" Giada questioned. "What purpose?" She looked at me for answers, her fiery anger igniting beside me.

A vicious chuckle tumbled from Naz's lips. "Oh, dear. Hasn't he told you? Did you think you were here on some sort of vacation? That this was some kind of … *love* connection?" He spat the words, all traces of the gracious businessman slipping away. Naz glared at her with oily disdain. "Primo here was supposed to retrieve one of your cousins as leverage. But now, it seems he thinks he makes the decisions around here and has brought *you* instead." He began to pace, hands clasped behind his back.

I had debated telling her the truth while I lay awake the night before, but I realized if I got to Naz first and explained things, there would be no reason to tell her. She would believe she was here with me voluntarily throughout her stay. It would make security far easier and would be just as effective getting what we needed from Giada's family. Eventually, she'd learn the truth, but after I found a way to explain. Instead, Naz had to check in and overreact, fucking over my plans.

"So, what is this?" Giada shot at me. "I've unwittingly gone off with my own kidnappers? I accepted candy from the unmarked van, didn't I?" She smacked her hand over her forehead and began to pace. "This is utterly perfect. Now, they'll all get to say *I told you so*. Motherfucker."

Naz paused his own mental tirade to watch her with a curious eye. He would quickly detect she was different than most women if he spent any amount of time around her, and I wasn't sure if I wanted that. He was married, but that didn't stop his voracious appetite for women. Just the thought of him growing interested in her caused my jaw to clamp down so hard I'd need a tire iron to release it.

Giada suddenly stopped her pacing and whipped around in my direction. "How long am I stuck here?" She bristled with injustice and outrage.

"As long as it takes," I growled.

Her green eyes blazed. "Excuse me, I think I've lost my appetite." Giada stormed off toward the stairs, leaving Naz and I bobbing in her turbulent wake.

"I wish you hadn't done that," I told Naz, knowing I was walking a fine line.

"And allow you to let some woman fuck up our plans? This has been in motion for years, Primo. *Years*. And you let your dick derail everything. That's inexcusable."

"Nothing is derailed. She will have the same bargaining power as one of her cousins, and you know it. You have a problem with her for some other reason. Why? You've never cared who I had in my bed before." I was treading on dangerously thin ice, but I couldn't hold back my words. I was already upset with Naz about my mother, which made it even harder to ignore his meddling in my affairs with Giada.

"I may not have cared before, but that was because you've never tried to fucking play house with the enemy before. Whatever has passed between you two has been too convincing to be a simple ruse. That woman is far too independent to have followed you here on a whim. You've developed feelings for her, and that has compromised you." He glared at me with the condemning black gaze of a man who survived entirely on suspicion and manipulation.

"You're wrong," I stated flatly, attempting to keep my tone devoid of any emotion. A fevered reaction would only support his argument. "I feel nothing for her. It was an entertaining challenge to see if I could get her here of her own accord, but that's the end of it. Now, I'll have to up security to keep her in line."

Naz eyed me, dissecting my every word and movement like a CSI detective. "That had better be the case. I have a meeting Wednesday with the Gulf suppliers. I'd like you to come by tomorrow so that we can discuss matters beforehand. Ten a.m., don't be late." With those parting words, he spun around and left, the black cloud he brought upon his arrival still lingering over me.

Sometimes I considered my relationship with Naz in terms of a foster father, but he'd always been more of a boss than a father. Requiring my education and training me were strategic maneuvers rather than guidance from a place of love. I'd always excused his harsh tactics because the results had benefitted me. I assumed he was doing the best he could and had cared for me, though his methods didn't always show it. Why else would he invest so much time and money into my development?

What I'd learned from his brother shook that foundation. I

was questioning everything about our relationship, and that uncertainty made overlooking his shortcomings far more challenging.

I'd spent ten years being raised by a devoted mother. I knew what it was to care for someone. To love and sacrifice. When I thought Naz was trying to achieve that in his own way, I excused a lot. Now, I was seeing him differently. More critically.

His controlling behavior looked far more abusive than misguided. And when his predatory gaze had trailed Giada's departure, I wanted to rip his lecherous eyes from their sockets.

A colossal storm was brewing. If I couldn't reconcile what I'd learned and continue to see Naz as an ally, our relationship would hit a breaking point, and that could have deadly consequences. Leaving his employment wasn't an option, and overthrowing him could mean war. I may have been an important part of his organization, but I was by no means the only player.

I would have to decide quickly what I could live with and where I had to draw a line. Taking a stand against Naz would be the greatest challenge I'd ever faced, and I wouldn't dare entertain it without thorough provocation.

FIFTEEN

Giada

WHAT A FUCKING SHIT SHOW. I WENT OUT ON A LIMB DEFYING MY family for him, and it was all just a goddamn ploy to get me out of the country. I barely managed to keep my tears at bay until I was out of their sights. Scalding, angry tears stained my cheeks with shame and heartbreak as I hurried up the stairs to my room.

I had to give him props. He'd played the long con better than anyone I'd ever come across. Who knew how long he'd been scouting my family, planning to snatch one of us.

Back in Vegas, when I'd caught him ogling the other girls, he hadn't been scheming how to get some action, he'd been plotting our kidnapping. Not ours. Hers. Alessia was the only cousin with me. She was who he had his sights set on all along.

I slammed my door shut and leaned against it as a shuddering sob had me clutching my chest. I'd always been a decent judge of character—how could I have been so wrong? I could understand my body lusting after a man who was pretty but toxic. Physical lust was chemical and rarely logical. But how could my heart yearn for someone who saw me as nothing more than a pawn? I'd never been so horribly wrong in my life.

I had started to believe Primo might actually have wanted me despite my flaws. That he had seen my imperfections and hadn't needed to change me—that he desired me exactly as I was.

But it was a lie.

As much as I hated to admit my terrible error in judgment, I had to get ahold of my family and tell them I was in trouble. Making the admission would hurt like a sonofabitch, but I had to do it. I needed someone to help get me out of Mexico. My wounded pride would heal. I wasn't sure I'd survive an attack from Naz or his guards.

He was terrifying.

My shock and anger had helped keep my fear in check, but I could tell the man was two Froot Loops shy of a full bowl. I half expected his eye to start twitching like a cartoon villain when he demanded answers to why his orders hadn't been carried out. A child throwing a tantrum, except this child was a grown man with adult weapons at his disposal.

I hurried to the bed and dropped to my knees, frantically lifting the bed skirt to resume my search for my missing phone. I felt around in the sheets, peeked behind my nightstand, and then emptied every article from my suitcase until the room was littered with clothes. That was when it hit me—

I wasn't going to find my phone. I was being held hostage; my phone had been taken.

No-no-no-no-no.

I slammed my fists against the ground, furious with myself. I was the physical embodiment of every dim-witted horror movie starlet, too engrossed in her own world to realize the dangers around her. It was pathetic. *I* was pathetic. A whirlwind of self-loathing consumed me, but I didn't give in to its battering assault.

I refused to be that girl—weak and pitiful.

No more wallowing. No more mistakes.

I wiped my tears away and scooped an armful of clothes back into my suitcase, clamoring to pile in as much as I could. I would find a way out of there. I would not be a fucking damsel in distress.

Thinking back to my brief journey through the house before breakfast, I couldn't recall seeing any landline phones. There had to be another way. Alma had been a kind older woman. Maybe she would sneak me her phone so I could get word to my family. I'd assured Matteo I was here of my own free will, and I needed to tell them I'd been wrong. It sounded like they would get word of my abduction soon enough, but it was important to try to get word to them myself—tell them where I was and give them any help I could offer.

As I collected the last pile of clothes, something fell to the ground, catching my attention. The lighter. It must have slipped from the pocket of the pants I'd been wearing the day before. I dropped the clothes in a messy heap and sank to the floor, my fingers numbly retrieving the innocuous silver object.

I rolled it around in my hand, my eyes almost losing focus in an unseeing trance. This tiny, worthless object had started it all. If I hadn't stolen the lighter, I never would have seen Primo again. But if that was the case, why was I there?

Like a ray of sunshine peeking through a storm, logic infiltrated my emotional haze.

If Primo had been instructed to get one of my cousins, why had he taken me instead? There'd been no mistaken identity. He knew exactly who I was and that I was *not* what his boss wanted. Getting me to go with him could have been some kind of twisted game, but I didn't get the sense that was the case. I was foolish after being deceived to believe I had any clue what Primo was thinking, but my gut told me his desire had been genuine.

Despite what I'd learned, I still couldn't imagine him hurting me. Maybe I was still drunk on the illusion of a whirlwind romance with him, but I couldn't see it. The way he looked at me like he'd go mad without a taste of me; no one could act that convincingly. There was truth behind his molten silver eyes.

The realization flooded me with calming reassurance. I hadn't been wrong. Primo may have had ulterior motives, but the connection between us had been real and substantive enough for him to justify defying his boss. He wanted me, and that just might be my ticket to safety.

I made my way out to the small balcony off my room. The midmorning sun shone from behind me over the house, casting teal and cobalt swaths of color across the water. Only the most delicate of trickling waves lapped at the sandy shore, and a gentle salty breeze tugged at my flowing white blouse.

The location was serene in a way I could only imagine Heaven would be. Trying to reconcile the predicament I was in with such divine surroundings was difficult. Almost disorienting. How could my life be at risk when I was nestled in paradise?

On the edge of the sand by the house, fluttering palm fronds swayed as if part of an invisible ocean current. Sandpipers scurried at the water's edge in search of breakfast, and an armed guard strolled through the sand in the distance.

Okay, so maybe it was a militant, prison-like version of paradise.

The task of getting to safety was daunting, even if Primo did have a weakness for me. I wasn't Maria. I couldn't fight my way out of there if things went awry. No, but what other choice did I have? I had to try. If I continued to slip beneath his skin, maybe he'd help me escape. I certainly wasn't going to cower in my room like a child. Primo brought me here for a reason, and I was going to get to the heart of it, then get my ass back home.

The door to my room clicked open, but I didn't turn to see who had joined me. I could sense Primo's brooding presence, come to me as if summoned by my thoughts of escape. He didn't join me on the balcony, choosing to linger in the doorway just behind me instead. It was probably best. I was still pissed at him for deceiving me. If I was going to play on his desire for me, I would need to appeal to him, but my temper was still too hot for that.

"I suppose I could be someplace far worse than this," I said sarcastically, allowing my words to drift back to him on the warm breeze.

"You won't be mistreated unless you give me reason to do so." His words were cold and clinical, detached from all emotion as if he'd lobotomized the human side of himself. He'd never been particularly warm or nurturing, but this side of him was even more robotic than I'd witnessed before.

Curiosity nipped and clawed at me until I turned around.

I needed to see this man who disobeyed his boss to keep me near him then professed his indifference toward me like so much mud on his shoe. Just like before, both at the casino and at my apartment, his casual stance broadcasted a careless apathy, but the raging storm in his gray gaze could not be silenced. He was a living, breathing cacophony of emotion compressed and pressurized behind an impenetrable wall of armor.

"Why did you bring me here?" I asked calmly, attempting to mirror his own impassivity. Bottling up my anger and seeking to confront him with the truth I'd already unraveled.

"Exactly as Naz explained. We needed leverage over your uncle."

"No. I want to know why *I'm* here and not one of my cousins like you were ordered to bring." Before I started an assault against his defenses, I needed to test for weaknesses. See how ardently he would fight against his desire for me. I wanted to hear him tell me himself that I'd meant nothing.

"Does it matter?"

"*Yes*. Tell me."

"Because you were easier to target," he shot back evenly, eyes narrowing just a fraction.

I took a measured step forward. *"Bullshit.* Tell me the truth." No matter how hard I tried to remain calm, I couldn't keep the rage from my voice.

"I saw you as a challenge. Kidnapping anyone is easy, but luring someone of their own free will was far more entertaining. Is that want you want to hear? That you were entertainment?" He stepped forward, slowly snaking his hand behind my neck and caressing my jawline with his thumb.

I wanted to yank myself away and lean into his touch at the same time. The push and pull made me feel maniacal, teetering on the edge of insanity.

I gave into a crazed smile. "It's exactly what I wanted to hear, but not for the reason you think."

"Oh, yeah? And what's that?"

"Because I can hear the lie in your words. You may fool your boss, and you may even fool yourself, but you can't lie to me."

Primo's jaw flexed, and his hand flinched momentarily tighter around my throat. "It doesn't matter what you believe. You're still going to be used to get at your family, and you will end up hurt if you give us trouble."

Finally allowing my anger to show, I glared at him and lifted my chin. "Then *do it,*" I hissed. "If that's how this is going to go, *hurt* me." I slammed my hands against his chest. "Show me what a monster you can be. Prove to me that you felt nothing when you were inside me, because until you do, I won't believe it."

He growled with rage, whirling us around to press my front against the wall with his body firmly behind me. "What you're asking for is a death sentence for both of us, and no matter how good your cunt tastes, I'm not willing to die for you. Stop this fucking bullshit now. You hear me?" His heaving breaths mingled with my own, his mouth just inches from mine.

The more adamant the refusal, the greater the admission.

He was battling against his desire for me. If he felt nothing, he would have shrugged and walked away, unaffected. Feeling the wrath of his frustration was all the reassurance I needed. My anger receded, and a calm, determined certainty took its place.

"I hear you, loud and clear," I said on a shaky breath.

Primo was just as affected by the connection between us as I was. If I could convince him not to shut me out, I might get far more than a ticket home. I was no longer interested in pursuing a simple escape. After feeling the fervent intensity of his emotions, I realized there was more on the line than my freedom. I wanted the man I'd come for, and I wouldn't settle for anything less.

Mistaking my response for submission, Primo pulled away, straightening his collar and exiting my room without another word.

SIXTEEN

Primo

I AVOIDED GIADA THE REST OF THE DAY. SOMETHING ABOUT HER riled me up more than anyone else I knew. Her words should have rolled off my back like the ocean breeze, but instead, they soaked straight into my bloodstream, making my heart rate skyrocket and my emotion spiral out of control. I had to stay away from her to have any hope of remaining sane.

The irony of the situation didn't escape me—the fact that I brought her to my home just to keep her at arm's length. It would have been far easier on me to have kidnapped her cousin as I'd been instructed, but I seemed to be harboring masochistic tendencies. I'd convinced myself I could enjoy her while she was here and combine business and pleasure.

That had been a naïve error on so many levels. Now, I had to deal with the consequences.

"I hope there were no issues with our guest," I prompted Santino when I checked in that evening.

"Not at all, actually. She's eating well and seems to have taken to Alma."

Of course, she had. She'd probably poison my housekeeper with the same alluring venom she'd used on me, and the next thing I'd know, Alma would be petitioning for Giada's freedom.

"I trust Alma has been warned about staying in line?" I grumbled.

"She has. I don't believe there's anything she could do to create problems. There are no phones in the house aside from yours and mine. She knows better than to cross you."

I grunted. "You don't know how compelling our little prisoner can be."

"So far, she's been rather compliant. She did ask to go for a walk on the beach this afternoon, but she stuck to the shoreline, swam for a bit, and hardly said a word."

I'd told Santino that Giada was allowed on the beach if he escorted her, but I was suddenly reconsidering that decision. The bitter taste of jealousy left a sneer on my face when I thought of Santino seeing Giada in a bathing suit, watching her perfectly rounded ass as she strolled along the sandy shore. I didn't want anyone else laying eyes on her body, even someone I trusted as deeply as Santino. He'd been a friend since my days on the streets and owed me just as I owed Naz. Hopefully, unlike my relationship with Naz, my friendship with Santino wasn't founded on a series of lies. As far as I knew, we were solid. I'd given no reason for Santino to be disloyal.

It's possible Naz would say the same about you.

True, but he was responsible for my parents' deaths. If he couldn't understand why that would be hard for me to accept, then he had issues of his own. I'd never done anything to hurt Santino and wouldn't let my fucked-up mental state bleed into other areas of my life. I shook off the self-doubt and shoved aside my jealousy.

"As long as she behaves, I see no reason she can't be on the beach, but you have to keep a close eye on her. She's brazen enough to try something stupid, and she's of no use to us dead."

Santino stared at me for a moment as if he were studying me. "I overheard your conversation with Nazario."

I glared at him, holding perfectly still. "I suggest you think very carefully about what you're going to say next."

"Are you telling me I can't speak openly to you? Because I would have thought we were past that at this point." He hadn't been upset before, but my warning had clearly triggered his temper.

I sighed and ran a hand through my hair. "Of course, you can speak."

"I can tell something's different with you since you got back. If I can see that, Nazario will too. He'll think she's getting to you."

"Why are you telling me this?" I asked warily.

"Because I've seen the way you look at her. I've known you too long and seen you with too many other women to believe she means nothing. As far as I'm concerned, good for you—there's no reason you shouldn't have a woman in your life—but I doubt Nazario would feel the same."

My gut reaction was to lash out in denial about my feelings for Giada, but Santino was only trying to help me. What he said was true on both counts, which was the reason I'd been trying to distance myself from her. Nothing good could come of being with Giada. And as for Naz, if I was going to get him off my back about the girl, I would need to give him another reason for my irregular behavior. I wasn't entirely ready to confront him about my mother, but it would seem I had no choice.

"I appreciate your concern, but there's no need to worry. I have Naz under control." *If there was such a thing.* Confronting him with what I'd learned would buy me some time to manage the situation with Giada. Once we received our shipment at the New York pier and got Giada back home, things could go back to normal, and I could get rid of this pounding headache.

I spent the next morning in the gym working out my frustrations. Often, I swam or jogged on the beach, but with Giada at the house, I didn't want to be out of reach if there were problems. I spent an hour on the heavy bag working combinations, then did some weights before hitting the treadmill for some low-key cardio to wind down.

Just as I started up the treadmill, Giada came strolling into the gym with a yoga mat under her arm and a grin on her face as if she were at a spa retreat.

"I hope you don't mind, Santino said I could use the gym," she called over the sound of my rhythmic footfalls.

I continued jogging, attempting to ignore her as she bent over to roll out her mat, showing off every curve and dredging up memories of her naked body beneath me.

Fuck.

Was I so weak-willed that I couldn't finish my workout in her presence? I trained my eyes ahead, staring at myself sternly in the mirror, but there she was in the background, my peripheral vision just making out her twisting form as she stretched. It was too much. I had to look.

Her stretching morphed into an array of artful yoga poses that taunted me as if I were a kid salivating outside an ice cream shop. She progressed through a series of movements once, then twice through. When she started again, I hit my limit. My restraint snapped. I slammed my hand against the emergency stop button and stormed from the room to prevent myself from wrestling her to the ground and fucking her into next week.

I took a long shower with water so cold I expected shards of ice to start bouncing off the shower floor. The chill helped cool my blood and focus my mind to prepare for my meeting with Naz. I couldn't afford to be distracted in his presence.

I managed to eat a quick breakfast without running into Giada, then made the short drive to Naz's house. It had always been convenient to live so near one another, but now I wished for a bit more space between us. At least with security, I had a few minutes' warning when he did surprise me with a visit, assuming they weren't slow like last time.

Naz's house was more like a fortress. He had more security at his place than there was at the border. I understood why, but I wasn't sure I'd ever want to live like that. I appreciated the luxuries this life afforded us, but when it came at the cost of freedom and privacy, it was no longer so alluring.

"Ah, Primo, you're here. Good, we can get started." Naz folded the newspaper he was reading and motioned for me to join him. I'd found him on his back patio overlooking the enormous pool on the side of his house and the ocean beyond it. He was still in a plush robe after swimming laps and had the remnants of a smoothie and coffee on the table. "Can I have Marta get you something to eat or drink?"

"No, thank you. I had breakfast before I came over."

He waved his hand in a gesture that said, suit yourself. "I trust our guest is adapting to her new situation."

"She appears to be more adaptable than most," I answered vaguely. From what I could tell, she still refused to see herself as a pawn, but I didn't want to explain that to Naz.

His lips thinned. "Now that we have her, it's time to reach out to Enzo and communicate our demands. The shipment will be reaching New York shores in a week, and we need access to that port. I take it they are aware we have her?"

"Yes."

"Good. Perhaps I'll contact him tomorrow. It would be helpful to us if he's given plenty of time to squirm before I speak to him." He looked out over the pool and beyond to the serene shoreline. "What other news do you have from the city?"

"The Chinese still haven't established new leadership. Two factions are battling for control and so concentrated on their internal struggle that they shouldn't be an issue."

"And the Russians?"

"I don't think they care as long as we stay off their territory. You know they're only ever in it for themselves and don't ally with anyone." Juan Carlos had initially tried to gain access to the Russian ports in order to avoid dealing with the Italians. He claimed he would be able to use his recently acquired contacts to smooth over a deal, but his efforts had failed. Naz's blind ambitions had made him overconfident about his brother's chances of success. I'd known we had a snowball's chance in hell, but I wasn't about to get my head blown off for voicing that opinion. The Russians never worked with anyone; there was no reason they would change their habits now.

Naz huffed in agreement. "That's the problem with these other organizations. They don't understand like we do in the south how to work together with your competitors such that both parties prosper. They're too busy fighting one another to see the bigger picture."

Seeing my opening, I took the plunge and confronted Naz about my parents. "Actually, on the topic of competitors, I did learn something interesting from a conversation I had with your brother."

Naz casually picked up his coffee mug and took a sip. He looked at me patiently, but he was stewing with curiosity beneath the surface.

"We figured out a surprising connection I might have had with Martín Alvarez, something that I don't believe comes as any shock to you."

He continued to stare at me but otherwise gave nothing away.

"Were you ever going to tell me there was more than simple charity behind you taking me in? That Alvarez was my father, and you had both my parents killed?" By some miracle, I kept my voice devoid of emotion. It would have been dangerous if Naz began to doubt my loyalty, so I had to broach the subject with the utmost caution.

"Is this what's behind your disobedience? Why you brought the wrong girl? Were you defying me because you felt betrayed?" He was wary—curious but not defensive—which was good.

"This has nothing to do with her." I had to deny it, but I was hoping that's what he would believe.

He studied me, picked apart every tiny detail to assess my

motives before he continued. "I didn't think Juan Carlos knew the connection."

"He didn't, at least not until our conversation." The two brothers had an interesting dynamic. Considering they were family and worked together, it would make sense to confide in one another, but that wasn't the case. Between their age difference and a strong competitive streak, the two were more like wary allies than members of the same team.

"How did you figure it out, then?"

"That's irrelevant, and you've not answered my question." My voice tightened with anger as I began to lose the battle over my control. "I want to know if you ever planned to tell me."

He lifted his chin indignantly. "No, I didn't. Your parents were the past; I was your future."

"Why did you do it? How did you know I was Alvarez's son?"

"There were rumors he had a bastard son. When I confirmed that a child had escaped the siege, I did some cursory searching. My efforts came up empty, so I let it go, but when I saw you at the fight, I knew it was you. You were the spitting image of him."

"That explains how. I also want to know why."

"Are you looking for me to tell you I felt guilt over what I'd done and sought to repent by taking you in? If that's the case, you're in for a disappointment. There's no generosity in my story." His words were a callous warning.

"I want to hear it anyway."

He lifted a brow and glanced back out toward the beach. "I never wanted children of my own because they make a man weak, but there's something to be said for having a protégé. Someone who can be molded into a proper successor. You became that someone. You had the required ruthlessness in your veins, and your years on the streets had brought that to the surface. You were the perfect subject, and look at what we've been able to achieve together." He lifted his arms to indicate the vast wealth around us. "I am the fucking king of this country, and you are poised to take over once I've tired of my reign."

He hadn't wanted a son; he'd wanted a mirror. A human experiment. Someone he could mold into his image without fear of injury or weakness. The explanation made sense when I looked at Naz from a different perspective—set aside the desires of a homeless orphan and looked at the man as he was. I couldn't say I was all that surprised, nor could I claim I wasn't glad he'd taken me in. He'd given me a far better life than I would have had on the streets. How could I hold that against him?

"I doubt your brother would be so thrilled to see me in control," I countered, curious if he truly intended to hand me his empire.

"Juan Carlos will do as I tell him, just as he's always done," Naz scoffed. "It's not up to him to decide the fate of my business." His eyes cut back to me, all traces of levity vanished. "But what happened in New York calls into question my faith in you."

"How can a man become a leader if he's not able to make his own decisions? I assessed the options, and in my judgment, I took the right path. She was unprotected by a mafia husband or boyfriend, and she made the job easy by coming with me willingly. Can you really not see why I might have altered my plans?"

He continued to stare down his nose at me. "That had better be the case. Should I decide that this woman has clouded your judgment in any way, I will take matters into my own hands." He finally broke eye contact and stood. "It's time for me to get dressed for my meeting. I'll be in touch." And with his parting words, I'd been dismissed.

The conversation hadn't been particularly good or bad, but just getting past it eased the tension in my chest. Naz would continue to watch me carefully, assessing my actions beneath his paranoid microscope, but I could still breathe easier knowing not all the scrutiny would be aimed at Giada.

My relief that she was out of the direct line of fire was not something I cared to analyze.

Instead, I spent the afternoon working away from the house and ignoring all things Giada until evening rolled around and I had to return home. As I strolled through the downstairs, I started to wonder if the house was empty when a peal of laughter trailed from upstairs. It was Giada, and her voice echoed with pure delight.

I was instantly enraged. What the fuck was Santino doing with her that would warrant that sort of sound? I hadn't specifically told him not to touch her, but surely he wouldn't be so foolish. Whether she was my wife or a prisoner, he was never given permission to lay hands on her.

I crept up the stairs two at a time, moving soundlessly through the house toward hushed voices and the crack of a pool stick striking balls. The game room. They were playing pool. I stepped into the doorway just as Santino bumped Giada with his shoulder playfully, then spotted my presence and hastily retreated.

His sudden change in demeanor caught her attention, and Giada looked my way as well.

"Perfect timing!" She grinned. "We were just starting another game. You can join us." She wore a pale blue strapless sundress and had her hair cascading down her back in loose waves, completely unaware of how fucking gorgeous she was and the seething anger I hid just below the surface.

Witnessing them together, laughing and flirting, I could hardly see straight from the vibrating fury inside my head. Santino was far more aware of how precarious the situation had become.

"Actually, now that Primo is home, I need to head out." He placed his cue stick back on the stand and nodded at me warily, only addressing me when he was close enough that she couldn't overhear. "She was bored, Primo. And nothing happened, so don't blow it out of proportion." Knowing he was walking on treacherously thin ice, he slipped out of the doorway and off to safety.

I turned my attention back to Giada, who assessed the balls on the table as if a tornado of trouble wasn't swirling right out her window.

"What the fuck did you think you were doing?" I growled at her, unable to hold back the savagery in my tone.

Giada stilled and lifted her eyes. Instead of the shocked innocence I expected to see on her face, she wore a victorious battle mask. "Entertaining myself," she asserted without an ounce of fear or hesitation. "What did you expect me to do? Stare at a wall all day?"

My fists curled so tightly my knuckles cracked. I prowled forward, eyes glued to the devilish woman sent to earth just to upend my life. "Santino is here for your protection and to guard you, not as your entertainment and certainly not as some fuck toy for you."

Her eyes flashed with a hint of her own sparking temper. "Why does it matter to you? I'm just here as leverage. It shouldn't matter who I talk to or if I fuck your entire army." She held her ground as she spoke, not giving up an inch as I rounded the table toward her.

"While you are under my roof, you will do as I say because every-fucking-thing on this property is mine." I closed the distance between us until we were toe-to-toe. "That means this sharp tongue"—I cupped her jaw and gently squeezed her cheeks—"is mine. And this…" I released her, snaking my finger down her neck, between her breasts and across her belly down to the apex of her thighs where I cupped her sex. "*This* is mine."

Her breathing shuddered on parted lips. "How am I supposed to know that when you won't come near me?"

"I'm telling you now. Stay the fuck away from my men."

"And what about you? Will you continue to hide from me?"

She was so fucking bold, and I wanted to both tear her down and protect her at all costs. Her maddening spell over me erased all logic and reset my brain to a primal level. Things like strategy and consequences were incomprehensible when I was in her thrall.

"What are you doing to me?" I breathed, my hand coming back up to wrap reverently around the delicate column of her throat.

"The same thing you do to me. Haven't you considered that this thing between us has complicated my life as well? You're not the only one who feels powerless. I would never have come with you if I'd felt like I had a choice, but I didn't. This pull is too great, and it fucking guts me when you push me away." Giada reached inside her soul and poured out its contents at my feet as if she had nothing to lose. She was in no position to challenge me, but that didn't stop her.

So fucking brave.

So fucking tempting.

I surged forward and nipped at her lower lip, drawing back with the sensitive flesh still pinched between my teeth before releasing her and trailing my tongue over the abused tissue. Giada lunged forward and tangled her tongue with mine, moaning into my mouth.

I felt the sound straight down to my cock.

She was a hurricane of desire and emotion, and I couldn't seem to escape her. If the winds didn't change and she continued to set her sights on me, her battering effects would forever change the landscape of my life. There was no avoiding it. Every second I spent with her drew me further into her orbit.

The thing that worried me the most was that I couldn't see through to the other side of the storm. The clouds were too dense to predict our survival. I spent years living with uncertainty, and I wasn't a fan. In fact, I did everything I could to avoid it as an adult, but with Giada, I wasn't sure I had a choice. She was the wildcard that threw everything into chaos.

As my mouth slanted over hers and I sought to possess her with ravenous abandon, I wondered if a little anarchy wasn't exactly what I needed in my life.

How could something that tasted so good be wrong? Was that what an alcoholic would say? They say addiction is when a habit disrupts the function of everyday life. I would have to be willing to upend my life if I wanted to give in to the craving for her. Was I becoming addicted to this woman?

I slowly pulled back from our kiss, meeting her wary gaze when she opened her eyes.

"Please don't push me away," she whispered up at me.

"You don't know what you're asking."

"I'm asking for you. Just you."

I breathed deeply to clear my head but had no answers. "Let's get some food. We'll both feel better once we've eaten." I stepped aside and set my hand on her lower back to guide her forward. Masculine satisfaction roared inside me when she followed my lead.

Maybe Giada and I could come to some kind of middle ground where everyone was happy. Where she didn't fight me, and my life wasn't obliterated by her presence. I briefly recalled the sight of Santino smiling down at her, and that wistful delusion was shattered.

Giada was all or nothing, and I had to decide what I could live with, and what I couldn't live without.

SEVENTEEN

Giada

Dinner with Primo was uneventful, which I took as a win. I was hoping that time together, no matter the activity, would help wear down the defensive wall he'd erected since we'd come to Mexico. After dinner, he made his excuses and walked me to my room. I didn't push him for more, not wanting to burst the bubble of our pleasant evening.

I went to bed feeling good about the progress we'd made that day, even though it had started on a rocky note, but when I went for breakfast the next morning, he was already gone. I found Alma in the kitchen and decided this would be a good opportunity to work on bonding with her. She was a short, older woman with heavily wrinkled skin and long hair, still mostly brown in color, that she kept swirled back in a loose bun. I found her to be very kind but quiet, which gave me hope she might be of use to me.

"Good morning, Alma. What delicious goodness have you been working on this morning?"

"Good morning, Miss Giada. I've got some pan dulce—sweet bread—and of course some eggs for Señor Primo because that's what he prefers." She brought over a plate with a large roll on it and a side of eggs. The bread had a white top coating that had cracked apart while baking and left an interesting webbing on the surface. It smelled utterly divine.

"This looks perfect, thank you!"

She blushed and waved a dismissive hand at me. "It's just some bread, mija."

I pulled off a piece of bread, which was still warm, and let the lightly sweet treat melt on my tongue. "Oh my God, you are amazing. If I stay here long, I'm not going to fit in any of my clothes."

The older woman giggled. "You don't want to be too skinny. Men like curves on a woman."

"Girl, I've got curves to spare, don't you worry."

"Oh, I'm not too worried about you. Somehow, I think you can take care of yourself."

I glared at her coyly. "You're not so helpless yourself, I'd say. I'd love to know how you learned to speak English so well."

"When Señor Primo first came to live with Señor Vargas, he was required to learn English. My duties as a housekeeper were expanded to include caring for Señor Primo, and since he was only allowed to speak English in the house, I had to learn along with him."

"So, you helped raise him?"

She dropped her gaze and smiled fondly. "I'm not sure I would say that. He was a very mature twelve years old when he arrived and didn't need much mothering, but I did what I could." It was clear the woman cared deeply for her boss, which spoke volumes about him.

"Do you have children of your own?"

Alma beamed. "Oh, yes. Three boys and two girls, all grown with families of their own now."

"Do you get to see them often?" I wasn't certain if she lived in the house or not, but she was definitely there for long hours.

"Well, they're all very busy, but we get together when we can. Aside from my sister, my entire family lives here in Guaymas, which helps." There was a melancholy tone to her voice, though she tried to hide it with her positive outlook, but I could tell she missed her family.

I offered her a tight smile, wishing there was something I could do.

"Don't you give me that sad look," she chided playfully. "This job has helped me provide for my family in ways I couldn't have otherwise, and Señor Primo is a good man to work for. I have no regrets." She accented her statement with a sharp nod.

"Good to hear." I chuckled. "What makes Primo a good boss? I'd love to know more about him."

Soft footfalls sounded on the tile behind me. "It seems I've arrived at the perfect time," Santino mused. "Alma, don't you have more important things to do than gossip with our guest?" He wasn't particularly harsh with her, but she made her apologies and hurried from the kitchen.

"Well, you're no fun," I pouted.

"Fun or no fun, I'd like to keep my head on my shoulders where it belongs. Now, what's on the agenda for today?"

"Do I have any options?"

He squinted as if deep in thought. "I have to be here at the house for the next hour, but if you'd like, I could take you on a drive through the area after that. There are some canyons nearby and a marina worth seeing."

"That would be amazing, thank you!"

"Don't thank me. I'm just trying to keep you out of trouble, for both of our sakes."

"I'm not sure why you seem to think I'm planning on causing a problem. Have I tried to escape or made any unreasonable demands?" I widened my eyes in my best puppy dog impression.

Santino eyed me suspiciously. "I'm not buying that for a second."

"Then you're smarter than you look." I gave in to a devious smile, drawing a huff of laughter from the young man.

"Just try to stay out of trouble until I'm done." He shook his head to himself as he walked away.

True to his word, Santino came for me about an hour later. We set out in his Land Rover but never made it to the canyon before he received a phone call from Primo instructing us to return to the house. The relaxed, carefree mood in the car became saturated with tension.

Santino was worried he'd upset Primo, and I was worried I'd gotten Santino into trouble. As much as I'd joked about causing issues for him, I didn't truly want him reprimanded on my account. By the time we got back to the house, I was ready to go to bat on his behalf and argue that he'd done nothing wrong, but my mental preparations were unnecessary. Primo merely nodded at Santino when we entered the house and instructed me to put on a swimsuit.

"Are we going out to the beach?" I asked cautiously, not wanting to poke the angry bear. He may not have been upset with Santino, but he was visibly tense about something.

"No, we're going out on my boat. Alma is packing us a lunch, so get whatever you need to be on the water for a couple of hours and meet me back down here when you're ready." He disappeared into his office, and I made my way upstairs to see what I could scrounge up for a boating date.

Twenty minutes later, I was back downstairs in a beach dress over my swimsuit with hat, sunglasses, and all the outdoor necessities. As of yet, I'd only seen Primo in suits and one glorious view of him naked, but never in anything casual. When he strolled in wearing a white linen shirt with the sleeves rolled up and a faded pair of jeans ripped at the knees, my legs threatened to give out.

He was raw, seductive masculinity—every schoolgirl's crush and every grown woman's late-night fantasy. Refined with a razor-sharp, jagged edge. A man so ruthlessly confident he had no need of stereotypical bad-boy attire. He was sophisticated, savage, and infinitely complicated—I was utterly dumbstruck at the sight of him.

I rolled my tongue back into my mouth and tried to string together a few coherent words. "Um, I'm all ready."

Primo slid a pair of sunglasses into his breast pocket. "I'll get the cooler from the kitchen, and we can go."

Fifteen minutes later, we were walking down the pier toward his boat on a gorgeous equatorial fall day. The temperature was closing in on eighty degrees, warm even for the moderate climate.

"Which one is yours?" I asked, scanning the long line of docked vessels.

"Second from the end on the right." He pointed at a moderately sized sea-faring boat that may not have been the largest boat in the marina, but what it lacked in size, it more than made up for in luxury. It looked brand new, and it was stunning.

"That's not a boat, it's a *yacht*!" I gaped.

"You see that behemoth across the way?" He motioned toward what looked like a small cruise ship. "That's Nazario's boat—now, *that* is a yacht."

"That's not a yacht, it's obscene," I muttered. Who could possibly need such a grandiose boat?

Primo just smirked and led me over the gangplank onto his craft.

A man already on board popped his head out from the interior and addressed Primo in Spanish. I could only assume he would be our captain, so while the two talked, I slipped around to the front of the boat and admired the posh leather seating and the ornate wood floorboards.

"I'd never want to leave if I had access to this boat all the time," I said when I sensed Primo join me.

"When the water is rough, you might change your mind."

"I don't know. I have a pretty strong stomach."

He motioned for me to join him on the bench seat. "Hopefully, we shouldn't test that theory today. Diego is going to take us down the coast a bit, and here in the Gulf of California, the water is rarely rough. I enjoy taking the boat out myself sometimes, but since someone has been rather insistent about having my undivided attention, I figured I'd leave the navigating to someone else." His tone was dry, but I could sense the sarcasm.

"Is that teasing? Do I detect a jokester hiding deep beneath all that stoic badassery?"

He scoffed. "Hardly."

"Santino has a lighter side, so if you put up with him, you must have a softer side in there somewhere." I leaned in, bumping my shoulder against his.

"Don't talk about Santino," he grumbled as the boat slipped from its mooring.

"I won't talk about him if you'll tell me how you two met."

Primo glared at me with resigned exasperation, a look I was more than used to receiving. "We met when I lived on the streets. He was a part of the same fighting circuit I used to compete in, but he was two years younger, so he wasn't fighting age yet. We looked out for one another while we were there. Once I'd been with Naz for about a year and was more comfortable with him, I asked if Santino could train to be one of his men to help get him off the streets. Naz agreed. We located Santino, and he was more than happy to join us. When I got a home of my own, it was natural that he would come with me as a part of my security team."

"The same way you brought Alma with you? I understand she's been a part of your life for a while."

"I think you need to stop snooping in other people's business." His words were a warning, but the tone conveyed little threat.

I had to fight to contain a smile. "I like learning about you, and it's not like there's much else to do at the house."

"That's why we're here. To distract you and keep you from meddling in other people's affairs."

"I'd like to think we're here because you wanted to be here with me. Although you certainly didn't seem too thrilled when we arrived at the house."

He tilted his head back and inhaled the salty sea air that tousled his waving sandy hair. "The situation with you is complicated, but it's also not the only problem I'm dealing with."

I adjusted to angle myself farther toward him and gave him an earnest look. "I know you're not a fan of sharing, but if you'd like to talk about it, I'm happy to listen. Contrary to popular belief, I can listen when the situation calls for it." I smirked, coaxing a small smile from him.

He reached out his hand and took mine in his, tracing the lines of my fingers and examining me as if I were foreign to him. I watched raptly, loving each delicate touch and forgetting to breathe when he brought my hand to his mouth and inhaled my scent. When he was done, he wove our fingers together and looked off in the distance, cradling my hand in his lap and ending the conversation.

I was entirely too awestruck to argue.

We sat quietly for a half hour, watching the coast drift by and spotting the occasional dolphin racing alongside the boat. When it was time to eat, we went inside to take a break from the sun and enjoyed the array of options Alma had packed for us. Primo pulled a beer for each of us out of a small refrigerator, and though I wasn't typically a beer drinker, it was the perfect accompaniment to a boat picnic.

Once our stomachs settled and we went back outside, Primo instructed Diego to take us into an isolated inlet where the water was especially clear, and there was a sandy beach along the shore. I discovered during our expedition that much of the coast was rocky, and while it was still beautiful in its own way, something about a white sandy beach was always magical. The most appealing part about this stretch was that it was completely unoccupied.

The boat slowed, and I stood to peer over the edge. We were only about a hundred yards offshore, and the entire area was sandy-bottomed and clear.

"How deep is it here?" I asked Primo.

He joined me at the railing. "Only about ten feet, which is why we can't go closer. It's a protected beach, no access on land, but there's a small dingy on the back of the boat. We can take it ashore if you want to check out the beach."

I grinned up at him, then removed my hat and sunglasses before lifting my dress over my head.

His eyes narrowed. "What are you doing?"

Instead of answering, I quickly stepped up onto the chaise lounge built along the side of the rail and hurtled myself over the edge, diving into the chilly water below. Being impulsive and a tad reckless filled me with elation. When I surfaced, I immediately sought out Primo and grinned up at him. "Or we could just swim there." I bit down on my lower lip, reveling in the begrudgingly amused look on his face, then turned and began to swim toward shore. The water was cold, but adrenaline kept me from feeling its effects.

Seconds later, a splash sounded from behind me. I glanced back to discover Primo had launched himself over the railing fully clothed. I squealed and kicked away with Primo in pursuit. He allowed me to reach the shore, slowly stalking after me as I stumbled in the sand and laughed. Walking backward, I openly gawked at the chiseled mountain of muscle hulking after me, wet clothes hugging his perfect body.

Without warning, he charged forward and lunged to scoop me over his shoulder. I lost myself in a fit of cackling laughter, not even pausing when Primo's hand smacked me on the ass. He took me to the tree line and lowered me down his body, pressing me back against the trunk of a palm tree.

"What am I going to do with you?" His rumbling voice vibrated from his chest into mine, wrapping its way around my heart. "I can't tell if you were sent as a curse or a divine reward, nor does it seem to matter. You could rain down havoc on my life, and I still don't think I could stay away."

"Then don't. Don't stay away." I licked a drop of salty water from his lips, drawing him into a deep kiss. My shaking fingers reached for the clasp on his jeans, fumbling to get my hands on his cock. I was seized with the needed to touch him—feel him inside me—more than I needed life itself.

"Tell me you're on birth control," he rasped.

I nodded rapidly. "I use the shot. It's still good for another month."

He instantly dropped down, wrenching my bikini bottoms to the ground. He then stood and finished unfastening his pants, removed his button-down shirt and instructed me to slip it on to protect my back. The second my arms were through the sleeves, he lifted me in his arms and ground the long length of his cock against my center.

We both moaned a chorus of inhuman sounds, slipping back to a place governed by primal, dark desires. A place only known to feral creatures of the night and the deeply depraved.

"Fuck, I missed this." He lay his forehead against mine, then angled himself at my entrance and rocked inside me. Just the tip at first, but with each firm thrust, he penetrated deeper into my core until I could feel him burrowing into my soul.

My head rolled back and around, lost in a sea of sensation. I buried my fingers in his wet hair and shrieked when he yanked my bikini cup down and latched his mouth over my aching nipple. Every breathless gasp and whimpered moan that slipped from my lips fed his insatiable hunger. The world spun in a dizzying whirlpool of pleasure until I thought I would hyperventilate from the coiling, clambering orgasm skittering along each of my nerves until it barreled into my pussy and exploded from my core.

A supernova of sensation blinded me from the inside out and stole my hearing, leaving in its staid a high-pitched ringing. I couldn't see or hear or feel my way around it until I released a shuddering breath and ordered my muscles to loosen one by one. Only then did I realize that Primo was also coming down from his own release, and I gently sank into the cradle of his brawny frame.

I eventually lowered my legs, centering myself on solid ground and retrieved my clothing. When I removed Primo's shirt, I discovered a slew of scratches and stains.

"I'm afraid this is ruined." I held the shirt up for him to see.

"It's just a shirt. Better it than you." He took the shirt in one hand and clasped the back of my neck with the other, pulling me in for one last languid kiss. "Let's get back."

We made the easy swim to the boat, and Primo helped me onto the back platform. Diego had placed a couple of towels on a nearby bench that we used to dry off. Primo instructed him to take us back to the marina, and we went up to the shaded top deck for the journey home.

He sat in the corner of the booth seating, and I curled up against him, knees pulled into my chest. I wasn't sure he'd meant for me to invade his space so thoroughly, but I didn't care. He curved his arm around me rather than pull away, and that was all that mattered.

"There's something I've been curious about from the beginning," he said, his thumb gently stroking up and down my arm. "Why do you steal things?"

I looked out over the water and tried to think of the proper words. I'd never talked about it to anyone, so it was hard to even know how to explain it.

"I'm not sure, exactly. The first time I did it, I was thirteen, and my aunt Vica was getting married. All six of us girls—my sisters and cousins—were flower girls. Our moms got us ready first at my grandparents' house, then ran around helping to make sure everything else went smoothly. I got annoyed with my oldest cousin, Maria, who always threw fits about family weddings, so I went off on my own and happened to find this small silver object in a hallway. When I wandered back into the fray, I discovered everyone was looking for a missing cuff link the best man had misplaced. I realized that must have been what I found, but as I watched everyone searching and thought of the tiny secret stashed in my purse, I couldn't find the words to tell them. The wedding would go on without it, and something was thrilling about knowing I had what they were all looking for." I glanced down and chewed on my lip as I finished. "I guess it sounds pretty petty and ugly when I say it out loud. Usually, it's not meant to be malicious, and I never go into a situation planning to do it. It just … happens."

He knew my dirty little secret, but I still hated to lay out the nasty details and expose myself further. I didn't want him to think I was spiteful or unworthy. More than ever before, I wished I wasn't so flawed.

"I told you before that I thought you wanted to be caught, and I still believe that. Has anyone else ever caught you or suspected?"

"No, you're the only person who knows anything about it."

He made a low humming sound deep in his chest. "I think you needed someone to see you for who you are, which is not the person you've portrayed yourself to be. I'm not sure why you didn't feel like you could be yourself, but that's what happened, and then you felt trapped."

I didn't understand how someone who had known me for such a short amount of time could see me so clearly, but he did. And giving credence to his assertion, knowing that he did see the real me and accepted me as I was, filled me with a resounding sense of inner peace.

"My family's not bad, but I've just never connected well with any of them," I admitted, then realized that all of Primo's family was dead. What an idiot I was. Who gripes about not connecting with their family to someone who had no family left? I felt like smacking myself in the head. I couldn't imagine if my entire family were killed. Just the thought brought a hollow ache in the pit of my stomach and made me realize that I did sort of miss them.

I peeked at him from the corner of my eye, but he didn't seem to be hurt by my careless words. Next time, I'd try to be more thoughtful. For now, our discussion about family was the perfect segue to a question I'd been mulling over.

"I don't know if you're aware," I started, "but Thursday is Thanksgiving back home. I was wondering if I might be allowed to call my family and check in with them. I'm sure it would mean a lot to them to know I was okay."

Primo peered down at me with an uncharacteristic softness to his gaze. "I think that could be arranged."

EIGHTEEN

Giada

WE HAD A PLEASANT DINNER TOGETHER THAT EVENING, BUT I could feel Primo pull away from me as soon as we got back to the house. I was a welcome guest, but no longer a lover or a girlfriend. Was he worried about someone seeing us together? His boss hadn't been thrilled I was there, but Naz wasn't at the house all the time. Why did it matter what we did in the privacy of his home?

When he excused himself for the night, leaving me alone in the living room, I moped all the way back to my room. I felt confused and dejected. As I got ready for bed, I analyzed his words and actions to a point of madness, then realized I was acting like a bystander in my own life. I wasn't a helpless witness. This was my damn boat, and I was the fucking captain. If I wanted the man, why didn't I just make the move? I was confident he wanted me too and likely wouldn't reject me if I pushed the matter, so why not go for it?

I slipped from my room in my silk camisole and matching shorts, eyeing the dark, unoccupied hallway. The chances I would see anyone were slim to none, but I still skulked down the hall to his room, quietly sneaking open his door and tiptoeing inside.

I could see his still form under the covers, and it gave me pause. I hadn't fully considered what I'd do if he was asleep. I stood stock-still, trying to determine if he was actually asleep and whether it would be imprudent to wake him. Then the covers thrust back on the side nearest me, and I could see in the dim light as Primo shifted to the middle, making room for me. Hurrying over, I slipped in next to him, curling on my side with my back to him. As I'd hoped, he wrapped his warm body around mine.

"Go to sleep, viborita." His drowsy rumble touched me deep in my chest, warming me from the inside out.

My happiness and relief manifested in a victorious grin. Having him welcome me into his bed thrilled me. My heart felt like it would burst, and I became almost giddy with energy—anything but sleepy. I tried to close my eyes, but my mind was whirring with activity. One question, in particular, kept rambling through my mind until I gave in to the compulsion and risked waking him again.

"Primo?" I whispered hesitantly.

He only grunted softly in reply.

"Back when we were in Vegas, you were there to take Alessia, weren't you?"

He sighed. "Not exactly. I was scouting, waiting for Naz to make the call. He didn't make the decision to capture her until after you returned home."

"But you knew we were going to be there. I've been wondering about that for a while. How did you know we'd be there?"

He squeezed my middle. "Why do you ask so many questions?"

I waited for a handful of heartbeats for him to continue. "You're not going to tell me, are you?"

"We have ways of getting information, just as I'm sure your family has sources of information on us. Now enough talking. Go to sleep."

I wasn't sure how I felt about the possibility of a rat in my father's organization. Someone close to us had leaked our travel plans, and that was scary. It hadn't proved deadly this time, but it could be dangerous in the future. I'd have to remember to tell my father when I had the chance, but until then, best not to annoy Primo by keeping him up.

I woke some hours later to a delicious warmth pooling in my belly and Primo's fingers deep inside my folds. The skill of his touch was diabolical, the eroticism intoxicating.

The moon was still high overhead, casting the room in an ethereal glow. I was on my back, Primo propped on his elbow above me with his shadowed gray gaze devouring me whole. Never in my life had someone looked at me with such ardent concentration.

I widened my legs, allowing him greater access to my center, arching and writhing under his touch. A harmony of sensation rippled beneath my skin, humming through my veins. When Primo lowered his mouth and grazed his teeth over my nipple through my silk nightie, a tidal wave of pleasure swept me away, drowning me in a flood of ecstasy. Liquid elation ran through my veins as my body quaked and quivered its release.

Primo slid his finger from my folds and drew a wet trail

up to my belly, then pulled me back against him again and pulled the sheet over us. I fleetingly wondered about him and whether he wanted a release, but the thought was quickly lost to my exhaustion and post-orgasmic stupor.

When I woke again, the sun was well into the sky, and Primo was gone. I would have enjoyed waking in his arms, but staying the night with him had been more than enough to start my day off right. I smiled and stretched, noting a delightful soreness in parts of my body no yoga could ever reach.

I skipped my workout and headed straight for the shower. A half hour later, I was refreshed and more than a little optimistic about my time in Mexico. Alma placed a heaping plate of food before me, and I dove in, hardly saying a word in greeting.

"Someone's got a healthy appetite this morning." Primo strolled in behind me, sweat-soaked from a session in the gym.

I just smirked. "I did a bunch of swimming yesterday—must have burned a lot of calories."

He hummed nonchalantly and plopped my phone next to my plate. "Who exactly were you wanting to call?"

I gulped down the bite of food I'd been chewing and wiped my mouth. "My cousin, Alessia. She's the person I'm closest to, and I'm sure she's worried sick."

"All right, but try not to sound too happy to be here." He stationed himself on the bar chair next to me and began to scroll on his own phone.

I clicked on Alessia's name in my favorite's list, and the phone only rang once when her frantic voice picked up.

"Giada? Is that you?"

"Hey, Al! It's me."

"Oh my God, are you okay? Have they hurt you? Where are they keeping you?"

"Al, one question at a time. I'm okay," I said, glancing at Primo. I wanted to reassure my family I was in no danger, but that wasn't exactly helpful to his cause. "I haven't been mistreated, so try not to worry."

"Not worry? They've called Dad and made demands in exchange for your return. I haven't been able to find out what they're asking for, but none of the guys seem too happy about it. Are you really okay? If not, say the word … peaceful, and I'll know you're in trouble."

"Al, really, I'm okay. How's my family?"

"Your mom is freaking out, lighting candles and not sleeping."

Well, that was surprising. Not necessarily that she'd light candles, but that my absence would cause her to do so.

"I figured she'd be glad to get me out of her hair," I scoffed.

"G, don't be dense. You know she loves you."

"God, you're right. I'm sorry. We argued before I left, and I'd hate for her to think it was her fault. Tell her I'm sorry for being such a pain in the ass and that me leaving had nothing to do with her."

A sniffle sounded over the line. "You tell her yourself when you get home," Alessia said, battling tears.

My own eyes began to burn. "Love you, Al. Promise I'll be home soon enough."

"Love you, too." Her voice was a coarse whisper, choked and ragged.

I hung up the phone and wiped at my eyes. When I glanced over at Primo, his posture had stiffened, and his eyes had clouded over with stormy intensity. His entire countenance had transformed from broody but playful to cold and calculating in a matter of seconds.

"You told her you're fine, but you know I can't guarantee your safety."

I gazed at him with the trust and confidence I felt in my heart. "There are no guarantees in life at all, but I know if anyone can keep me safe, it's you."

I'd intended to reassure him, but judging by his flared nostrils and speedy retreat, my aim had missed the mark.

NINETEEN

Giada

PRIMO WAS IN A MOOD FOR THE REST OF THE DAY. I GAVE HIM space until bedtime when I again let myself into his room. He welcomed me into his bed, but this time, there were no middle of the night extracurricular activities. He was up and off to the gym before I woke, but I didn't have time to dwell on his absence.

The day before, while Primo was off working and brooding, I'd made plans with Alma to prepare a Thanksgiving dinner as a treat for Primo. Well, maybe not just for him, since he wasn't used to my kind of Thanksgiving. We roasted a turkey, and I made potatoes, but we also cooked a couple of traditional Mexican celebratory dishes. There was far more food than our little household could eat, precisely as it should be on Thanksgiving.

I tried to get Alma to join us at the table, but she adamantly refused. Santino, on the other hand, had no qualms with participating in our dinner. The three of us made a serious dent in the food and even did some laughing, although Primo didn't stray far from his stoic nature. It was a lovely afternoon and a great chance to pretend life was normal—that I wasn't technically a captive and the man I was falling for wasn't conflicted about being with me.

The next day, Primo skipped his normal workout and left early on a work-related outing. I took the opportunity to do some yoga on the beach at sunrise with Santino sipping coffee and grumbling behind me. I wasn't technically a morning person, but yoga on the beach was worth rising early.

After I was thoroughly stretched and grounded, we went back to the house to start our day. I had no idea what exactly I was going to do all day to entertain myself, but I got cleaned up and ready regardless. I was glad I did because not ten minutes after I came downstairs, Santino informed me that I had a visitor.

"Mr. Vargas's wife, Haley, just passed through the gates and is here to see you."

"Haley?" I tried to picture the older man with a woman named Haley, but it just didn't compute.

"I believe they met in Vegas. They've been married about five years," he explained.

The picture he painted was an unfortunately accurate representation of reality. Haley couldn't have been more than a few years older than me, which meant Vargas was easily old enough to be her father. She was bleach blonde, had large fake breasts, a toned, lean body any woman would kill for, and a gleaming white smile that died before it reached her cornflower blue eyes.

My heart hurt for her.

"Hey, Giada!" she greeted me warmly. "I'm Haley. I thought I'd see if you wanted to do some Black Friday shopping with me. I don't need to scout for deals, but there's still something fun about the frenzy of Black Friday."

"Oh! That sounds like fun, actually. I didn't realize they had Black Friday down here."

"Well, they call it 'El Buen Fin,' but it's the same thing. It's a good excuse for some girl time—grab your purse, and we can head out." It was sweet of her to try to befriend me, but it felt odd. Did she know I was technically a hostage?

I looked at Santino in question, not sure how I was supposed to answer. He knew I wasn't exactly clamoring to get away, but he still might not have wanted me leaving the house. His narrowed eyes cut from Haley to me and back, the grim line to his lips and rigid posture giving off an uneasy vibe that I found to be infectious.

"Does Mr. Vargas know about this shopping trip?" he asked Haley.

"Of course!" She flashed a glamour shot grin. "He's the one that suggested it. He understands us girls have to get out and enjoy some retail therapy sometimes."

Her response didn't seem to ease Santino's concern. In fact, he looked fiercer than I'd ever seen him when he turned his attention back to me. "I suppose if it's under his instruction, then you should go."

I didn't like any of this one bit, but it didn't sound like I had much of a choice. "Are you coming with me?"

"No need," Haley piped in. "We'll have two of my men with us to keep us safe. You'll be in excellent hands. Promise, we're going to have a great day."

"Sounds like a plan." I tried to sound excited, but I couldn't rid my voice of worry.

Santino's hard gaze followed me out the front door, and then I was alone with strangers. While I'd been in Mexico with Primo, I hadn't once felt like a real captive until getting in the car with Haley. The severity of my situation came crashing down around me, and it was terrifying. I had zero control over what happened to me, and Santino's state of alarm told me there was a real threat of danger.

Primo's boss wasn't thrilled I was there, but he needed me for leverage, right? Wouldn't it be counterproductive for him to kill me? Of course, death wasn't the only terrifying prospect out there…

I slammed the door shut on my spiraling thoughts. They weren't helping.

Haley and I situated ourselves in the back of a stylish black Mercedes with two men in suits and sunglasses seated up front.

"So, where are you from?" Haley asked. There was a sincerity to her voice that indicated she was genuinely interested in getting to know me. She seemed nice enough, and it would be helpful while I was in Mexico if I had at least one friend, so I tried to be open-minded where she was concerned.

"Born and raised in New York City. What about you?"

"Originally from the Midwest, but I met Nazario in Vegas." Her smile faltered, and her gaze dropped down to her hands. Something about that statement bothered her, but it could have been anything. My instinct that it was Naz that bothered her may have just been my prejudices. Maybe she had family she missed back home, or maybe she was just embarrassed about what she'd been doing in Vegas when they met.

"Do you go back home often to visit?"

"No, I didn't get along great with my family. When I left, it was for good. Are you close with your family?"

"Yes, I guess so, although not as much as I'd like. I'm kind of the black sheep in my house."

"Well, that's the great thing about moving somewhere new and starting over. You can be whoever you want to be." Her smile was too broad. Unnatural. I wondered if she was with Nazario by choice or if circumstances forced her into it. Or maybe it had been by choice, but she'd come to regret that decision. Either way, I got the feeling she wasn't happy.

"What do you like most about living here in Guaymas?" I steered our conversation into what I hoped was a safe topic.

"Probably being on the water. Whether we're on one of Naz's boats or just enjoying the view from the house, I've never felt more peaceful than I do by the water."

"I could definitely understand that. We went out on Primo's boat the other day, and the views were amazing."

She smiled wistfully. "I could lose track of time for days on the water. And the weather's great year-round here, so there are lots of opportunities. Maybe we'll find a cute swimsuit or two while we're out—you can never have too many of those around here."

Our escorts took us to an outdoor shopping district in town that looked almost like an old town square. In the center, a large grassy area contained a raised gazebo that looked like it might be used for public functions. Kids ran around and played, and a couple of people walked dogs on leashes. The perimeter of the square was lined with shops and restaurants, all cozied under covered awnings extending from the brick buildings. The entire area had been constructed decades before but was well kept as if a treasured piece of the town's culture. Not exactly the mall I had envisioned, but definitely appealing in its own charming way.

As expected, people were out in droves to take advantage of the holiday weekend discounts. The street between the park and the shops was filled with parked cars and a row of frustrated motorists attempting to drive through the busy square. We parked a couple of blocks away and walked, one guard leading the way, and the other behind us.

Shopping with Haley was unexpectedly enjoyable. We tackled one-quarter of the square before we decided to break for lunch at a cantina grill. Situated on the corner, it had a surprisingly large outdoor seating area with metal tables stretching out onto the sidewalk.

"We should definitely eat outside on such a gorgeous day," Haley noted. The weather had been beautiful, slightly cooler temps with a warm sun that made walking in and out of the shade remind me of being a kid and jumping back and forth between a hot tub and a pool. I was chilly in the shade and hot in the sun, but quick trips between the two was the perfect medium.

"Sounds good to me. Table for four?"

"No way, this is girl time. The guys can eat on their own."

"I'm not sure there are enough tables for them to sit by us." I scanned the busy patio, only spotting one or two open tables.

"One of them can go grab food while the other watches us, just as long as they can still see us. Nothing to worry about. Now let's eat, I'm starved." She led the way to the hostess station at the front, and we snagged the only two-seater table available. Our escorts leaned against a car not far away, and I soon forgot about them.

I was surprised to discover Haley spoke perfect Spanish, helping me to communicate with our server and decide on my lunch order. "Did you know Spanish before you met Nazario, or did you pick it up after you moved here?"

"I learned once I moved. The guards and staff all speak Spanish, so it wasn't too hard when you hear it all the time. It's good to know what the people around you are saying." Her eyes flew to mine, and then she smiled as if she said something she wasn't supposed to and was trying to smooth it over.

It seemed obvious to me you would want to know the language of the country you were living in, so I wasn't sure why she would be wary of me knowing that. I'd enjoyed our day so far, but the mental and emotional gymnastics I'd had to perform were going to leave me exhausted by the time I made it home. Shopping with Haley was enjoyable but far more taxing than a stop into Nordstrom back home.

"I think I'm going to run to the restroom," I told her, scooting out of my chair.

"No problem, you can leave your stuff here if you want."

I thanked her and made my way inside to the back of the restaurant where the single-stall water closet was located down a hallway past the kitchen. I did my business and debated telling Haley that I'd hit my shopping limit and ask to go back home after lunch. It had been a decent morning, but I'd been on edge the entire time, and my stress levels were maxed.

As I stepped out of the restroom, a hand wrapped around my mouth, and I was yanked to the back of the hallway and out a back exit into an alley. Sticky nausea filled my belly, curdling into a thick mass of fear and helplessness. My heart leaped into a frenzied pace, forcing its way from my rib cage and up into my throat. I tried to pull in a lungful of air past the finger under my nose and only got a paltry breath tainted with the stench of grease.

It was a man's hand and strength that assaulted me, but I couldn't see him. He stayed out of view behind me, pressing me against the wall once we were outside. I tried to squirm and fight, but it was impossible once he had me against the wall. He hissed at me in Spanish, mouth next to my ear, and yanked my dress up around my hips.

Every molecule in my body crawled with disgust and terror.

I couldn't understand a word he said, but I didn't have to. His voice dripped with the bloody promise of violence.

Oh God, no. This can't be happening.

Tucked in a corner next to an overflowing dumpster, I screamed against his hand, my voice muffled by his meaty palm. Reason and logic escaped me as I succumbed to terrified panic, thrashing and hyperventilating against his hand. If I passed out, at least I wouldn't have to live with the wretched memory seared in my brain. But before it came to that, the man was yanked off me, sending me stumbling to the ground.

I looked up in time to see Santino pull out his gun and put a bullet right in the man's forehead. His head shot backward, a spray of blood splattering the brick behind him, and a deafening bang ricocheting off the walls of the alley. Totally unfazed, Santino slid his gun back in its holster and helped me off the ground before the man's body fully came to rest.

I clung to him as relief sucked all the strength from my legs and had me shaking like a newborn fawn. "You're here. You saved me … he was going to … but you saved me." My words tumbled out past my quivering jaw. I wasn't crying. It was shock that had my body rebelling.

"I've got you. I told Primo I'd keep you safe, and I meant it." He directed me toward the mouth of the alley just as one of Haley's guards came jogging back, gun in hand.

He shouted something at Santino in Spanish, to which Santino shot back an equally mystifying, rapid-fire response so scathing it would have withered paint off the wall. Not allowing a reply, he turned his back to the man and led us to his car parked a block away.

"What did that man say to you back there?" I asked, still trying to process everything that was happening.

"He asked me what I was doing following them. I told him not to fucking question me when he couldn't even do his own damn job." Santino helped me in the car gently, but his voice was deadly sharp. He was furious. When he got into the driver's seat, he texted out a quick message then started homeward.

"I thought we were safe with them around. I knew you were worried, but I couldn't imagine anything happening with two guards watching us." My head slowly shook back and forth, recalling how fast a simple bathroom trip had spiraled into the unthinkable. Were the streets of Guaymas really that unsafe?

"If they'd had any intention of keeping you safe, it wouldn't have been an issue."

My head snapped in his direction. "What are you saying?"

His jaw flexed and contracted. "Nothing. I'm not saying anything except that I'm glad I followed you back to the restroom." He ended his statement with a finality that communicated he would say nothing further on the matter.

We drove the rest of the way home in silence, the first pangs of homesickness aching in my chest.

TWENTY

Primo

I HAD TO GO INTO HERMOSILLO FOR THE DAY, AN HOUR AND A half drive from Guaymas. Most of our operations were run from Hermosillo, but we preferred to live on the coast. I had several meetings to conduct, one of which was at a strip club we owned. That's where I was when I received a text from Santino informing me of Haley and Giada's impromptu shopping trip.

My initial response was immediate worry, which steamrolled straight into anger. Why the fuck should I be worrying about Giada? First, she was with Naz's men, and he knew we needed her alive just as much as I did. Second, where exactly did I think my little fling with her was going to go? We weren't living some white collar, fairy-tale life. I killed people for a fucking living, and her family would kill me if they could get close enough. Continuing this idiotic charade was only going to end in disaster.

I'd stepped out of the office and into a hall when I got the text, ready to tear ass out of there if needed. As I processed the situation, frustration bubbled to a boiling point inside me, and I swung my fist, putting a hole in the wall.

The office door creaked open, and my day manager leaned against the frame. "If you were anyone else, I would beat your ass. But since this place is yours to tear apart, have at it."

I shook out my now screaming knuckles, hoping I hadn't broken anything. "What else do we need to go over before I get the fuck out of here?"

"Nothing that can't wait." He paused, eyeing me warily. "If you need to work out a little tension, several of the girls are getting off the morning shift now." The club was open twenty-four-seven, and while sex wasn't officially on the menu, it was far too lucrative of a trade to pass up.

I wasn't one to sample the product, but for once, I wondered if that wasn't just what I needed. Maybe getting my cock wet would help get Giada out of my system. I was willing to try just about anything to free myself from the compulsion she cast over me.

"I think I'll just take a look around before I go," I murmured. I wasn't sure I would fuck one of the girls or not, but if I did, it was no one's business but my own.

He extended his hand in invitation toward the back of the club. "You need anything, just let me know."

I walked down the hall to the employee backstage entrance. Pulsing bass from the music up front could be heard throughout the building. When I'd first arrived, there were a dozen customers—above average for ten a.m. on a

Friday, but not surprising for a pseudo-holiday. Things would kick up significantly toward lunch and be packed by dusk.

Several girls were in various states of undress in the prep area, totally unfazed by my presence. A couple of others stretched to get ready for their routines. I took in each of them, debating if any were sober and clean enough for me to even consider putting my dick into them.

One of the girls at the back of the room sat at a makeup mirror removing a set of false eyelashes. She was a petite thing, young enough that she wasn't worn down or overly enhanced. She had long black hair and smooth coppery skin that shimmered with an ample dusting of body glitter.

I made my way over to her, ignoring the curious glances from the rest of the girls. When she realized she had company, she peered up at me and smiled. I rarely talked to the women, so they didn't necessarily know who I was specifically, but only management was allowed backstage.

"Can I help you?" she asked with only a hint of trepidation.

I let my eyes roam over her high cheekbones and full, pouty lips. "Are you interested in making a few bucks?"

She smiled, stood, and took my hand, leading me toward the private rooms. They were small, sparce rooms designed for one purpose with a pole on one side and a disgusting vinyl loveseat on the other. Overhead, a disco ball spun in slow circles and reflected the LED colored lights throughout the room.

She selected one of the rooms and closed us inside. I refused to go anywhere near the loveseat and chose to stand as she began to gyrate on the pole. She was decent at her job. I'd seen my share of strippers dance and could honestly say there was a level of skill involved. This girl could move, but I viewed her in a clinical fashion, as if judging an audition rather than trying to get off.

She was attractive, nearly naked, and grinding on a pole—why the fuck wasn't I aroused?

There was only one answer, and she had venomous green eyes and an intoxicating personality that made me forget who I was. Forget my obligations and responsibilities. Forget the dangers and consequences of being with a woman like her. When it came to Giada, I was more drugged out than any of the girls dancing at the club, and it made me fucking furious.

I was powerless, like a pawn in a chess match I'd never agreed to play.

Wanting to rip myself free of the web I'd landed in, I charged over to the girl and pressed her back against the pole. Her chest rose and fell in hurried, jittery movements as she peered up at me fearfully. All I could see was Giada's challenging gaze, as green as the palm fronds above her, when she practically begged me to fuck her against that palm tree.

No matter how badly I fought against my developing feelings for Giada, there was no denying them. I could fuck every woman from here back to Guaymas, and not one would dim my thirst for the Italian who snuck into my bed at night. Nothing would stop me from worrying about her or keep me from being jealous when another man looked at her.

I could try to ignore it, but I'd only make myself insane. So where did that leave me? I couldn't have her, but I also couldn't keep myself away.

I was well and truly fucked.

I growled out a savage roar of frustration, shoving myself away from the petrified dancer and storming from the club. I had thought I couldn't get any more upset. That my emotions had risen up and unleashed a full-on coup against me until I was a prisoner at their mercy. For hours, I walked through the motions of my day, conducting meetings and discussing business under constant threat of losing my shit. Of becoming a conduit for my emotions rather than their master.

It wasn't until I received a text from Santino just after lunch when I realized just how wrong I'd been. I'd had the strength to take control of my emotions—I'd just needed the proper motivation. Fear had kept me immobilized, but I was stronger than my fears.

Giada was attacked. She's uninjured but shaken up. I'm taking her to the house.

The second I learned Giada had been in danger, I shattered through my flimsy glass prison and locked down my emotions with the ease of a lion crushing the life from a helpless rabbit. I was a polished steel blade, ice cold and ready to dole out retribution.

I completed my remaining tasks in Hermosillo with mechanical efficiency, but still didn't make it back to Guaymas until after dark. Santino was watching television in the living room alone when I arrived home. He took one look at my face and knew explanations would have to wait.

"Upstairs," was all he said.

I took the steps two at a time, first checking her room and finding it empty. I then went to my room and thought it was empty as well before I spotted her head poking up over the back of a chair on the balcony. I prowled over and found her curled in a ball, bundled in a blanket to ward off the chilly evening air.

When her eyes lifted to mine, her face flooded with relief. She bounded from the chair and into my arms, where I held her tightly against me. I lifted her legs around my waist and carried her inside, the tension in my shoulders easing for the first time that day. I could feel her breathing shudder against my neck, and her solace at being in my arms made me harder than any stripper could ever achieve.

"Shhh, I'm here," I murmured into her hair as I sat down on the bed. "I'm not letting you out of my sight again. Either you're here at the house or you're with me. Okay?"

She nodded, then pulled back and met my eyes, her green gaze iridescent with unshed tears. Even after being attacked, her strength was astounding, and I wanted to devour it one courageous tear at a time. Our lips came together at the same time, ravenous for one another.

That was how it was between us.

Cataclysmic. Elemental. An inescapable force pointless to resist.

Within seconds, we were naked and on the bed, my cock pushing deep inside her. What passed between us that night in the darkness of my bedroom wasn't just sex; it was a promise. An apology. My unspoken word to her that I would protect her at all costs.

When she came apart in my arms, the cool certainty of resolve snapped its whip and aligned the two warring factions inside me. I realized that protecting this woman came before anything else. Once that was decided, all the other pieces slipped into place. I was no longer conflicted.

Giada Genovese would be mine.

I just had to figure out how to make that happen and keep us both alive in the process.

TWENTY-ONE

Giada

From the second I ran into Primo's arms, the dynamic between us shifted. Whatever doubts or conflict he'd been wrestling with had disappeared. His gaze was reverent, and his touch was possessive. He opened himself up and allowed me to see the depths of his desire for me. Like a balm to my soul, each caress and kiss soothed my hurt and made me whole again.

As we lay entwined with one another, the frantic beating of our hears easing back to normal, I debated asking him what had changed. I didn't want to push him away or disturb the blissful bubble around us, but if we had any hope of having a relationship, we needed to be able to talk openly. He'd proven he wasn't put off by my forward manner. I needed to trust that I could be myself and speak up when I had something to say.

"Today was the most scared I've ever been in my life," I admitted softly. The room was still, but the faint hum of lapping waves gave movement to the darkness.

Primo held me tighter, his hand cupping the back of my head. "I'm so sorry you had to face that."

"I had no idea it would be so dangerous in town. I could tell Santino was worried when I left, but I never imagined…"

"The problem isn't the town." His words were eerily quiet with an undercurrent of murderous rage that had my heart rate quickening. "I had a feeling from the beginning that Naz wouldn't take well to you, but I'm afraid it's worse than I anticipated."

Lifting my head, I searched his face, but his eyes stayed fixed on the ceiling above. "You think Naz was responsible for my attack? That doesn't make any sense; he needs me as leverage. Plus, if he wanted to hurt me, why not just do it rather than plan a secret attack?"

"He thinks my attachment to you weakens me. We do need you, but not necessarily untouched. Should something happen to you that appeared to be a random accident, neither your family nor I could fault him. I don't know for sure that he was responsible for what happened, but that's what my gut is telling me. This is exactly why I've tried to keep myself from you. Everything about my life is dangerous."

"It is, but don't you think I should have some say? What if I think you're worth the risks?"

"You may think you can make that decision, but you don't know my life and all it entails."

"I think I got a pretty good tutorial today, and it doesn't change the way I feel about you."

He was quiet for several minutes, lost in his own

thoughts. "When Santino told me what had happened, all I could think about was getting back to you. It made me realize that I'm only making things worse with my indecision and weakness. I either needed to send you home or embrace this thing that exists between us. Since I can't seem to stay away from you, that leaves me with only one option."

"So … you feel stuck with me?" I suddenly felt like the fat kid no one wanted on their team in PE.

"That's not what I said. I want to protect you, and the best way to do that would be to send you home, but I'm too selfish to do that. Aside from fucking over our plan, I'd never see you again, and I just can't make myself do it. I want you too much to send you away."

Joy exploded in my chest. I'd gone from crying tears of anguish alone on his balcony to floating on air, all because of this mercurial, complex man who cradled me in his arms like a precious gem.

"You can't fathom how happy it makes me to hear you say that you feel it too."

He kissed the top of my head. "It would be far less dangerous for you if I didn't. Naz would have no reason to doubt me, and I could send you back home in one piece."

I shook my head against his chest. "Not one piece. My heart would be shattered."

"But you'd be alive."

"In the sense that I'd be breathing, but that's it. I was drawn to you from the moment I saw you, and once that connection was made, I don't think it could ever be severed. Not without devastating heartbreak. You are the life that I want, whatever that means. Whatever the consequences."

I listened to his steady, even breaths for long minutes, wishing life could be as simple as it was there in his bed.

"It's going to take me time to figure out a way for us to be together," Primo said after a while. "I'll have to convince Naz you aren't a threat to me and to our operation."

"I don't understand why he thinks I'd be a problem. He has a wife. Why would you having a woman be any different?"

"I'm still sorting it all out myself. While I was in New York, I learned that Naz was responsible for my parents' deaths. My mother worked as a housekeeper for a wealthy family. I never knew, but the man of the house had an affair with my mother, and I was the product of that relationship. When I was ten, the house burned down while I was at school. Everyone inside was killed. It was only after talking to Naz's brother than I learned Naz had been responsible for the fire and that I'd lost not only my mother that day but my father too. Naz took me in knowing who I was. Knowing that my father was the rival he'd killed. When we got back, I confronted him about it and tried to figure out his motivations. From what I could gather, I was an experiment to him. A living doll he could craft in his image without being weakened by having a true family. He may have a wife, but she is nothing to him but a warm body. I have been his life's work for over a decade, and he doesn't want me to derail what he sees as my destiny. To him, your death would be a small price to pay to keep me strong and aligned to his cause."

What he told me gave me a whole new perspective on the dynamic between the two men. It also made me realize how much more Primo had been dealing with in the past week than I'd realized. He'd learned that the man who helped raise him had been responsible for his parents' deaths. Hell, he'd only just learned who his biological father was, and I'd been frustrated about him keeping me at a distance. Even on the best day, that would have been hard to process.

My insides twisted to think of how much turmoil he had

to be in. I felt horrible he'd had to learn what Naz did but also incredibly grateful that he'd shared it with me. Knowing now what he'd been dealing with strengthened my respect and admiration for him.

On the other hand, what I'd learned about Naz was revolting. He was a sociopath—what other way was there to describe a man who would kill his son's girlfriend to keep his son all to himself? Primo may not technically have been Naz's son, but close enough.

It was madness.

"He's crazy. You know that, right?"

My head rose and fell as he took in a deep breath. "I suppose to some extent I knew, but I never realized how bad it was." He sounded weary, and I could only imagine the terrible burden of his situation. I didn't want to add more discomfort to our already delicate conversation, but there was something I still needed to address. We'd taken our blossoming relationship to a new, more intimate level, and that meant there was no excuse not to confront him with the accusations my family had presented. "I have something I need to ask you. It scares me to know the truth, but it's too important to ignore. I know my family is involved in all kinds of illegal activities, but they claimed the cartels are far worse. That you guys participate in sex trafficking and bombing civilians and all kinds of terrible things. Is that true?"

"Not long after my mother died, I was almost picked up by some men who stole children and women off the streets. They nearly had me in their van when another man confronted them and saved me. I was absolutely terrified. I'd come a breath away from untold terrors, and the memory of that helplessness and crippling fear never left me. As I got older and grew to take on more responsibilities with Naz, I learned about the more unsavory aspects to his businesses. I was always more of an enforcer than a business partner, but I still knew more than most. Excluding myself from participation in his trafficking practices was one of the only ways I have every refused Naz anything. He wasn't pleased, but I have remained firm in my stance. I can't tell you that the cartel doesn't involve itself in that kind of activity, because it would be a lie, but I can assure you that I've never approved. There are some lines that should never be crossed, and that is one of them." The harsh finality of his words spoke to his conviction.

His participation in an organization that trafficked innocent people wasn't ideal, but I believed in his distaste for the practice and sensed his remorse for allowing himself to remain aligned with Naz for so long.

"Naz doesn't have a conscience at all, does he?" I couldn't imagine how someone could do that to other human beings.

"He sees life in a much more animalistic fashion. Kill or be killed. So no, he doesn't feel bad when he profits from the destruction of others."

"Is his brother as bad as he is? Maybe he could help?"

"Juan Carlos has hated me since the day Naz brought me home. There's no way he'd help me stand against Naz."

"Did he know who your parents were? Is that why he hated you?"

"Surprisingly, no, he didn't know. I think just the fact that I was an outsider at all rubbed him the wrong way. He wanted the money and power to stay in the family."

"If neither of you knew, how did you figure it out?"

"I was at his house and happened to see a broken figurine I recognized. As it turned out, Juan Carlos led the siege that killed everyone in the house—the fire had only been a coverup and a statement to all other potential rivals. Juan Carlos took the figurine as a souvenir of their accomplishment, but he had no idea it was my mothers. I knew immediately because it had been representative of a treasured memory for my mother and me."

"Are you glad you know the truth?"

He couldn't undo the past, so knowing who was responsible didn't change what happened. It only complicated his life, and I would understand if he wished the truth had remained hidden.

"I'm glad I know. It's helped me see my situation more clearly. To see Naz more clearly. I wish I hadn't left the figurine back at Juan Carlos's house, but that's my only regret about learning the truth. The Lady of Guadalupe is the only piece of my mother that still exists."

"Could you ask him for it?"

"Now that he knows what it means to me, he'd never let me have it. He'd rather burn it that give me the satisfaction. It's not the end of the world. I have my memories of her, and that's always been enough."

I smiled, glad he at least had a mother who had loved him. "Tell me about her. I'd love to hear more."

His chest vibrated with a deep rumble. "She loved to play games—cards or checkers or bingo—anything we could find. If it wasn't a school night, she'd let me stay up late so that we could play games for hours. She made the best empanadas I've ever had, and she used to sing all the time when she did chores. Even when she was working, she was always singing."

"She sounds lovely," I whispered, a ball of emotion clogging my throat.

He lifted up on an elbow and peered down at me. "Why do you sound like you're crying?"

"I just wish you could have had more time with her. No child should have to lose their mother."

"I'm glad I had her as long as I did—long enough to remember. Had she died a few years earlier, I might have been too young to have any memories of her at all." He rolled me onto my back, and his eyes grew hooded. "Enough talk about things we can't change. I want to see that beautiful smile again, and I know just how to find it."

He kissed his way down my body, then licked and sucked at my core until I thought I'd pass out with pleasure. He may not have found my smile, but he did bring tears of pure bliss to my eyes.

It was only fair I returned the favor.

We fell asleep that night wrapped in one another's arms, our fates more entwined than ever, and my heart dangerously close to being irreconcilably his.

The next morning, Primo explained that our time together had to be limited to our nights in his bedroom. He didn't want to give Naz reason to lash out while he figured out our next move. If any of the staff or guards told Naz we were seen in any kind of intimate expression, it might force his hand.

I wasn't thrilled, but at least we had our nights together. The weekend passed quickly. After my scare on Friday, I was more than happy to have a boring, uneventful couple of days.

Monday resumed the routine we'd begun the week before. I did yoga in the gym while Primo finished his workout, then he left for work, and I kept Alma company while she buzzed about the kitchen.

"What's on the menu today?" I asked cheerily.

"Good morning, mija. I'm making tamales today. They take a while to prepare, so I wanted to get an early start."

"I'm not a huge fan." I wrinkled my nose. "The one time I had some, they were awfully pasty."

She waved a maize-soaked hand at me. "This is my sister's recipe, and she makes the *best* tamales, not that I'd ever admit that to her."

I smirked, all too familiar with the joy of having sisters. "Are you two close?"

"We were when we were younger, but it's been hard to stay in touch as we've gotten older. Luz is my younger sister, and I have two older sisters along with four brothers."

"Good Lord, that's a lot of kids."

Alma chuckled. "It seems normal to me."

"I have two sisters, and we fought enough to make my parents crazy. Having eight kids in a house sounds like a nightmare. At least the boys wouldn't be constantly at each other's throats."

"Oh, they were a handful in their own way. One time, two of them got into such an intense wrestling match they rolled themselves out the front window of the house. I thought my father was going to kill them."

"Yeah, none of this is making me want to ever have kids."

"Ah," she scoffed at me. "You don't mean that."

"I do. I've never really felt that maternal instinct. Just not my thing."

"You're young. Who knows what the next few years will bring. You might find you feel differently." She smiled warmly at me, and I returned the gesture, but it felt empty.

I truly didn't think I'd ever want kids. It never seemed like a big deal to me before, but I suddenly felt anxious. Would Primo want children? If he did, was that something I could give him?

Good grief, I'm getting carried away.

"All right, Alma. I think I better go get cleaned up." I clapped my hands against the granite counter and slid from my chair.

"Hold off," Santino said from behind me. "I just got word that Naz is here."

"But Primo's not here."

"He's here to see you."

My eyes stayed locked on his as a chill skittered down my spine, and my legs suddenly became molten lead welded to the floor. I had faith that Primo would keep me safe from Naz, but he couldn't do that if he wasn't around. Why would Naz come to see me? Would Santino protect me, or was his loyalty to Naz?

I finally dropped my gaze and nodded shakily. "I'll be in the living room."

Breathe, Giada. You're a badass mafia princess, remember? This guy can't scare you.

I gave myself a mildly effective pep talk, then sat stiffly in an armchair. There was no greater way to stretch out time than waiting for evil incarnate to pay you a visit. My heart took the opportunity to climb its way into my throat, and my palms were so clammy I could have passed for dead. But I gave myself credit because when Naz finally walked through that door, I channeled my cousin Maria and made sure I was one hundred percent, grade A badass. No matter how I felt on the inside, he wouldn't get even the faintest whiff of fear from me.

"Hello, Naz." Chin high, shoulders back, bitch face on.

"I heard what happened last week and wanted to check on you. I've told your father you're being well cared for, and I wanted to make sure I hadn't misled him." He gave every appearance of being a caring, fatherly figure. It was more than a little disturbing because he was almost convincing. If I hadn't known that he was likely the culprit behind my attack, I might have believed his act.

"Isn't that kind of you," I offered, dripping saccharine sweetness. "It was fortunate Santino was there to rescue me."

His eyes narrowed, but his smile was unnaturally fixed. "Why don't you accompany me onto the back porch? We can talk and enjoy the beautiful morning."

I nodded and led the way, feeling his oily gaze on my back with each step. We sat at one of the dining tables near the pool, and Alma brought two glasses of water before scurrying away.

Naz sipped from his glass and gazed out toward the beach. "I'm not sure what your life was like in New York, but I would not hesitate to say it was far different than life is down here." He paused, fingering the condensation that began to form on his glass. "You think Primo is perhaps like the men you grew up with. That he has feelings for you and wants to make you happy. Primo is far more complicated than you could imagine. He killed a man for the first time when he was only thirteen and has only ever known a life of violence."

I wanted to lash out. To scream at Naz that whatever Primo had experienced was a direct result of him poisoning Primo's life. Vicious, hateful words slithered under my skin, a rattlesnake coiled and ready to strike. But I wouldn't allow it. I wouldn't believe his lies, and I wouldn't screw up any chance Primo had at breaking free from Naz by spewing my frustrations. Instead, I clamped my jaw shut and played the role required of me.

Naz pulled something from his breast pocket, studying it before placing it on the table and sliding it toward me. It was a photograph. Dark but dotted with specks of light illuminating two people in the middle—Primo pinning a mostly naked woman against what looked like a stripper pole.

"That was taken Friday from our security cameras in the Hermosillo club. While you were being attacked, Primo was fucking another woman. You mean nothing to him, so don't pretend to make him into something he's not." Icy hatred slipped into his voice, betraying the depth of his emotion on the subject.

It hurt to see the photo. I recognized the dress shirt Primo had been wearing Friday, and while that didn't necessarily mean the photo was taken that day, it was enough to cast suspicion.

I had to hand it to Naz. He was good. His words may not have done the job, but the photo was hard to overcome. That was, except for the fact that he was desperate to scare me away from Primo. If that was the case, and he had cameras in a room where Primo allegedly fucked another woman, why hadn't he brought me a picture of them in the act?

Naz may have been a good actor, but I was better.

I allowed a single tear to slip from my lashes when I slid the photo back to him. I was raised with two sisters in a strict Catholic family; I could summon tears like other people blinked. It had been a necessary life skill to master in our house.

Naz took the bait as I'd hoped and grinned mournfully at my visible heartbreak. "What you need is another woman to talk to. Haley said you two had a lovely time together Friday before things … took a turn. I'll send her over after lunch, and you two can have some time together." He slid the picture back in his pocket and rose from his chair.

I stayed seated, choosing to use my heartbreak as an excuse not to see him out.

He clasped a hand on my shoulder in mock support. "It's

best you knew before you made a terrible mistake. Your uncle and father have agreed to our terms, and this entire little episode will be over in just a few days. We'll have you back home soon, and you can put this whole ugly mess behind you." He patted me gently and walked away, totally oblivious to the ten different ways I envisioned breaking his hand.

I hated every minute I spent with him, but if I bought Primo some time, it was worth every nauseating second.

True to his word, Naz sent Haley over that afternoon. I didn't let my loathing for him bleed onto her, so I was happy to have her company. She was a tool in Naz's fucked-up game just as much as I was, at least, I hoped. I couldn't stomach the notion that she might have knowingly participated in my attempted rape.

"I'm so glad to see you're okay. I was horrified when I heard what happened." Her face was creased in genuine remorse, reinforcing my belief that she was innocent of wrongdoing.

"It was pretty terrifying. I don't even want to think about it." My lips formed a thin line of unease.

"I can totally understand. Let's do something fun instead. Interested in a walk on the beach?"

"That sounds perfect. Let me change out of my yoga gear, and I'll be right back." I hurried upstairs and put on fresh leggings and a comfy sweater, along with some sunscreen. The days had gotten progressively cooler since I'd arrived, but the sun still packed a punch.

When I went back downstairs, I located Santino first and let him know our plans, then found Haley gazing out the window at the beach. "I'm all ready. Do you need any sunscreen or anything?"

"Oh! Nah, I'll be fine without. I'm used to the sun." She

slipped her shoes off but kept her purse clutched in her hands. "All ready!"

I smiled and slid the glass door open, Haley and Santino following me out and down the patio steps toward the sand. Once we started toward the shore, Santino hung back and allowed us our space. The beach was unoccupied except for a few individuals here and there in the distance. We made our way in the stiff ocean breeze to the hard-packed sand just beyond the water's edge and walked for several minutes before I broke the silence.

"Do you have many friends here in Guaymas? It seems like being the boss's wife might be a bit lonely—I mean, not to be rude. I was just curious." *Smooth, Genovese. Real smooth.*

Haley smiled, thankfully unbothered by my forwardness. "We have company for dinner on occasion, and I enjoy visiting with one of the housekeeper ladies, but no, it's not the same as having girlfriends. I never really had a lot of friends, though, so it's not something I miss."

"I've always had so many cousins and sisters around me that I never had many outside friends either. Having so many women in my life just gave me a headache anyway," I teased, not wanting Haley to feel bad. Too many women could be annoying, but being alone would be far worse. With a husband like Nazario, it had to suck balls.

"Have they told you when you'll be going back?" she asked quietly, the first acknowledgment I'd heard from Haley that I wasn't just a long-term houseguest.

"Soon, I think." I kept my thoughts on that to myself. I wasn't sure how much of what I said to her was fed back to her husband. If I told her how much I cared for Primo and that I didn't want to leave him, Naz could find out. It wouldn't surprise me at all if he interrogated her about our conversation when she returned home.

"That's good. I'm sure they—oh!"

A strong gust of air caught the thin scarf she was wearing and swept it right off her shoulders.

"I've got it!" I cried, leaping after the shimmering blue fabric and snagging it just as it hit the ground several feet away. It was a gossamer fabric more for fashion than warmth and airborne as quickly as a kite. "There we go." I gently shook off the scarf and presented it to her with a smile.

"Thanks. I'll have to tie this silly thing this time." She reached out to take it from my hands, but I pulled it away before she touched it, my eyes glued to the band of purple bruises circling her neck.

"Oh, Haley," I breathed, my horror-filled words carried off in the wind but still rung loudly in my mind.

Her face hardened, and she snatched the scarf from my hands. "Please, just leave it alone." Her brittle whisper barely penetrated above the ambient noise and the blood whooshing in my ears. She sounded defeated and hollow, nothing like the cheery woman I'd thought I was befriending. How miserable was her life? Was there any way she could get out?

"I'm so sorry." My voice broke along with my heart, bleeding for this poor woman alone and friendless in Mexico with a monster for a husband.

She lifted her eyes to mine, blue like the endless sky and equally empty. Haley was a shell of whoever she used to be. Broken and tragic. "Don't be sorry. Just go home, Giada, and never look back." The words were spoken without a hint of emotion; her features eerily detached.

She turned without another word and began to walk back toward the house, leaving me frozen in shock, the wind whipping through my hair and tugging at my sweater. A clamp squeezed down around my heart, and the burn of grief smarted at the back of my throat.

Haley was in so much pain, and there was nothing I could do.

I was no longer in that alley being attacked, but I felt equally as powerless as I had then. As women, we had a duty to help one another when it came to our safety. No woman should have to be scared in her own home.

Three hours later when Primo came home, I was curled up in the living room still thinking about what I'd learned, haunted by the ghost of Haley's agony.

"Everything okay?" he asked, using his fingers to lift my chin and bring my gaze to his.

I gave him a thin smile. "Yeah, but we need to talk."

Primo's face hardened. He nodded in understanding and sat in the chair opposite me. I told him all about my visits from Naz and then Haley. He listened without comment, allowing me to purge the thoughts and emotions that had been festering all day.

"I'm not happy about it, but I can't say any of this surprises me," he finally said, leaning back in his chair.

"You should have seen her, Primo. It was heartbreaking."

"I've never pried into their relationship, but I knew if he dealt with his wife the way he handled raising me, he likely used his fists to communicate. He was a strong believer in physical lessons. Not the most civil means to teach, but effective, nonetheless."

"I wish there was something we could do to help her."

He did a brief scan of the room, ensuring we were alone. "Me severing ties with him will be hard enough. I don't think there's anything I can do for her that won't enrage him."

I nodded, my gaze drifting outside to the sun sinking down past the horizon, coating the landscape in thick swaths of tangerine and fuchsia. "Can you tell me about the picture?" I asked, unable to bring myself to look at him. "He said you fucked her. I let him think I believed him so that he wouldn't be suspicious, but it didn't make sense. I need an explanation."

"The picture was taken Friday, he hadn't lied about that. And I was going to fuck her. That was my plan."

His admission was a knife straight to my gut. Whether he went through with it or not, just knowing he'd planned to was still painful. I kept my gaze trained outside, even when I heard Primo rise from his chair and close the distance between us.

"I told you that I had hoped to send you home. To push you away in order to keep you safe. But when it came down to it, I couldn't." He reached down and slid his hands beneath my armpits and lifted me until I stood before him. Then he placed his hands on either side of my face and demanded my attention. "You aren't just on my mind; you own my every craving. Nothing smells as sweet as your hair on my pillow. No wine could ever taste as sweet as your lips on mine. No paltry sunset could ever mesmerize me like the flecks of gold that dance in your emerald eyes. You have become my reason for breathing—the thought of another woman is comical compared to what I feel for you."

His eyes burned my face as they drank me in, then his lips molded against mine. A kiss so deep and devastating it stunned my senses. He stole my breath and gave me his own with the sensual glide of his lips and the roll of his tongue against mine. His hands, rough and warm and familiar, held more of my heart in their strong grip with every caress of my face and tug of my hair.

Not my heart. His.

The jittery, excitable organ in my chest no longer beat for the sole purpose of pumping blood through my veins. It beat for him. Sang for him. Lusted for him.

Like a compass pointed north no matter its location, my heart would forever yearn for this one captivating man. All I could do was follow its lead and hope my heart knew best.

TWENTY-TWO

Giada

"You do that in here just to torture me, don't you?"

I peered between my legs, ass high in the air, to where Primo was jogging on the treadmill and smirked. "I have no idea what you're talking about. This is a gym. I'm doing yoga. Seems perfectly reasonable to me." I spread my legs from a downward facing dog pose into a standing straddle forward bend, hands on my ankles and body wide open for his viewing. I may have been wearing leggings, but it felt seductive as hell, and I loved it.

Primo slammed his hand down on the emergency stop button, and the whirring of the treadmill rapidly slowed. He stalked over to me, sweat molding his clothes to his chiseled body. The scalding heat of his ravenous stare engorged my clit until it pulsed with anticipated pleasure. I rocked my hips gently from side to side, a tasty treat to lure the hungry wolf.

As his feet stepped within reach, strong hands clasped my hips and pulled my center roughly against his throbbing erection. "This is what you do to me. Whether you're bent over in my gym or eating fucking breakfast in my kitchen, you make me so hard I can't think straight." His voice scraped across my skin like the gravelly sand from the beach outside our window.

My cheeks flushed, and my breathing stalled as one of his hands slipped down to cup me. I was so wet I was sure he could feel it. A deep, masculine groan poured from his throat, but before he could make another move, his phone began to ring.

"*Fuck.*" He tore himself away from me, the loss of his touch making me feel achingly empty. "Yes," he answered in a clipped tone. "Overnight? What about the girl?"

I stood and turned toward him, meeting his angry gaze.

"Yes, Santino can manage her … alright, I'll see you at the airport in an hour." He ended the call and glared at me, but I wasn't the source of his frustration. "Naz wants me to go to Vegas with him for a couple of meetings. We'll be gone overnight."

I smiled reassuringly. "Not a problem. If Naz is with you, I should be fine, right?"

"I suppose, but I still don't like leaving you here when I'm so far away."

I walked over and placed a hand on his chest. "I'll be fine, promise. I won't leave the house until you're back. You better get upstairs and get ready. We don't want to give Naz any reason to doubt you."

"Fine, but we're finishing what we started in the shower. I wasn't done with you."

"But I only just started my workout," I argued in mock protest.

Primo grinned wickedly. "I'll give you all the workout you'll need. Now, *go*." He spun me by the shoulder and smacked my ass.

I yipped and giggled, then did what I was told.

An hour later, Primo was gone, and I was left to my own devices. I occupied myself successfully for a few hours but grew bored by midafternoon and sought out reinforcements.

"Come on, Santino. You have to be just as bored as I am." I'd found him scrolling through his phone in the kitchen and invited him to play pool, but he declined. Unfortunately for him, I rarely took no for an answer.

"Bored, yes, but alive. Primo finds out I played with you, and he just might kill me."

"Psh," I scoffed. "One, he won't find out. Two, we're in a better place now, so he won't freak out like he did the last time. Trust me. It's either that or we do each other's nails. I think you'd look amazing in a rich coral shade."

Santino rolled his eyes to the ceiling and shook his head. "I can't believe I'm doing this."

I did my best cheerleader impression, clapping my hands and bouncing on my toes before hurrying upstairs. The ironic part was, I sucked at the game. I never played much growing up, but I enjoyed it when I did, and it was far better than spending another hour doing nothing.

"I feel kind of funny that I don't know this already, but do you live in the house?" I asked as we started our first game.

"Yeah, I have a room by the garage."

"Do you like living here? It's not like you can bring girls home or invite friends over."

He shrugged, then bent to aim his next shot. "That's never

bothered me. I know what it's like to live on the streets; living here is hardly a sacrifice."

I felt like an insensitive prick. Primo had told me about their rough beginning—of course, Santino wasn't going to be bothered by something as petty as impressing girls. He was a good man. The more I got to know him, the more I could understand why Primo had gone back for him.

"Well, I'm glad Primo has you to watch his back." I smiled even though I completely muffed my shot.

"You have a funny way of showing it—trying to get me killed playing pool with you."

"Please, drama queen. Just play the game."

He glared at me wryly, then sank the game-winning eight ball without ever taking his eyes from mine.

It was remarkably quiet in the house at night when everyone was gone. I wouldn't have thought there would be much difference, but once Alma left and Santino retired to his room, the Spanish-style mansion felt empty. I called it a night early and retreated to Primo's room, where his comforting scent still lingered in the air.

On the nightstand closest to the door, I found my phone plugged in and waiting for me. I wasn't sure when he'd had the chance to set it out before he left, but he'd done it intentionally. It was a statement of his trust in me and showed that he was more concerned with my safety than preserving the illusion of my captivity.

I scooped up the phone and snuggled into bed, breathing deeply over his pillow. I could smell the earthy cologne he wore mixed with his natural musk, enveloping me in visions of sunrise and sex on a tropical beach. Exotic. Sinful.

Thank you. I added a lipstick kiss emoji and hit send, hoping he was near his phone. A minute later, my phone dinged.

It was the least I could do. Were you able to keep yourself occupied today?

I bit down on my lip and grinned. **I did. I managed to rope Santino into playing pool with me.** Seconds after hitting send, the phone rang.

"Hello?" I answered coyly.

"You know that didn't go well the last time." His voice rumbled across the line like a dog's feral growl, but he didn't scare me.

"Don't you dare be mad at him. He put up a fight, but you know how persistent I can be. I swore to him it wouldn't be a problem."

"And how could you possibly make that promise?"

He wasn't there to see the color in my cheeks or the soft smile on my lips, but he could no doubt hear them in the vulnerable tone of my voice. "Because you trust him, and you trust me, and I know you'd never hurt either of us."

Primo only grunted, making me giggle.

"How is Vegas?" I asked, redirecting our conversation.

"Pointless. There's no reason for me to be here. We have one more meeting in the morning, and then we'll be back by lunch." His voice was ragged with fatigue and frustration, so I tried my best to cheer him up.

"Just a few more hours. If you'd like, I can even save my yoga until you're home. Give you a little demonstration of all my favorite poses."

"That's excellent motivation to get back. In fact, our flight is scheduled for eleven, but we should be done with our meeting by nine. I'll call first thing in the morning and see if I can get it moved up."

I grinned, already contemplating which of my workout bras was the sexiest. "Sounds like a plan, and maybe next time you go to Vegas, I can come with."

"I'd enjoy that, but we'll have to be careful. I hear the pickpockets in casinos are terrible."

My smile spread from ear to ear. "G'night, Primo."

"Sweet dreams, viborita."

TWENTY-THREE

Primo

"I'D LIKE TO MOVE UP OUR FLIGHT BY AN HOUR," I INSTRUCTED our pilot as I rose from bed the next morning. Naz had a private jet we used almost exclusively. When I went to New York to retrieve Giada, we'd decided it would be best to charter a plane that wasn't connected to us. Having our own plane at our beck and call was far more convenient.

"That shouldn't be a problem if I jump in and fly back there now."

"What do you mean fly back? Didn't you stay here with the plane?"

"I thought you knew," the pilot stuttered. "Señor Vargas had me fly him home last night. It's not a problem, though. I'll head to the airstrip now and fly up."

My ears began to ring with a rush of blood from my thundering heart. He'd gone back, and he hadn't told me. Naz didn't want me to know he was back in the same city as Giada with me hundreds of miles away. It hadn't made sense when he'd asked me to go with him. The meetings were routine and shouldn't have required my attendance. On the flight over, he'd told me he wanted to make sure I maintained relationships with all the suppliers in case something happened to him, but that was bullshit. It was all just a scheme to separate me from Giada.

"I need you to come get me as fast as you can," I barked at the pilot.

"Yes, sir. I'm on my way." He hung up, and I barely kept myself from throwing my phone across the room in frustration. I could be back home in just a couple of hours, but considering the circumstances, that felt like an eternity.

Taking several deep breaths, I unclenched my grip on my phone and dialed Naz.

"Primo, I was just going to call you," he answered in a jovial voice that made my skin crawl.

Not knowing what he was up to, I had to force myself to act as unaffected as possible. "I reached out about moving up our flight and heard you'd gone back. I hope nothing was wrong."

"Not at all, just a bit under the weather. I'm getting older and that happens sometimes. Hopefully you don't mind handling the meeting on your own."

"It's not a problem. I'll be back later today to let you know how it goes."

"Sounds good. Safe travels." The phone clicked dead, and my teeth ground together.

I never imagined Naz would make a move so quickly. I'd given him no reason to be suspicious more than he already was. If he thought he was going to keep me in line by hurting Giada, he was gravely mistaken. I owed him in many ways, but even I had limits. If he laid a finger on her, I'd raze his fucking empire to the ground and watch him burn among the ashes.

TWENTY-FOUR
Giada

"Naz and Haley are on their way up to the house," Santino called over to where I was reading by the pool.

"What? I thought Naz was with Primo."

"I didn't want to worry you, but Primo texted earlier saying Naz came back last night. I have no idea what he's here for, but if he's got Haley with him, it shouldn't be a problem." His words conveyed one message, but his coiled muscles and murderous gaze said another.

"I think I'll come inside." I stood and followed him back into the house, frantically debating why Naz would pay us a visit. I sat perched on the edge of the sofa while Santino went to the front door and greeted the boss of the Sonora Cartel. A man who wanted me dead and regularly beat his wife into submission.

Naz's noxious voice seeped into the room like a deadly gas, infiltrating every corner and making it hard to breathe. I tried to remind myself that he wouldn't bring Haley over if he planned to kill me, but no amount of convincing would settle the panic flooding my bloodstream.

As their footsteps neared, I stood, and for the first time in my life, I couldn't muster even a millimeter of a smile. Something about smiling implied that everything would be alright. It calmed and soothed people. I desperately wanted to be able to smile and banish the insidious fear clamoring through my veins.

Like the moon crossing before the sun, Naz sucked every bit of light and hope from the room. He was a monster and my mortal enemy. He hated everything about me and was vicious enough to rip me to shreds, merely for existing.

I was utterly terrified.

When Naz turned his callous gaze my direction, my voice abandoned me alongside my courage. I stood across the room, mute and petrified in place. I had no idea what he wanted, but some innate sense inside me told me his presence at the house was wrong. There was a reason he'd insisted Primo joined him on his trip to Vegas then snuck back early. A reason during those few hours of Primo's absence he'd found his way here. That reason was clear in the venomous smile he shot in my direction.

I tried to tell myself he wouldn't do anything in front of Haley, but why not? She knew how violent he could be. Why hide his nature around her? But why bring her in the first place. If he'd come to kill me, there was no reason to drag her along.

Confusion and uncertainty weren't enough to make me

feel better, but they helped thaw my brain from its fear-induced lockdown. Freaking out wasn't going to help me survive this situation. I needed to be strong. I needed use of all my faculties, and cowering behind a wall of fear would only cripple my defenses.

"Santino, I want to have a word with Giada," Naz mused in an eerily placid tone. "On the way over, Haley discovered she'd left her phone at home. I need you to run her back to the house while I visit with our ... guest."

The command gave Santino little option, but as a testament to his courage, he took a stand. "With all respect, sir, my orders were to stay with Giada."

I glanced at Haley. She stared at me wide-eyed and terrified. Was she afraid of what he'd do about the fact that she'd left her phone at home? Had he threatened her when she realized the device was missing? It was heartbreaking to know that Haley had to cope on a daily basis with the sickening terror I was now experiencing.

Naz went inhumanly still, his eyes narrowing with barely restrained savagery. "Don't you *dare* defy me!" he raged, an ugly blue vein bulging from his forehead. "Do as you're fucking told, or I'll send your severed head back to the filthy street where I found you."

As he spoke, the tremors of his fury resounded through the room, and my eyes danced back and forth between Haley and Santino. Both of them were in danger when all Naz really wanted was me. I appreciated Santino's efforts to protect me, but I couldn't stand by and watch at Naz hurt him because of me. I'd rather risk my own death than live at the expense of someone else's life.

. . .

"*Go,*" I blurted, drawing everyone's attention. "You should go with Haley. Mr. Vargas and I can have a quick visit while you're gone." My gaze pleaded with him, and though he was visibly reluctant, he finally acquiesced.

"Of course. I'm sorry for any disrespect, sir. We'll be back shortly." He led Haley from the house, leaving me alone with a monster. The front door clicked shut like a cage closing a harmless sheep in with a hungry lion. In an instant, the air thickened with menace.

I had been trying to protect the others, but I started to regret my decision as fear and weakness muddied my resolve. My eyes drifted to Naz in time to see his smile twist smugness into cruelty.

He clasped his hands behind his back and began to pace slowly. "Did you honestly think you could weasel your way in here and take him from me?" His black voice wrapped around my throat and squeezed.

"I didn't ... I'm not taking anyone." I tried to give strength to my words, but the fear he cast over me was too crippling to overcome.

"Did you think I didn't have ears inside this house? That you could stand here in this very room and discuss severing ties with me like I was the fucking *cable* man?" His voice grew to a roar, face contorting with rage as he stepped closer.

How could he have known? No one was left in the house unless they'd been hiding. Then my stomach took a sickening plummet as the realization hit me.

He'd been listening.

He had microphones in Primo's house. It was the only way he could know exactly what we'd said two nights ago. He'd heard every word, so there was no denying it. He knew our plans and was livid. Homicidal. And I was the target of his wrath.

I didn't think; I just ran.

Darting behind the couch, I grabbed a vase and tossed it as hard as I could at him, but he was far more nimble than I could have imagined. He ducked and lunged, grabbing a handful of my hair and yanking me viciously backward. I cried out in pain, reaching back to grasp for his hand in a futile attempt to ease his grip.

"I don't care if I send you back to your fucking father in tiny fucking pieces," he hissed by my ear, spittle spraying my cheek. "I'll sink the entire fucking shipment—ten million at the bottom of the ocean—before I let Primo throw everything away for a goddamn Italian *whore*." He released me and spun me around, allowing me the briefest window of false relief before his fist collided with my face.

Pain exploded into my eye as I tumbled to the ground, a ragged cry ripping from my throat. That was when it hit me that if Santino didn't come back to save me, this madman was going to kill me. I'd always been so fucking optimistic that the true nature of the dangers around me had never fully sunken in.

Naz was completely and totally unhinged, and he wouldn't be happy until he choked the last breath from my body.

The rancid taste of regret mixed with the coppery tang of blood on my tongue. I suddenly wished I'd done so many things differently, but I refused to give him the satisfaction of seeing me weep. See me break and shatter into a million pieces on the Saltillo tile floor.

I drew myself up to my feet, standing on trembling legs, and glared at death. "You think you're going to win by killing me? My family will destroy you, but only if Primo doesn't do it first."

His lip pulled up in a snarl. "If you live, you ruin everything I've worked for anyway. I might as well see you suffer." His arm lashed out, backhanding me across the opposite cheek.

This time, I remained on my feet, using the motion after his strike to lunge to the side and grab a wooden statue of a naked torso. I immediately swung around toward him with perfect aim, striking him square in the head. He lurched to the side, hand reaching for his temple where blood began to trickle from his skull. When he turned back toward me, his eyes lit with rabid insanity.

He charged at me, tackling me to the ground with the bulk of his weight on my chest. I felt a sickening crack, and a searing pain ratcheted out from my rib cage. The agony was so severe that it stole the breath from my lungs, leaving me wheezing and gasping for air.

Naz sat back on his knees and peered down at me with twisted satisfaction just as the front door flung open. Thundering footsteps rang down the hall until Santino was standing in the entry to the living room.

For a second, time stood still.

Santino and Naz stared at one another while I struggled to breathe. Then everything happened at once. Santino reached inside his jacket at the same time Haley appeared out of nowhere, distracting him just long enough for Naz to reach for his own firearm.

A single shot blasted through the room, and I watched in horror as Santino stumbled backward into the wall. He slid to the ground, gun in hand, a bloody stain trailing behind him.

My lungs tried to gasp, but the resulting pain made my head swim.

This couldn't be happening. It was worse than a nightmare. How could this wretched man win? It wasn't fair.

Angry tears dripped from my eyes, and my vision blurred as I peered up at Haley, standing dumbstruck next to Santino.

"It seems you've poisoned everyone around here," Naz said to me, turning his back to his wife. He slowly stood and dusted off his slacks.

While he was distracted, I caught Haley's attention and pointed at Santino's gun. I begged and pleaded with my eyes for her to pick it up and shoot Naz. I only had a couple of seconds to get my point across, but she clearly glanced between me and the gun. Then her eyes drifted to her husband, and she stilled, almost as if going catatonic.

My face crumpled in crushing disappointment. He'd conditioned her in fear to a point she wouldn't even fight back. She was too terrified that if her attempt didn't work, her pain would never end.

Naz looked up in time to see me realize my defeat and glanced back at his broken wife, chuckling at her fragmentation. "I am king in this country," he said, leering at me as he pulled out his gun and cocked it. "I don't care who your family is or how love-sick Primo is for that wet cunt of yours. No fucking woman is going to take me down." He lifted the gun and pointed it at where I lay, a sickening grin twisting his face.

My eyes fluttered shut just as the shot cracked through the room.

TWENTY-FIVE
Primo

"I DON'T CARE WHAT NAZ OR GIADA SAY," I YELLED INTO THE phone at Santino. "You get back there and stay with her. I chartered a flight and came straight back, so I'm in town and on my way to the house. I'll be right behind you." I hung up the phone and slammed my foot down on the accelerator of the car I'd just coerced from the airport manager.

My instincts had screamed at me to get back home as fast as I could. I skipped the meeting and paid twice the normal fare to charter an immediate flight back to Guaymas. When Santino called and told me about Naz's appearance and his instructions to take Haley home, I lost it. I understood why Santino felt that he had to comply, but fuck if I was leaving Giada unprotected.

Once I got to the house, there would be hell to pay with Naz. I'd wanted to find a way to part on good terms—having the Sonora Cartel after us would make life incredibly difficult—now, I wasn't sure peace was an option.

Santino had only been gone from the house for a few minutes. I held onto hope that he could defuse the situation until I got there and that I could still work through my differences with Naz.

I made the twenty-minute drive at breakneck speeds, running lights and only coming to a stop once when I nearly hit a boy running after a ball. I hauled up my long driveway and came to a screeching stop at the front entry. Just as I reached for the car door handle, a gunshot rang out from inside the house.

For two thudding heartbeats, I froze, and time around me ground to a halt. A wave of emotion threatened to crash over me, but I refused to let it drown me if there was any chance Giada was still alive.

I wrenched open the car door and raced for the house. The front door was already wide open. Raising my gun, I cautiously stepped inside. The sight that greeted me across the foyer stunned me.

Santino lay bleeding against the wall, and Haley stood over him with a gun pointed into the living room. I could hardly make sense of what I was seeing. What the fuck was Haley doing with a gun? Had she shot Santino? How the hell had everything devolved in such a short span of time?

"Haley, put the gun down," I ordered smoothly, my own weapon trained on her as I eased forward.

The delicate blonde didn't move a muscle aside from a tremor in her outstretched hands. She didn't startle or look my direction. She kept her eyes glued on her target.

Three more shots rang out in quick succession.

I charged forward, seizing the gun from her hand. Haley crumpled to the floor as if it had taken all her strength to fire those last shots. Inside the room, Naz lay in a bloody heap, riddled with bullet holes. Next to him was Giada, curled protectively inward, nasty bruises blossoming across her olive skin. Her eyes lifted to mine, and my vibrant warrior began to sob. She was hurt and upset, but alive.

Relief coursed through me as I rushed to her side. I started to lift her in my arms, but she winced and shook me off.

"I'm fine, but I think he broke a rib or two." Her chin quivered as she looked past me to Santino, large salty tears running into the blood from her cut lip. "He came back and tried to save me. Help him, please. Don't let him die."

I placed a tender kiss on her forehead and hurried to assess Santino's condition. He'd been shot but high enough in the shoulder that he might survive. I placed a call to my doctor, then grabbed a clean dish towel from the kitchen and pressed it against the wound. He stirred at the discomfort but didn't fully wake.

I was only two years his senior, but he seemed so much younger to me. We'd both accepted the dangers of the life we'd chosen, but I'd still felt responsible for him. Seeing him bleeding out after following my orders gutted me.

"Hang in there, man. Doc is coming, and we'll get you all stitched up." I gritted my teeth, hating to admit that he needed more than a doctor. Hospitals complicated everything, but I couldn't let him die if there was any hope of saving him.

Hunched protectively around her middle, Giada came up behind me and lowered herself to sit next to a quivering Haley, who had curled up against the wall with her knees pulled tightly against her chest. Giada grimaced, face taut with pain as she wrapped her arms around the other woman.

"You did so good," she cooed to Haley like a mother comforting a small child. "I'm so proud of you. We'll help get you back to the US, and you can start over, okay? Everything is going to be so much better, I promise."

Haley's trembling morphed into wailing sobs that echoed through the entry until the doctor arrived. He rushed over when he spotted us all clustered on the floor. When his eyes fell on Naz, he stilled, gaze turning warily back to me. The muscles in his throat flexed as he swallowed down his fear. Naz's death would rain down chaos in our world, and the doctor knew it.

"Santino needs the most help. I'm afraid we'll need to get him to the hospital. I'm not sure there's much you can do," I explained.

He examined the wound briefly. "He needs to get to an operating room as soon as possible."

"That's what I thought. Have a look at Giada and then I'll help get him in your car. I'll need you to take him to the hospital."

The man had been on our payroll for years, so he knew the drill, nodding and moving on to Giada. He did his best not to hurt her, but any movement at all was clearly torturous.

"I'd say you need an X-ray to look at those ribs, but most likely, there's nothing that can be done but allow time to heal. I don't hear any wheezing to indicate there's a punctured lung, so that's good, but like I said, an X-ray would be wise. She's mildly concussed, nothing to worry about there, and all the other damage appears superficial. I'd say right now, a warm bath and lots of rest is the best course."

"Let me help you get Santino loaded up, and then I'll attend to her."

We gingerly lifted Santino and carried him out to the

doctor's car, maneuvering him into the back seat. The doc jumped in the driver's seat and was off without further instruction. When I returned inside, I walked to Haley, who'd been staring at Naz vacantly. I took her hands and lifted her to stand, commanding her attention. "I want you to go upstairs. The first room on the right is a guest room. You can go and clean up or rest, whatever you need. You can't go back to your house now, you understand that, right?"

She nodded in quick, jerky movements.

"Good. Like Giada said, we'll get you taken care of soon enough. Rest for now." I stepped back, allowing her to retreat upstairs away from the carnage, then carefully lifted Giada in my arms and carried her up to my master bath.

"What will you do now?" she asked once we were alone.

"I'll have to deal with the fallout. I'll take the blame for his death. If Juan Carlos learned that Haley killed his brother, he'd never let her live." I set Giada on her feet and eased her jeans down her hips.

"What about you? Will he come after you?"

"Possibly, but first he'll need to come back here to claim his brother's throne. Before he does, we'll be long gone."

"Where will we go?"

"To New York and the safety of your family." I looked at her long-sleeve shirt and realized we'd need to cut it off. "Let me run downstairs and get some scissors."

"Wait," she said, reaching for my hand and grimacing. "My family thinks you kidnapped me—they hate you. I'm not sure they'll ever get over that."

I gently swept a tendril of her hair back behind her ear and admired the determined spirit of this woman. Even broken and bloody, she was thinking about someone other than herself.

"It's a risk worth taking to get you to safety. Besides, there is information I can offer to help gain their trust. Try not to worry about that. First, we need to get out of here before Naz's men discover what's happened." I lifted her hand and kissed the tips of her fingers, then hurried downstairs to find scissors.

On my way back from my office, scissors in hand, I spotted Alma staring agape at Naz's bloody corpse. She'd been a part of my life for so long, I could hardly imagine her betraying me, but she'd worked for Naz before I ever arrived. I needed to give us as much time as possible, and that meant ensuring no one alerted Naz's loyal soldiers before we had the chance to flee.

"Alma, can I speak with you?"

She jumped at the sound of my voice, hurrying over. "I just went to the market for food, and when I got back … what happened? Where is Giada? Why is there blood on the wall?" She was frantic with worry.

"Giada is all right, but Nazario tried to kill her. Santino was shot trying to protect her. I got here in time and killed Naz. We'll need to get out of the country, and I need to know if I can count on you to stay quiet until we do. We need a few hours to get away before Nazario's men come for us."

Her wrinkled face softened, eyes crinkling in the corners. "Mijo, you were like one of my own. Of course, I'll do whatever I can to help."

I squeezed her hand, desperately relieved I didn't have to hurt her. "I'm afraid this means you're out of a job, though. I'm sorry for that."

"Don't worry about me. You take care of that lovely girl of yours. All I've ever wanted for you was to see you happy."

I placed a heartfelt kiss on one cheek, then the other. "The battle's only just begun, but I'll do my best." And that was the truth. Naz may be dead, but our struggles were far from over.

TWENTY-SIX

Giada

My head felt like it had been batted around by two semi-trucks, and my ribs screamed every time I moved, but it was all manageable, knowing how close I'd come to death. Haley was the reason I was still alive. I'd closed my eyes, resigned to accept my fate, but when the gun went off, I didn't feel a thing. No slamming force or searing pain. I opened my eyes, wondering if I'd died and my mind just didn't know it yet. Then Naz crashed to the ground beside me.

I thought he'd broken her—beat her and caged her until she had no fight left—but I'd been wrong. Her blue eyes, wide and feral, were locked on Naz's motionless body as though he might reanimate and come after her. As if she were replaying every excruciating, humiliating thing he'd ever done to her. It was no wonder she put three more bullets into him.

A half hour later, up to my neck in a tub full of steaming hot water, and I still couldn't believe all that had happened.

"I grabbed some food for you," Primo said when he came back to the bathroom. He'd let me soak for a bit while he'd made some calls and managed things downstairs. I'd needed the time alone to process.

"I wouldn't have thought I'd be hungry after what just happened, but I'm famished."

He placed a tray with a sandwich and a pile of grapes next to the tub and sat beside me. "That's your body recovering from the adrenaline and shock. You'll have a little more energy once you eat, but I'm afraid these injuries are going to take some time to heal, and we don't have that luxury. The next twenty-four hours aren't going to be easy for you."

"I'll be fine. It's only pain, right?" I tried to smile and lighten the mood, but the pull at my lip made me wince.

Primo's brows were drawn, lips pursed in a thin line of concern and residual anger. I may have been the one in physical pain, but he was shouldering an enormous emotional burden. I hated to see him hurting.

"I'm sorry about Naz. He was a horrible human being, but I know he was kind of a father figure to you. It can't be easy to lose him, no matter how crazy he was."

He dropped his hand down to the water and swirled his fingers beneath the surface. "I just can't believe he tried to hurt you. That his mind had become so warped he thought killing you would help further his fucked-up plan."

"He heard us talking," I said softly. "In the living room. He has microphones somewhere and knew everything we'd said."

Primo's head slowly shook side to side. "As much as I

hate to admit it, Naz's death was inevitable. I just hope I don't lose Santino as well."

"Have you heard from the doctor?"

"Yes. He got Santino to the emergency room, and they took him immediately back to surgery. I wish I could be there, but we have to leave as soon as possible. Once we get you dried off, I have a plane waiting for us."

I nodded. "I'm ready. Help me out, and we can go."

Primo helped lift me to my feet and out of the tub, then retrieved a towel and patted my body dry with tender care. Before he could step away to find me clean clothes, I grabbed his hand to get his attention. Warmth spread throughout my chest when his stormy gray eyes met mine.

"I know we haven't known each other long, and I don't want to scare you away, but I almost died today, and it made me realize that I want you to know that I … I love you."

His hands raised to either side of my face, and his forehead came to rest on mine. "Don't say that," he whispered. "You see what a life with me is like."

"I see loyalty and devotion. I see tenderness and strength. I see a man worth standing beside, even if it means we have to walk through hell together."

Primo's lips found mine in an achingly sweet kiss, featherlight but more ardent than a thousand other kisses combined. "You've been through a lot today. We'll get you home, and then we can discuss what comes next."

"I'm not going to change my mind, you know."

His lips curved into a resigned, mournful smile. "Let's get you dressed."

He helped me into a dress and panties—there was no way I was putting a bra on my aching ribs—then brushed my hair and packed a bag for each of us. I managed to ease myself down the stairs while Primo carried our bags.

Haley joined us on the way down. She had composed herself, but her eyes were still bloodshot and puffy from crying.

"Where are we gonna go?" she asked, her gaze fixedly avoiding the place where Naz still lay.

"We're going to New York," Primo said. "From there, you can go wherever you like."

I wasn't sure how much Primo knew about Haley's background, but I had gathered that she didn't have family she could turn to for help. "I'd be more than happy for you to stay with me until you sort things out," I offered quickly. I owed her my life, so the least I could do was give her someplace to stay.

"Actually, I have a cousin in Missouri. Maybe I can give her a call once we're on the plane?"

I smiled warmly, relieved there was someone in her past who cared for her. "Of course."

Primo led us out front where Santino's Land Rover was still parked. He helped me inside, then went to put our luggage in the back when a black sedan started up the driveway.

"Stay in the car," he barked at us, pulling his gun out and sliding it into the back of his pants.

The car stopped around twenty feet away. To my amazement, Maria and Matteo exited the vehicle. They both held guns and stood behind their open car doors as if preparing for a shoot-out. Primo lifted his hands in the air and said something I couldn't make out, but Maria and Matteo didn't ease their threatening posture.

I panicked.

They thought Primo was a danger to me. I had to convince them to calm down before they tried to kill him. I was so worried about stopping them that I forgot to consider what they would think when they saw my bruised and bloodied condition.

I flung open the car door and climbed out to stand next to Primo. "Please don't hurt him," I cried, my eyes pleading with Maria.

She took in my battered appearance, her face contorting in disgust. "You *sick* motherfucker," she spat. Her arm lifted, and I moved on instinct.

It all happened in a handful of seconds.

My lunge. The gunshot. Pain rocketing through my body.

"Giada, *no!*" screamed Primo, catching me as I flew back into him. "*Shit, shit, shit.*" His voice dripped with panic as he lowered me to the ground. "What the fuck did you do?" he screamed up at my cousin.

Maria rushed to my side, her arctic blue eyes coming into my field of vision, more panicked than I'd ever seen her before. "Oh, *God*, Giada. Why?"

"It wasn't him," I tried to explain in breathy gasps. "Don't … hurt him. It … wasn't him."

The pain was overwhelming.

I could see the three of them above me, but they grew blurry and distant. The more I drifted, the less my body hurt, so I allowed myself to be carried away. To float along on a river of numbness until the world went dark, and there was nothing.

TWENTY-SEVEN

Primo

FIRST SANTINO, THEN GIADA. MY WORLD WAS BEING RIPPED apart, shredded and mutilated until it was unrecognizable, and there was nothing I could do to stop it. All the power and wealth I'd accumulated meant nothing if I couldn't save the people I loved.

My heart pounded like a piston in my chest, but I refused to let panic consume me. I yanked my shirt over my head and pressed the wadded fabric against Giada's shoulder to stem the bleeding.

"What happened here? Who did this to her?" Maria demanded, still struggling to understand.

"My boss, Nazario Vargas, but that fight is over. He's dead. We were on our way to the airport for New York. I needed to get her out of here before Nazario's brother and loyal soldiers find out I killed him. She's not safe here, even at a hospital. I know it won't be easy, but I think we should take the flight and get her help once we land." I looked at Matteo for support, knowing he would be far more logical than his wife in this situation. She was clearly distraught and still struggling to trust me.

Matteo motioned for me to lift the compress off Giada's shoulder so that he could assess the wound. "It's not bleeding too badly, and there's no exit wound. Small caliber at a distance so minimal tissue damage. She'll need surgery to get the bullet out, but I think she should survive the trip if we hurry."

"Help me get her in the car. You two can follow me."

"Fuck, no," Maria snapped. "I'm staying with her."

"We don't have time for this shit," I growled back. "I don't care where the fuck you ride, just help."

The three of us maneuvered her into the back seat while Haley moved to the front. I was glad Giada wasn't awake because the pain would have been unbearable. We raced down the driveway, not one of us acknowledging the dead guards beside my open gate. It looked like their throats had been cut in an ambush attack. The men weren't necessarily bad people, but I wasn't close enough to care about their deaths. All I cared about was getting Giada to safety.

We made it to the airport in record time and were in the air shortly thereafter. A terse silence blanketed us throughout the flight. Haley sat alone in the front row, her body wracked in silent sobs the moment we lifted off the ground. Matteo made a brief call to Giada's family, explaining what had happened and making plans for them to meet us at the New York airstrip.

During the entire flight, I held Giada on a small sofa,

keeping her secure and maintaining pressure on her wound. I could hardly fathom that this woman who I had bullied, tricked, and endangered had taken a bullet for me. I was abandoning everything to keep her safe, but her sacrifice made mine look meaningless. She'd surrendered her life to protect me. There was no greater pledge of love and devotion a person could make.

I couldn't imagine I was worthy, but knowing Giada, my thoughts on the matter would be irrelevant. As constant as the sun rising in the east and equally as captivating, Giada was the most confident, headstrong woman I'd ever met. She bounded through life with charismatic purpose, enriching the lives of everyone around her.

To lose something so precious after I'd only just found her was unconscionably cruel. Surely, if there was a God, he would not be so vindictive. So unjust and merciless.

It had been years since I had cast my voice to God in prayer. After my mother's death, I lost my faith in many things. I still wasn't sure how I felt on the matter, but in a moment of crushing desperation, I was not above begging for help. With my eyes closed and my heart flayed open, I pleaded with God to save Giada. I swore if she lived, I would endeavor every day thereafter to be worthy of her love. To cherish and protect her with my life.

"It would appear your time together has been rather transformative."

I opened my eyes to find Matteo's calculating gaze assessing me. He'd likely been watching me the entire time, but I'd been too distracted to notice.

"They've been eventful, that's for sure," I murmured in response.

"She told her cousin she was safe and wanted to be there with you, but under the circumstances, we felt confident she'd just been manipulated. Duped into going quietly. But she was telling the truth, wasn't she?"

I gazed at Giada's pale skin, normally so radiant and healthy, and felt my heart contract. "It wasn't supposed to be like this. I was supposed to get her cousin, Alessia, but when she approached me at the casino, she derailed everything. I was completely taken with her."

"I hope you're aware that her father isn't going to give a rat's ass how much you care for one another."

I looked back at the man who had saved my life years before—a man who was honorable and highly influential—and I laid all my cards before him. "Our slate was wiped clean, you and I. You have no duty to help me, but I'd happily be in your debt again if you could bring yourself to speak on my behalf. Talk to Edoardo and Enzo and give them pause to at least consider the possibility that I am worthy of her."

He offered no reaction. Not even the slightest clue to his thoughts on the matter. "I can't make you a promise when I have no idea how this will play out when we arrive."

The grinding sound of the landing gear lowering resonated throughout the cabin.

"I suppose if they kill me as soon as I touch the ground, there's little need to plead my case."

"We're about to find out. Just hang onto her and keep your cool." His wary tone gave me a glimmer of hope that he just might have my back.

I secured Giada against my body to prepare for landing and schooled myself for what was to come. We'd made the normally five-hour flight in half the time, which was exceptionally quick but still felt like a lifetime knowing each second could be Giada's last. If our circumstances hadn't been so precarious, I would have had the pilot take us to Texas or somewhere closer, but we'd be vulnerable anywhere but New

York where her family could protect her. Their influence at the airstrip would prevent a customs nightmare and keep her safe once she was transported to a hospital.

Despite my anxiety over dealing with her family, there was a large part of me that sighed with relief when we touched down on the runway because we were that much closer to getting Giada help. I resigned myself to whatever the outcome, so long as she survived.

The pilot taxied the plane to an air hanger instead of the main building, under instruction from her family to keep the authorities out of the picture. Inside, an ambulance was waiting along with several black SUVs with dark tinted windows.

Matteo helped me maneuver Giada out of the narrow doorway and down the stairs. The paramedics met us with a gurney, and she was quickly secured and wheeled away. I abhorred not going with her, but her family would never allow it. Instead, Maria leapt into the back of the ambulance, leaving me surrounded by half a dozen angry mafia men.

I pulled Haley out from behind me, resting my arm around her back. "This is Haley. She was another victim of Nazario and a friend of Giada's. Before we address my crimes, I'd ask that you allow her into the safety of a car. She doesn't need to experience any more trauma today."

Enzo nodded at one of the soldiers behind him, who approached us and coaxed Haley to leave my side. Once she was in the car, somewhat protected, I addressed the group on my behalf.

"I know you have a lot of questions and probably want me dead, but before you jump to any conclusions, understand that I love Giada, and killing me will only hurt her further." I stared at Enzo Genovese, the family boss and ultimate decision maker.

His eyes flicked over to Matteo.

"He's not a threat at the moment," Matteo conceded. "Let's get to the hospital, and we can sort him out later."

Enzo glanced back at me but only spoke to his men. "Take her to a hotel. Make sure she has whatever she needs. The rest of us will head to the hospital."

Two of the soldiers took my arms and ushered me to a vehicle. Matteo joined us inside, much to my relief. We all caravanned to the hospital and were taken to a small interior waiting room where emergency patient families were allowed to wait. Giada had been taken directly into surgery, and we wouldn't have any word on her condition until the procedure was complete.

"There's an unoccupied consultation room open," Enzo pointed out before we had a chance to sit down. "I suggest we take a few minutes to talk before the ladies arrive."

I nodded and followed Enzo with Matteo and Edoardo behind me. The tiny room was only about six feet square and contained four chairs and a small Formica table. Making the space feel even more confined, Matteo closed the blinds on the small window, secluding us from view.

They weren't going to kill me there at the hospital, but that didn't make the scene any less intimidating. Edoardo looked like he wanted to rip my head from my shoulders and put it on a spike on his front lawn. I couldn't blame him. Giada wouldn't be on an operating table if it hadn't been for me.

"I appreciate you allowing me the opportunity to explain," I started.

"I don't see why he should be allowed to say anything. He shouldn't even be breathing at this point." Edoardo glared at me. Luckily, his brother wasn't swayed by the show of emotion.

Enzo lifted his hand in warning. "There's always time to do things right. Killing him before we know what happened would be imprudent. Let's hear what you have to say."

I launched into the tale, describing the evolution of my relationship with Giada from our first encounter in Las Vegas to the showdown with Naz. I bent the truth slightly, taking credit for Naz's death, but only to protect Haley. The only people who knew the truth were the three of us that had been in that room, and it would stay that way.

"I know it may be hard for you to believe," I continued, "but I've given up everything for Giada. I love her and want to be with her, and she put her life on the line to save me. Don't make those sacrifices worthless by keeping us apart, please."

Enzo looked at Matteo. "Do you have anything to add?"

Sleeves rolled to his elbows, expensive gold watch at his wrist, Matteo leaned forward with his elbows on the table. "I have a bit of history with Primo. I don't know him all that well, but from what I've witnessed, I'd say he's honorable. I also know, after watching Giada jump in front of him to take a bullet, that if something happens to him, she'll never forgive those responsible."

Edoardo wasn't thrilled with what he'd heard, but he had set aside his bloodlust long enough to truly listen. "What exactly do you expect to happen? You aren't family—you're not Italian, and you have way too much history with the cartel to be any part of our organization."

I met his hard stare, not letting an ounce of weakness show through. "I don't have to be a part of your mafia family in order to love your daughter. I could be a valuable asset in many capacities, should you be interested in working with me, but even if that never pans out, what matters is Giada. The only thing that will ever matter to me is Giada."

Enzo nodded. "It sounds like there's going to be much to discuss in the coming days. I'll allow you to remain here unharmed, but it will be on a probationary basis. Should I get word that you have maintained your cartel connections or stepped out of line in any way, you will receive no leniency. Understood?"

"Perfectly. Thank you, Mr. Genovese, for your trust in me. I will prove to you it's not misplaced." I held out my hand and was rewarded with his firm grip.

"All right, let's get back out there," Enzo said wearily. "The women have probably already arrived, and I can only imagine it's going to be a long night."

TWENTY-EIGHT

Giada

THE MELODIC LILT OF A WOMAN'S VOICE DREW ME FROM THE hazy grip of sleep. I tried to push away the sound because with it came an insistent throbbing from my neck to my navel as though an elephant had found its way onto my chest. The louder the voice grew, the more pronounced the pain. I desperately tried to flee back into my numbing wonderland to no avail.

A man's voice joined the woman's, both right beside me, and sirens sounded in the background. Growing ever more curious, I forced open my heavy eyelids and blinked away the cobwebs.

"Lucifer?" I asked groggily, eyes squinting at the television above me.

"He's not a bad character—does what he wants when he wants—and women fall at his feet. There are far worse programming options at five a.m., trust me." Filip smirked at me and clicked off the TV. "Welcome to the land of the living," he said softly.

I glanced around the room, quickly realizing I was in a hospital. A swell of memories toppled over me, catapulting my heart into overdrive and triggering the heart rate monitor alarm. The insistent buzzing brought a nurse to the room who turned off the alarm with a gentle smile and helped me incline the bed so I was more upright. She informed me she would tell the doctor I was awake and left us alone.

"Where is everyone? How long was I out? Wait ..." I glanced around before looking back at him in confusion. "Am I back in New York?"

He chuckled, coming to sit on the edge of my bed. "You're back home and were taken into surgery yesterday afternoon. It's now five fifteen a.m., so you were out for the better part of twenty-four hours. And as for your family, the ladies stepped out to the cafeteria to get coffee, and Primo just slipped away for a bathroom break. You managed to wake up during the brief window of peace and quiet in here. Aside from now, none of them have left your side."

I nodded, relieved to know they were near. "Don't take this the wrong way, but what are you doing here?"

"I'm on guard duty. Your family didn't want you left unprotected. Unlike last time, I'm not letting you out of my sights." He glared at me playfully, but he had to have been upset I left my apartment without telling him when I met up with Primo. Filip would have been in trouble for not keeping me safe, and that wasn't fair to him. Any scolding I received was justified.

"I'm sorry about that; I really am. I know that put you in a bad spot and endangered myself. Granted, I still would probably do it again, but that doesn't mean I wouldn't feel bad about it." My lips pulled up in a lopsided grin I hoped was endearing enough for him to forgive me.

He rewarded me with a chuckle. "Nobody's perfect. Fortunately, this particular escapade seems to have worked out in the end." His reassurance was swept away on a flurry of activity as my entire clan of female relatives returned. Filip slipped out of the room as my sisters and cousins swarmed my bed.

"Giada! You're awake!" Alessia cried, rushing to my bedside. She scooped my hand up and hugged it to her face. "We were so worried about you. Don't you ever do something crazy like that again, you hear me?" Tears swam in her eyes, making my throat knot with emotion.

"I'm so sorry, honey. I never meant to worry any of you."

Val and Camilla stepped forward and gave me gentle hugs, mostly comprised of pressing their cheeks to mine since my shoulder and one arm were firmly bandaged.

"Once you're feeling better, I want to hear every detail of your adventure," Val informed me with far more authority than should be possible for the youngest person in the room.

"Absolutely." I grinned. "As soon as I don't feel like I've been hit by a truck, I'm all yours."

Camilla pulled Val a step back, and her eyes darted nervously up at Filip. "Now that we know you're okay, we can let you rest. The hospital staff has had an absolute fit that we're all here."

They began to shuffle backward toward the door, all but Maria, who stood leaning against the wall, staring at me. "I can't believe you almost let me kill you," she chided in a gentle tone I wasn't aware she possessed. "I never would have forgiven you if you'd died."

"I never would have forgiven you for killing Primo," I teased back.

Maria rolled her eyes. "I wasn't aiming to kill him. It would have been a perfect shoulder wound to incapacitate him if you hadn't jumped in the way."

I gaped at her. "How was I supposed to know that?"

"Well, next time, you'll know."

"No. No more next times. This hurts way too fucking bad for a next time."

She handed me a cup of ice water from the tray next to my bed. "I really am sorry, G. You know I never would have hurt you on purpose."

"Thank you for coming for me." My voice cracked with emotion. "It didn't play out as you expected, but I appreciate that you were there to help me."

"You may annoy the shit out of me, but …" Her breathing hitched, and her arctic eyes grew suspiciously watery. "But we're family." Her words were forced out on a breath, raw and so saturated with emotion that my heart constricted. "Goddamn these hormones," she hissed, wiping at her eyes.

I smiled but was unable to laugh from the pain. "I'm surprised Matteo let you go with him to Mexico. How far along are you now?"

She scoffed. "*Let* me? Please. As if he could stop me if he wanted to. Besides, I'm only a few months along—just enough to make me tired and hormonal."

"I'm glad I'm here to see the rest of the pregnancy. Seeing you round and waddling is going to be the greatest entertainment ever."

"All right. On that note, I'm out of here."

"Wait, I have another question. Did you and Matteo really plan to storm Primo's house all alone? That seems awfully risky."

Her lips curved into a devious grin. "What made you think we were alone? We came prepared and weren't leaving without you."

My throat tightened. "Thank you, Maria. That's just about the sweetest thing anyone's ever done for me."

Maria teasingly bumped her hip against my bed, uncomfortable with my show of emotion. "Just try not to get into any more trouble. I'm not flying my ass to Mexico for you again. Now, I really do have to get out of here." She gently squeezed my thigh, gave me a tender smile, then nodded to my mom on her way out.

The room was suddenly painfully quiet. My mother looked utterly shattered, hair disheveled without a stitch of makeup, a broken weariness mapped on the lines of her face.

"Hey, Momma," I whispered.

Her eyelids drifted shut for a second, tears streaming down each of her pale cheeks. When she opened her eyes again, a spark of life returned to her face. She closed the distance between us and sat on the edge of my bed, taking my hand in hers. "I'm so glad you're okay, Sweet G."

It was the name she used to call me when I was little, instead of the term sweet pea. She hadn't used it in so long that hearing it buried me deep in a mountain of feelings.

"I'm sorry I worried you," I said in a shaky voice so weak it was foreign to my ears. "I guess you always knew I'd get into trouble."

Mom looked down at our clasped hands, mine cupped inside the both of hers. "It may shock you to hear this, but I've always been hard on you because you remind me of myself. Back when I was younger, much younger, I lived my life very differently. I was bold and vivacious. Carefree and longing for adventure. When I was only sixteen, I met a boy who made me feel like I was walking on air. I've never told you girls because there was never a right time, but I think that time has come."

My brows furrowed as the mood in the room shifted. We'd gone from remorseful and apologetic to something even more vulnerable. I wasn't sure what my mother was about to say, but I sensed it was going to be big.

"We only dated for a few months," she continued, "before I got pregnant."

The words ricocheted in my head, too amorphous for me to grasp them. Pregnant? My mother got pregnant before she met my father? My devout Catholic, never a misstep mother had a teen pregnancy? I couldn't make sense of it. I would have had an easier time believing her if she'd told me a nuclear war had started while I'd been unconscious. My mother an unwed mother? Not a chance.

"What happened?" I asked dazedly.

"Things quickly deteriorated with the boy, but I refused to abort the baby. Five years before you were born, I had a son who I gave up for adoption."

A brother. I had a half-brother somewhere out in the world. It was inconceivable.

"Does Dad know?"

She smiled. "Yes, your father knew from the beginning. That was never an issue, and while I think about the child sometimes, I know he was better off with parents who could care for him properly. I was a junior in high school and totally unprepared to be a mother." She paused and lifted her eyes to mine. "The reason I tell you this is so you'll know why I've been so overbearing. Those years after I gave him up were the hardest of my life. I desperately wanted to protect you from the pain I endured, but I'm starting to realize that each of us has to carve our own path and learn our own lessons. My need to keep you safe has prevented us from being as close as I would have liked, and I'm hoping you'll give me a second chance to fix that. I thought I was going to lose you forever and—" She sniffled, bottom lip quivering. "It made me realize how wrong I've been. How much I love you just the way you are and would rather have your smart mouth keeping me on my toes than never to hear your voice again."

The revelation about her son had shocked me, but her remorse over our relationship blew me away. It was everything I'd ever wanted to hear from her. The love and acceptance. The forgiveness and compassion. My mother wanted to be my friend, and nothing in the world would make me happier.

"I love you, Momma, so much. You don't know how much that means to me." My breathing shuddered on the cusp of a sob, but a stabbing pain in my ribs enabled me to rein in the turbulent emotions.

She leaned forward and pressed her cheek to mine, her hands clasping my arms in a makeshift hug. "I love you, too, Sweet G. More than you'll ever know." When she pulled back, her face lit with a smile that shone with adoration. "There's a man out there waiting patiently to see you. He hasn't left your side, despite a gaggle of us ladies swarmed around you."

"He's a good man, Mom. I know our relationship had an unusual start, but I hope you guys will give him an honest chance. I love him so much, and I don't want there to be bad blood between my family and the man I love."

"The men have talked and seem to be making progress. I think it's all going to work out fine, but if it helps, I'll make sure to light a candle about it at mass." She winked.

My mother was joking about Mass.

I was still unconscious. That was the only explanation.

The conversation I'd just had with my mother was so entirely surreal, there was no way it could have been reality.

I gaped at my mom so long that she giggled before standing up.

"I'll go get Primo. I'm sure he's dying to see you." She kissed my forehead once more before leaving me alone in the room.

Well, not exactly alone. I could see Filip through the window, standing guard outside my door. The showing of affection and concern I'd received upon waking up in the hospital was greater than anything I could have imagined. I was incredibly lucky to have such an amazing family, and I wondered if my sometimes flippant behavior could have been construed as unappreciative. They meant the world to me, and it was my job to make sure they knew that. I wasn't planning to completely rework my personality, but there was always room for improvement. It wouldn't kill me to be a tad more considerate.

I mentally solidified my second-chance-at-life resolution—it was kind of like a new year's resolution, only more profound. Life was precarious. Living each day to the fullest should have been more than a slogan on a coffee mug.

The smile blossoming on my face stalled when a pair of broad shoulders blocked the entry to my room. Primo stood in dress slacks and a white undershirt, hands in his pockets, and his eyes deeply shadowed. Even worn-out and blood-stained, he was breathtaking. His angular jaw was lined in scruff, and his hair tamed back in thick clumps as if he'd been running his hands through the wavy strands all night. His perfectly proportioned lips were fixed in an even line, and as usual, only his expressive, gunmetal eyes gave any hint at the thoughts ruminating behind his stoic façade. That tiny window into his soul was all I needed—relief, worry, frustration, adoration—they were all present in his tumultuous stare.

"Hey," I greeted softly. "Thanks for getting me home and for staying with me."

He prowled into the room, eyes locked on mine until he was only a breath away. "Don't you ever scare me like that again," he rumbled before pressing his lips firmly against mine. Fingers tangled in my hair, his intoxicating kiss made me forget about the condition of my ailing body.

Primo wasn't so easily distracted.

When I leaned into his touch, he eased himself away, drawing our kiss to a close, but he didn't end our contact. His soft lips found their way to my cheek, then to the delicate skin below my ear. "I thought you were going to die, and I've never been so terrified in my life." His whispered confession danced across my skin before filling my chest and warming me from the inside out. "I never imagined I could lose my home and my job—nearly everything recognizable about my life—and still be so perfectly relieved. None of it matters without you. I'm so fucking in love with you, Giada Genovese. I'm sorry I didn't tell you that before."

I couldn't breathe. My heart had swollen so completely that it left no room for my lungs. "Kiss me," was all I could force out between my trembling lips.

He granted my wish, allowing me to indulge in a languorous kiss.

"I hate to interrupt," came a voice behind us, "but I heard my patient had come around." A man in scrubs carrying a clipboard strolled into my room with a lopsided grin. "I'm Dr. Carter. It's good to see you feeling better."

My cheeks heated. "Thank you."

"We're going to need to take a look at you and run

through some questions." He peered at me with a quizzical look then glanced at Primo.

"I'm not going anywhere," Primo asserted.

"Not to argue with you, but it's also time for her pain meds. She'll probably be asleep for the next couple of hours."

I squeezed Primo's hand. "How about you just run to my apartment for a quick shower and come back? I can tell you're exhausted, and while I appreciate you being here, it won't hurt for you to take a short break. You'll feel so much better, then you can tell me about everything I've missed." It was sweet that he wanted to stay with me, but I'd only feel guilty seeing him in such rough shape.

He glanced at the window where Filip still stood guard. "All right, if you're sure you're okay. I'll run by your place and come right back. You want me to bring you some food?"

The wattage on my smile could have powered a small village. "That would be amazing. A burger. With cheese." Even if I was asleep when he got back, I'd eat my burger cold as soon as I got up. A taste of home and normalcy sounded incredible.

"It's six a.m. You want a cheeseburger?"

"Mmmm … and fries."

He shook his head and tapped the end of my nose with his knuckle. "See you in a few; and stay out of trouble while I'm gone."

"Why does everyone keep telling me that?"

He arched a brow at me. "Do I really have to answer that, viborita?"

"Yeah, yeah," I rolled my eyes. "Go get my burger."

TWENTY-NINE

Primo

The elevator doors opened to the hospital lobby, and I stepped out feeling like I could breathe for the first time in a week. Giada was alive. Her family hadn't killed me. We were in New York with the potential to make a new start. Things had played out differently than I'd expected, but I was starting to think it was for the best.

I'd been able to learn that Santino was recovering from his gunshot wound. I hated that he'd been injured, but it would help keep him safe from suspicion of being party to my treason. Juan Carlos might have wanted me dead, but he shouldn't suspect Santino's involvement.

It was still dark when I stepped through the sliding glass

doors of the hospital entrance. The bustle of people coming and going when we first arrived at the hospital was now absent. The loading area was empty of cars, and the designated smoking area was limited to a single middle-aged man, hands tucked into his armpits as he puffed on a cigarette.

My breath left my lips in a white cloud, but it was owed to the frigid morning rather than a nicotine habit. The temperatures had plummeted overnight, as if I'd needed any further reminders how far I was from home and how much my life was changing.

I'd had enough foresight over the years to prepare for the possibility that I would need to make a new start. I'd tucked away plenty of money in offshore accounts. I might have only had a suitcase of clothes in New York, but I was far from destitute.

Speaking of my suitcase, I wished I'd thought to take a jacket out before Matteo dropped our luggage at Giada's apartment, but I'd been too distracted. Once I made it to the subway, I'd be fine, but until then, I lowered my head against the cold and tucked my hands in my pockets. Just as I stopped at a street corner, the hard barrel of a gun pressed against the back of my head.

"Get in the car," a man growled in Spanish behind me. One of Juan Carlos's men.

If I went with him, I was a dead man.

I didn't budge, keeping my hands in my pockets while eyeing the black sedan that pulled up next to me. "What's this about?" I figured playing stupid was as good a tactic as any. It would buy me much-needed time to figure out an escape.

"*Callate tu pinche boca*. Get in the car before I splatter your fucking brains all over the sidewalk."

That was the thing. He hadn't simply shot me upon sight, which meant either he didn't want to kill me on a public street or Juan Carlos had ordered him to bring me back alive. Either way, it gave me something to work with. If he'd wanted me dead, my blood would already be crystalizing on the frozen ground.

My stalling angered him, and without warning, I took a punch straight to the kidney. I bent to the side, my hands ripping from my pockets in response to the excruciating pain.

The man clutched my shirt and pressed his mouth close to my ear, gun still trained against my head from behind. "Last time I'm telling you, puto. Get in the *fucking* car."

A thud sounded behind me, and the man collapsed into a puddle at my feet. I spun around to find Edoardo Genovese with a brick in his hand and wrath on his face.

"Fucking pigs, think they can come into our territory and push us around." He kicked my assailant in the back, far harder than I would have thought the older man capable.

Realizing the attack had been thwarted, the man in the car sped off, leaving his associate unconscious on the ground.

Edoardo pulled out his phone and called for the man to be collected and detained, then dialed who I assumed to be his brother, Enzo.

"We have a problem. The cartel is already making their move against Primo—we need to address this now before it touches Giada or anyone else … Be there in ten." He slid his phone back in his coat pocket and finally acknowledged my presence. "It's a good thing hospital parking sucks."

I huffed out a relieved chuckle. "I appreciate the help; I should have been paying better attention."

He lifted his chin, not about to argue. "As much as I'd like to go up and see my daughter, this is more urgent. Enzo and his wife have a hotel room here by the hospital. We're heading over there to sort this shit out."

Fifteen minutes later, I was in the living room of a hotel suite with half a dozen mafia men, including Matteo and a couple of his soldiers. Enzo gave a brief explanation of the situation, then directed everyone's attention to me.

"What can you tell us about the cartel presence in the city?" It was so much more than a question, and I could feel it in every calculating stare. This was the moment when I chose sides, and whatever I decided, there would be no going back. In my mind, I'd already made the commitment, but these men didn't know that. This was my opportunity to prove my allegiance.

"Juan Carlos Vargas is Nazario Vargas's brother. He moved to the city three years ago to start infiltrating the territory."

The room stirred with shifting bodies and startled intakes. These men had no idea such a powerful enemy had been amassing an army right beneath their noses.

"The port access Nazario needed to receive his shipment was only the first of his plans to start running drugs along the East Coast in a systematic expansion down to Miami. The initial shipment, worth ten million, was a sort of trial run with a new supplier. He needed the transaction to go smoothly in order to gain the supplier's trust and gain more business with him. While we supplied much of our own product on the West Coast, it was more cost effective to outsource production for the East Coast."

"That doesn't make any sense," Edoardo cut in. "Did he honestly think we'd allow him to continue doing business in the city after he'd kidnapped my daughter?"

"He believed the leverage of a hostage was necessary to negotiate a permanent foothold in the city, which he planned to demand after his initial shipment arrived. It doesn't necessarily make sense, but nor did his expansion. I did what I could to make him see reason, but he was hell-bent on seeing his schemes actualized. One of the biggest problems was that Juan Carlos was feeding him questionable intel and encouraging the delusions of grandeur. I think Juan Carlos may have been hoping something exactly like this would happen, and he'd inherit the empire."

"And what kind of force did he have in place to move that large of a shipment?" Enzo asked.

"At first, it was only him. Little by little, he brought in men and moved people quietly so his actions wouldn't make waves. He's been making connections and learning the climate in the city and neighboring states over the past three years. Nazario wanted to use New York to connect his Kansas City distribution channel with his designs on the East Coast, making a complete circuit through the US."

Enzo nodded sagely as if nothing I said was news to his ears, even though I knew it was. "Now that Nazario is dead, what do you expect Juan Carlos to do?"

"First, he'll need to go back to Mexico to ensure no one else tries to usurp his leadership position. Once he has established his rule, he'll continue with his brother's work. He was a firm believer in the expansion mission, which was why he volunteered to move his family to the front lines."

"Family?" asked Matteo.

"He's got a wife and daughter, but I doubt they'd be much use as leverage. He's not as devout a family man as he portrays himself to be."

"Exactly what kind of man is he?"

"Ruthless. Egotistical. Intelligent but lacking foresight. He and I have never gotten along, so I'm sure he'll be eager to watch me die."

Enzo stood and walked to the window, fingers smoothing his salt-and-pepper beard. "I suspect he believes you're an easy target. A fish out of water. I suggest we confront him directly while he's still disoriented over his brother's death—address both his infringement on our territory and his attack on you." He turned and held my gaze. "You know where he lives?"

"I do."

This time Enzo looked at Matteo. "You're welcome to join us or not. I understand that this isn't your fight."

"Are *you* going to explain to Maria why I stayed home while her father and uncle confronted the cartel? Our families are united. I have no intention of allowing you to face this kind of threat alone. Let's get this done before she finds out and insists on joining us."

"Wouldn't it be easier to just include her from the beginning?" asked Enzo wryly.

"Probably, but it's still not happening."

Enzo chuckled and shook his head. "It's been a pleasure knowing you."

Subdued laughter lightened the atmosphere in the room as we packed up and prepared to confront the enemy. It took over an hour to drive to Juan Carlos's house on Staten Island. I rode with Enzo and his brother while the rest followed in two more cars.

"I can't believe he's been living five goddamn miles from my house for the past three years, and I had no idea." Enzo strangled the life from the steering wheel when we parked out front of our destination.

"Actually, he's only been in this house since August, so about six months. And he's been intentionally flying under the radar so he wouldn't be noticed. It's not your fault you didn't know he was so close."

"Moving into my backyard could hardly be considered flying under the radar."

"Keep your friends close and your enemies closer. Plus, I think it was a statement. His proximity was meant to show you that you weren't invincible."

"The message has been well received. Intelligence efforts will have to be reassessed in the coming months," he growled.

The house wasn't gated, so we didn't have to worry about security until we arrived at his front steps. Two armed men stepped from the house, hands on their weapons. It was after eight by the time we arrived. Early, but not so early that everyone would still be asleep. Our appearance would certainly jumpstart their day.

Enzo stepped forward. "Tell your boss Enzo Genovese is here to speak with him."

The men exchanged glances before one slipped back inside the house. A few minutes later, Juan Carlos stepped outside, flanked by his two guards. At only forty-two years old, he was far younger than his brother but had cultivated a well-honed shield of impassivity. Every detail of his posture and manner dripped with dispassionate indifference. If he was unaffected by our presence, it elevated him in the power equation; however, his bravado was a show. Two of the most powerful men in the country stood on his doorstep—only a fool would disregard the dangers.

Juan Carlos was many things, but he was no fool.

"Gentlemen, to what do I owe this honor?"

"I understand you've been in the city some time now," Enzo began, "but it seems we've never been properly introduced. My name is Enzo Genovese, and this is my brother, Edoardo. We are here with Matteo De Luca and several of our associates on behalf of the Lucciano and Gallo families. You are familiar with those names, Mr. Vargas?"

"I am."

Enzo smiled. "Excellent. Then you should be familiar with the fact that this is our city. Our state. And we don't take kindly to people infringing on our business here. I certainly wouldn't hang a shingle south of the border and disrupt your operations, and I would expect the same courtesy in return. As it stands, your family has kidnapped and assaulted one of ours on top of infiltrating our city and disrupting business. Tell me, would you tolerate that type of treatment?"

Juan Carlos swallowed, a small glitch in his serene mask. "I was actually just preparing for my flight back to Mexico. You may have heard; my brother was murdered yesterday." His eyes briefly strayed from Enzo to glare at me.

"Yes, I imagine you have many matters to attend to back home. The thing is, once those affairs are settled, you need to understand that your presence will no longer be overlooked, and any interference in our operations will be addressed in full force. As for your choice of homes, I doubt there was anything coincidental about your proximity to my own home. I expect a for sale sign up immediately." Enzo strolled over to me and placed his hand on my shoulder. "You should also know that this man is under our protection. Any attack or slight on him will be seen as a direct attack on our families. There are all types of organizations that exist peacefully in this city alongside us, but there are protocols and boundaries that must be respected. This is your one and only warning that you have overstepped your bounds. Go back to Mexico, Mr. Vargas, and I strongly recommend you consider staying there."

Juan Carlos was outnumbered, not only at our makeshift meeting but also throughout the city. "I understand." His words were clipped, shoulders now tense with anger. He had no room to argue, and that only frustrated him more.

Enzo turned his back on Juan Carlos, his message received, and led us back to our cars. Once we were out of sight, Enzo shook Matteo's hand. "I appreciate your show of support."

"Judging from what I just witnessed, I think this may end up involving all of us. The Commission will need to be informed."

"Agreed. He's not about to go quietly into the night, but that's a fight for another day. At least we know the threat and can prepare."

"Keep me informed."

"Of course." Enzo turned to me as Matteo got back in his car with his men. "You should be safe for now, but if you suspect he's up to anything, let us know."

"I will, and I'm sorry to have brought this trouble to your doorstep."

"When money and power are at play, there are always rivals seeking to challenge us. That's nothing new."

"All right, you two," Edoardo called from inside the car. "I have a daughter in the hospital I've yet to talk to since she woke up. Let's get the hell out of here."

We made the drive back to the city, and they dropped me at Giada's apartment building so that I could shower and change. Once I was cleaned up, I managed to find a place where I could buy a burger before eleven and made my way back to the hospital. I found Giada upright in bed, watching television when I arrived.

"You're awake. I thought you might be asleep after taking your pain meds."

"I told them no narcotics. I missed so much already in the past two days; I didn't want to sleep through more." She smiled up at me, but her eyes didn't hold their usual light. She was in more pain than she let on. I wished I could convince her to take the meds, but Giada wasn't about to do anything she didn't want to.

"Did you get to see your dad?"

"Yeah, he and Mom just left. How did you know he was here?"

"Did he tell you about our morning?"

Her brow furrowed. "No, what happened?"

Her father might have preferred to insulate his daughters by keeping them in the dark, but Giada wasn't my daughter, and I didn't want our relationship to be founded on secrets. I told her all about how I'd been attacked and the resulting meetings. Maybe it was the lingering effects of the drugs, but she absorbed everything I told her as though I'd outlined a trip to the supermarket. She listened and nodded, but there was no freaking out or overreacting.

I thought back to seeing her join me at the coffee shop with her suitcase, to the time she confronted me about being used, and the way she coddled Haley despite being bloody and beaten. It wasn't the drugs. Giada was simply remarkable. She might have been somewhat confrontational but in a calm, confident manner. She knew her mind, stood up for herself, and was dependable when times got turbulent. I couldn't imagine a more perfect woman.

"I'm so relieved my dad and Uncle Enzo have accepted you," she said, taking my hand and holding it in her lap.

I wished I could lay with her and hold her in my arms, but she was in too delicate of a condition, and the bed was entirely too small. "It's more like I'm on probation."

"They offered you protection. That's good enough for me."

"Hopefully, it won't be necessary, but I have a feeling Juan

Carlos will be back. It's not my ideal scenario, but if the families unite against him, he won't stand a chance. I'm not too worried. I'd almost prefer he continues to challenge the mafia, then I'd get my chance to kill him and take back what belongs to me."

"I don't even want to think about a war right now." She visibly shuddered, making me feel bad for bringing it up.

"It probably won't even happen." I ran my fingers down the side of her face and around to her chin. "You know, it's strange. I always hated him. He was abusive and difficult. Always made my life a pain when he was around. But your light outshines those shadows so completely that I can't even see them with you in my life. I don't care if he lives or dies or whether it rains or snows. All that matters is you."

A single tear slipped from the corner of her eye. "I love you, Primo."

I stilled, a sudden revelation barreling into me. "Javier. My name is Javier Valencia; my mother called me Javi. Naz renamed me Primo. While it means cousin in Spanish and made for a good way of denoting our close relationship when he first took me in, he explained that primus in Latin meant first, and since I was to be his first in command, the name Primo would also signify my station. It was all a part of his sick plan of succession, but that's not who I am or where my life is headed. I think it's time I returned to being Javier."

Like a rainbow after a storm, she smiled through her tears. "Kiss me, Javier Valencia."

I pressed my lips to hers, unable to deny her. I would have razed cities and bled myself dry for her. For the love of a woman. And not just any woman. A mafia princess.

My trajectory had been drastically altered twice in my life —both instances revolved around a woman's love. The loss of my mother derailed my life and cast me down a dark path.

For years, I didn't care about anyone but myself, and that was a dangerous place for a man to be. When Giada thrust herself into my world, she righted my path. Grounded me and made me see past my own two feet. She may have taken a bullet for me, but that wasn't the only way she'd saved me. I owed her my life in more ways than one.

THIRTY

Giada

"YOU PUSHED YOURSELF TOO HARD TODAY," JAVI FUSSED AT ME from beside the tub where I soaked up to my chest in bubbles. My gunshot wound was healing nicely, but it wasn't allowed to be submerged yet, so I kept my shoulders above the waterline. He'd taken excellent care of me while I healed, and I relished our time together, even if I did call him by the wrong name a time or two. Now, having Javi in my life felt as essential as breathing.

"No, I didn't. Besides, it's only a few days until Christmas, and I wanted some decorations out. It's depressing not to have decorations at Christmas."

"You could have waited until I was home."

"It's been two weeks since I was shot. My shoulder and

ribs are both much better, and I didn't lift anything heavy." Having had enough of the conversation, I gingerly rose to my feet, suds drifting down my wet body. "Help me dry off?" My voice pitched low. Husky but feminine.

Javier grabbed a towel and helped me from the tub, all the while eyeing me suspiciously. I stood in place, encouraging him to pat me dry—something I could have done myself. It had been weeks since we'd been intimate, and I was desperately in need of his touch. He'd been adamant about not initiating anything to prevent me from being hurt.

It was time to overcome that little hurdle.

He swept the towel slowly down one of my legs then back up the other, methodically drying me and getting an eyeful of every square inch of my body, just as I wanted. When his hands swept the towel beneath my breasts, I arched a fraction and released a breathy moan.

"What game are you playing, viborita?" His voice was winded and rough, affirming that my plan was working.

"You know exactly what I'm getting at. I know you think you'll hurt me, but I'm well enough, I promise. And I know you can be gentle. Please?" I reached out and palmed the bulge in his pants, loving the way he jerked and hissed at my touch.

"Fuck, you know I can't deny you anything." His lips descended onto mine.

Delicious warmth quivered through me. My heart danced, skipping over beats and rushing blood to my swollen center.

Javi took my hand and walked us backward to the bedroom then gently lay me down. "Tell me if I hurt you." He removed his clothes, and the feel of his naked body caressing my skin sent a buzz to my head stronger than any drug.

I wasn't able to hold him and participate like I would have preferred, but just getting to be with him, connecting with him physically and emotionally, was the best Christmas gift I could have received. He worshiped my body with the methodical determination of a painter perfecting his canvas.

His hot breath.

His velvet tongue.

They lay siege to my delicate skin until all of my nerve endings sang for him, pleaded for his touch, and hummed in anticipation of his every movement. When he finally sheathed himself inside me, the spinning cogs and gears whirring in my brain came to a stop in perfect alignment, and my life suddenly made sense. The sense of being empty and unfulfilled was because somewhere deep down, I'd been saving room in my life for this man.

My love was too big to take a back seat to a career or other commitments. When I found the man who would capture my heart, that love would consume every fiber of my being. Loving Javier was my purpose, which was not to be confused with him completing me. I was the first girl to insist that women did not need a man to complete them, but I was starting to realize that the philosophy didn't preclude a woman from choosing to prioritize her relationship. He didn't complete me, but my partnership with him would give my life a new meaning.

I wasn't just me; I was his. The same as he was mine.

The dawning insight acted like kindling for the crackling flames dancing in my core. In an instant, the fire exploded through my web of nerves, igniting my entire body in an inferno of pleasure.

As it was between us, he followed where I led, and I came when he called.

My climax coaxed Javi over the edge. His cock jerked and pulsed inside me, his arms battling not to crush me with the intensity of his release. He groaned into my neck, his breath ragged and warm. We were two independent, competent individuals completely powerless over the invisible force that linked us together.

We recovered in one another's arms for several long minutes before Javi rolled to his side. I could only lay on my back, so he perched over me, one large hand splayed over my stomach.

"Are you okay?" he asked, kissing my shoulder.

"Mmmm … I'm more than okay."

His lips widened against my skin, which tickled and made me squirm then wince. The pain in my shoulder and ribs was muted while having sex, but the moment it was over, I was back to being an invalid.

"Okay, huh? Seems like maybe that's an exaggeration."

"It's nothing, really. Oh! I forgot to tell you that I got a call from Haley earlier. It sounds like things are going well with her cousin. She talked about looking for a job after the holidays and sounded optimistic about her future. I'm so incredibly happy for her."

Haley had ventured to St. Louis to stay with her cousin who was married with a young child. She was having to start from scratch, but being out from beneath Naz's control gave her the perspective to appreciate any new opportunity.

"That's good to hear. Maybe once you're feeling better, we can fly out and visit."

"We?"

"After everything that's happened, I'm not letting you out of my sight for a while."

He wasn't entirely unjustified in his concern, so I wasn't going to argue. I actually liked knowing someone wanted to look out for me. I'd always been so independent that a boyfriend clocking my every move had sounded revolting, but with Javi, it wasn't like that. He provided the perfect safety net to allow me to live freely. And in that vein, there was something I'd been wanting to talk to him about but knew he wouldn't like.

I turned my face and peered up at him. I figured hitting him with my idea when he was sex drunk was my best bet at getting his approval. "I've been thinking about everything that happened over the past couple weeks."

"Oh, yeah?"

I nodded. "My parents' housekeeper Lucy. She was one of your informants, wasn't she?"

"She's Alma's sister," he admitted.

"Did Alma know Lucy was with my family?"

"No. She had no idea where her sister was working, just that she was stationed somewhere for Naz."

My eyes fell to his chest where I traced lines on his smooth skin. "You know we have to tell my dad. She can't work there anymore, which breaks my heart because I don't want her out of a job."

"Honestly, I had completely forgotten about her, but now that you mention it, you're right."

"The good news is, I think she can help us." My eyes flitted back up to his.

"What do you mean?"

"I need you to hear me out, so try to keep an open mind. I think I know how to get your statue back."

His face hardened into chiseled granite. "I'm not going to like this, am I?" he mumbled.

"I'm guessing she knows the people who work in Juan Carlos's house?"

"Yes, some of them are family of hers, I believe."

"Lucy could get me into the house as a cleaner, and I could get the figurine back."

"Absolutely not," he barked, raising up off the bed. "It's entirely too dangerous."

I eased myself upright and crossed my legs. "*Listen.* He won't have bothered to know what us girls look like. Besides, he's in Mexico and probably won't come back to that house anyway since Uncle Enzo demanded he move. I'll slip into the house, clean just like anyone else, and then I'm out."

He jerked his legs into his briefs and began to pace. "There's no reason to risk you like that. The figurine is just an object."

"Javier Valencia, *look at me*," I demanded, all traces of pleading gone from my voice. "I'm not saying today, since clearly I'm not ready, but when the time is right, I want to try it. You know I'm capable, don't cage me for your own peace of mind."

Javi held my gaze, his features softening as I spoke. When I finished, he came back to the bed and sat next to me. "I almost lost you once; I never want to feel that again."

I ran my fingers through his hair. "I know, but you have to trust me. I can do this, and I want you to have that piece of your mom back. Let me do this for you."

"Fuck, you drive me crazy. I'm never going to win a single argument, am I?"

"Probably not, so you might as well get used to it."

He shook his head, then snapped his teeth at me playfully. "Fine, but we do it on my terms—when and how I say."

"I think I can agree to that. See, I'm not totally uncompromising."

His lips twisted into a wolfish grin. "As soon as you're all healed, we're going to test that and see just how *flexible* you can be."

I smirked in return. "Mmm ... an experiment. I always was a fan of science."

THIRTY-ONE

Giada

"Are you sure you want to do this, mija? I think maybe I should be the one instead of you." Lucy wrung her hands as she looked me over in my housekeeper's uniform.

Making the staff wear uniforms was a bit archaic, but Juan Carlos seemed to think otherwise. I wore a pale blue knee-length dress belted at the waist with short sleeves and a collar starched to a point of petrification. It wasn't totally unappealing. In fact, with a thong and garter underneath, it might just make a perfect Valentine's gift for Javi.

I tucked that little idea away for later.

"No, Lucy. It has to be me. Juan Carlos's people know you and would be suspicious if you showed up. It has to be someone they wouldn't recognize. None of them would ever in a million years imagine I'd do something like this. Besides, I live for this kind of stuff." I winked.

Lucy looked at the heavens and crossed herself. "Aye, Dios mío. All right, at least Señor Vargas is still in Mexico; otherwise, I would not let you do this. My cousin will vouch for you as a substitute. Do what you need to do and get out of there. If anything happens to you, I'd never forgive myself."

"I'll be fine, and you'll be back on a plane in no time, you'll see."

After a remorseful apology to my father, Lucy had gone back to Mexico and reunited with Alma and the rest of her family. The two women were in the process of opening a bakery in Guaymas with the severance money Javi had given Alma. He might have considered himself a hardened criminal, but it was gestures like helping Alma that gave away his softer side.

"I'm just glad I can help. I still feel terrible for giving information about you girls to Nazario. If it wasn't for his threats to hurt Alma and my family, I never would have done it."

I wrapped my arms around her in a warm hug. "I know, honey. Naz was a nasty man, but now we're all free of him."

Lucy pulled back, her brow knitted in a maze of skin. "His brother isn't much better. Maybe even worse. You be careful, okay?"

"Careful is overrated." I flashed a devious grin.

"Aye!" She swatted a hand at me. "Let's get you to my cousin before I change my mind."

Lucy's cousin drove me to Juan Carlos's house and introduced me to the guards as a substitute housekeeper for the day. They looked me over more than I would have liked, but the attention was owed to my curvy figure rather than any heightened suspicion. He'd left a skeleton crew on guard with his wife and daughter still living at the house. I wasn't sure what his efforts to sell had entailed, but there was a sign in the yard. My family wasn't too concerned since he'd remained in Mexico, but if he returned to New York and didn't vacate the house, I wasn't sure what would happen.

I'd been given a rundown of the cleaning procedures and told we started on the upper floor then worked our way down. I was instructed to tackle the toilets first. I'd never cleaned a toilet in my damn life. Lucky for me, everything already looked virtually spotless. I splashed around some water, used some cleaner to give the air a fresh, clean scent, then moved to the next room. I would have gone directly for the office if it wouldn't have raised an alarm, but the cleaning staff had a strict protocol, and my departure from their routine might have drawn attention. Instead, I was stuck going room to room, pretending to clean.

The far end of the second floor contained a suite of rooms tastefully decorated in mint green with elegant gold accents but lived in and decidedly feminine. I gave the bathroom a Giada treatment, then peeked into the adjoined living area and saw something that made me nearly drop my entire bucket of cleaning supplies.

A young woman sat on the couch watching a movie and sitting with her was my sister, Val. My legs sprouted roots and anchored me in place. My heart thundered in my head until I could hear nothing else. I was terrified but didn't want to put either of us at risk by outing myself.

I was mostly behind them, so they didn't notice me having a nervous breakdown on the other side of the room. The two girls giggled and scrolled through their phones, only half paying attention to the movie. Just how long had my baby sister been cozied up to the daughter of a cartel boss? Did she know how dangerous this family was? Did he know who his daughter had befriended? And why wasn't she at school? I thought about what day it was and realized it was MLK day, and she likely had a holiday. Had my mother brought her to the house? My father never would have allowed it, so he either kept my mother in the dark about Juan Carlos or hadn't been told about Val's new friend.

Shaking myself free of my shock, I left the suite of rooms through the bedroom. I would deal with Val later. It was time to head downstairs and wrap up this little *Mission Impossible* adventure.

I wandered in search of the office, dusting and jostling my supply bucket on occasion to look like I was busy. When I poked my head around a corner and discovered a vacant office, I breathed a huge sigh of relief. I continued with my cleaning charade, scanning the shelves for my target. I recognized it from Javi's description the moment I saw it. Aged with chipping paint and three broken prongs, the Lady of Guadalupe stood humbly next to a black abstract sculpture on a shelf.

As much as I wanted to make a beeline for the figurine and race from the house, I forced myself to dust my way over, then adeptly slipped her down into my bucket. I couldn't imagine Juan Carlos would have cameras in his own office, but just in case, I wanted to cover my tracks as best as I could.

When I finished with the shelves, I drifted into the hall and toward the back door where we had entered the house. I retrieved the figurine, dropping it into my dress pocket, then left the house in no particular hurry. Javi sat in his car waiting for me two blocks away. My feet picked up rhythm of their own volition, urging me to safety.

"Aside from our plane ride to New York, that was the longest couple of hours of my whole fucking life," Javi grumbled when I flung myself inside the car.

"You're telling me. I'm the one who had to pretend to clean toilets." I grinned impishly. "But it was worth it because look what I got." I held up the statue, relinquishing it into his possession where it always should have been.

Javi turned the figurine around in his hands with such careful reverence, my heart became a puddle of melted butter. To anyone else, the cheap souvenir would have been worthless, but to Javi, it meant the world. It was his last connection to his mother. A piece of his past and a cornerstone for his future.

"You can't fathom how much this means to me," he rasped, voice heavy with emotion.

"I'm just glad I was able to get it back for you."

"This statue is only the tip of the iceberg. You've given me my life back." He lifted his stormy gray gaze, so penetrating that my skin blossomed into goose bumps. I was already riding an adrenaline high, and seeing him so affected did strange things to my insides.

I grinned, unable to rein in my mirth. "Ditto, baby."

His lips curved into a feline, predatory grin. "Time to get you home so that I can show you just how grateful I am."

I unbuckled my seat belt and peered up at him through my lashes. "Why wait?"

It was all I could do not to call Val the day I saw her at Juan Carlos's house. I had to wait until two days later when I was back on Staten Island for a family dinner to talk to her. It wasn't a conversation for over the phone.

I arrived at the house early and found my mother in the kitchen. "Hey, Ma. Need any help?"

"No, I was just cleaning up. The lasagna's in the oven, and everything else can wait."

"Mmm, homemade lasagna. Special occasion?" The hearty aroma of tomato sauce, garlic, and herbs saturated the air.

"Just happy to have my family together. I thought … maybe it was time I told the other girls what I told you. It needs to be out in the open, and now that you're better, it's time we had a family chat." Her voice wavered with nerves. She didn't look at me as she spoke, instead keeping her eyes intently averted to her unusually dedicated cleaning efforts.

"Momma, you know they'll understand. And I think it's good to tell them—for you and for them."

She dared a glance over at me and sent me a shaky smile. "Thank you, sweetie. Tell me, what's been going on with you? Physical therapy going well?"

"It's going great, actually. My therapist said that my yoga had me in such good shape that I shouldn't need the full length of recommended recovery. This week I went back to the yoga studio and saw they were having instructor certification classes. I'm not sure why it hadn't occurred to me before, but I realized I'd love to teach a class. You know me; I'm not interested in being a full-time instructor, but I wouldn't mind doing one or two classes a week."

"G, that's wonderful! I think that would be perfect for you."

There was no greater feeling than hearing pride and excitement in your parents' voice when they spoke about you. Not to be judged or questioned. No matter how much I had schooled myself in the past not to care what they had thought about me, it never stopped hurting when my ideas were constantly met with criticism. I didn't want to crave their approval, but some things just couldn't be changed. Children would always hunger for the love and support of their parents.

I smiled at her with a grin that could light up a room. "Thanks, Momma. I'm going to head upstairs and chat with Val. You need help down here, let me know."

She waved me away, her eyes suspiciously bright. "Go on. Your sister will be excited to see you."

I found Val upstairs on her computer, a textbook and highlighters next to her keyboard. "Hey, there. You got a minute to talk?"

"Yeah, I was just working on some homework. What's up?"

I sat on her bed, crisscrossing my legs and fiddling with the fabric of her duvet. "I know this sounds a little weird, but I saw you on Monday over at a girl's house. I haven't told Mom and Dad, but that family is seriously dangerous. You have to stop going over there." I figured it was best if I was vague about how I'd seen her. She could assume I'd seen her walking inside as I drove by.

"Please, G, you can't tell them," she pleaded with me, scooting to the edge of her desk chair. "Dad will make me break off the friendship, and I can't do that. Her dad is awful, her mom is an alcoholic, and now she's having to move. I can't just abandon her."

"He's not just awful, Val. He's a cartel boss and Dad's *enemy*," I whisper-yelled.

"I know, okay?" she hissed back.

"You *knew*?" My voice pitched so high I probably summoned the neighborhood dogs. "Then why the hell were you over there? *How* did you get over there? Doesn't Dad have someone protecting you?"

"Yes, he has some thug shadowing me. I had the muscle head drop me at another friends' house, and I snuck out the back. Look, if I promise not to go to her house again, will you please not tell Dad? She can't help who her father is, and she needs me. *Please*."

I plopped back onto the bed, sighing in exasperation at the ceiling. "Now I know how Alessia felt," I grumbled.

"Huh?"

"Nothing. Okay, I'll keep my mouth shut, but I expect you to swear on your life that you will not go back over to that house. And she needs to know that she cannot tell her father who you are. That man may have gone to Mexico for now, but that doesn't mean the threat from his cartel is over. We don't know what will happen, so we have to be safe." I rolled off the bed feeling like a total pushover.

Val jumped up and circled me in her arms. "Thank you, G. You're the best!"

We'd see about that. After witnessing Naz's merciless depravity, I wasn't about to let my little sister walk into that same trap. I'd keep an eye on the situation. If she was in any danger, I'd rat her out in a heartbeat.

Hypocritical? I was aware.

One little near-death experience, and I was a certified snitch. Although, I did just sneak into a cartel boss's house to steal from him, so my badass card hadn't been totally revoked. I was still Giada Genovese, mafia princess and fashion goddess, just with a touch more perspective.

Life was far too uncertain to be careless with the people who mattered most. Javi and my family were everything to me, and I would fight for them, no matter the odds.

EPILOGUE

Giada

"I APPRECIATE YOU GIVING US A RIDE EVEN THOUGH THAT'S NOT your job anymore." I met Santino's eyes in the rearview mirror and grinned. I still wasn't entirely used to seeing him again. He'd recently made the move from Guaymas to start a security business with Javi. They had already snagged a couple of high-profile clients and were well on their way to making a name for themselves. I couldn't have been more proud.

"Traffic in the city sucks; I'm glad I could help." He pulled the car up to the curb outside the ornately carved entrance to Gramercy Tavern. Aunt Lottie was hosting a birthday dinner for Sofia and had reserved a private dining room for our party of around twenty. The tavern was a perfect combination of fine dining with a relaxed atmosphere. The food was amazing, but there was also a bustling bar and a cozy atmosphere.

"We'll catch a cab home. Thanks again!" I slid from the car, Javi exiting behind me, and did a full body shiver. "Man, I'm tired of the cold." The restaurant didn't call for formal dress, so I'd worn pants and long sleeves, but I'd left my heavy coat at home since we'd only be outside between the car and the restaurant.

"It's still just February. You have a ways to go until it warms up."

"February is nearly over, then it'll be March and spring," I asserted.

"And it'll get warm overnight?" he teased.

"A girl can be optimistic. Now quit pissing on my parade and let's get inside," I grumbled, my teeth already beginning to chatter.

We were directed back to the private room where we were greeted by Sofia and her husband, along with her parents and a number of others who had already arrived. I was engaged in conversation more than Javi, but he did his share of talking, and I adored seeing him interact with my family. He'd been accepted into the fold remarkably well.

I caught myself sneaking glimpses of him at every opportunity. The way his lean muscle mass filled out a suit jacket perfectly, or the corded strength of his neck that revealed itself when he spoke. He was assertive and confident, and I couldn't get enough.

"You keep staring at him like that, and I'm going to have to wipe the drool from your cheek." Camilla tapped my wineglass with hers and took a sip.

"If something that scrumptious was yours, wouldn't you want to lick the wrapping?"

She huffed a laugh, causing her to choke on her wine, which sent me into a fit of giggles. I patted her back, which did absolutely nothing but still felt like the right thing to do. Once it was clear she was going to survive, I looked up at the source of a chorus of voices welcoming a late arrival.

"Check it out. Filip just showed up, and he's got a gorgeous redhead with him."

Camilla didn't respond, drawing my gaze back to her. She glared at Filip like she wanted to flay him open from neck to groin and hang his entrails from the rafters. Her seething fury was so palpable, I had to do a double take, my eyes drifting over Filip and his date to see what I might have missed. When I looked back to Cam, her features were perfectly schooled, as if I'd imagined the whole thing.

I leaned close and whispered, "Is something going on between you and Filip?"

She cocked her head to the side and scrunched her brow. "We hardly know one another. Besides, look at how cocky and … and smarmy he is. He's probably with a different woman every night." She dove into her wineglass, taking a healthy swig.

Thou doth protest too much.

Interesting. Very interesting.

"Now that we're all here," Aunt Lottie directed over the hum of voices, "let's take our seats."

The room was outfitted with a private bar on one wall and an elongated oval dining table throughout the center of the room. Several small floral arrangements adorned the center length of the table with place settings for twenty-two lining the outer edge. Aunt Lottie and Uncle Enzo sat together on one end while Mom and Dad took the other, leaving everyone else to fill in the middle.

Once we were settled, an assortment of appetizers

distributed throughout the table. Silverware clinked and heartwarming chatter filled the room. After the noise settled, Sofia and Nico stood at their places to address the room, Sofia taking the lead.

"I just wanted to take a minute to thank everyone for coming tonight and thank my mom for arranging such a lovely evening. I'm not normally one to be the center of attention, but this was the perfect opportunity to tell everyone …" She paused and glanced at Nico with a beaming smile. "We'll be expanding the family in late August."

Jaws dropped, and the room burst with cheers and congratulations. Aunt Lottie was especially giddy, jumping up to hug her youngest daughter. I was thrilled for my cousin. She and Nico had been through so much over the years; they deserved all the happiness in the world.

Dinner was exquisite, and there wasn't a single lull in the conversation. I kept my eye on Camilla throughout the evening to see if I could learn anything more about what might have upset her. Every now and then, her spine would straighten, and her smile would grow brittle. I couldn't make out the source of her agitation until Filip's date released a particularly riotous peal of laughter, and Camilla stood, announcing she had to go. That was it. The woman had a cackling laugh, and every time it carried over the buzz in the room, Camilla had a visceral reaction.

"What? They haven't even served dessert." I pleaded for her to stay, but her clenched jaw brooked no argument.

"Sofia, I'm so sorry to cut out early, but I told someone I'd meet up with them tonight." She gave our cousin a hug, keeping her eyes carefully trained away from Filip and his guest, then excused herself and left.

I'd also observed Filip on occasion during dinner and found him to appear completely untouched by Camilla's distress until she cleared the room. His playboy smile withered and died faster than streamers in a rainstorm.

There was definitely something going on.

A quick glance told me no one else had noticed the incident. Conversation carried on, and wineglasses were refilled. A few minutes later, Filip spoke up, addressing the group.

"We seem to be missing an earring over here. Anyone see it on the floor around you?"

His date held up her hand, dangling a long silver earing for show. "It looks like this."

Everyone pulled out their chairs and scanned the floor, coming up empty. After a cursory search, we concluded the earing wasn't to be found and continued with dessert. While the table fell into soft murmurs as everyone indulged in their sweet treats, I sensed Javi's eyes on me.

I leaned in, bringing my lips next to his ear. "It wasn't me, I swear. That kind of thing doesn't hold the same appeal anymore."

He pulled me in and kissed my temple. "With a laugh like hers, I wouldn't blame you if you did," he joked softly, making me chuckle.

Five minutes later, one of the staff brought in the earring, explaining that it had been found in the bathroom by another patron. I couldn't help but shoot an I-told-you-so glance at Javi.

His eyelids lowered to half-mass, shadowing those molten-metal irises with a promise of delicious torture. "Tell your family goodbye. It's time for us to go." He rasped the words for my ears only. His arousal heightening his accent, sending a cascade of chills down my spine.

I cleared my throat and stood. "All right, everyone. It's time for us to head out."

As soon as he was able, Javi ushered me from the room,

but instead of leading me to the front of the restaurant, he yanked us inside the first doorway we passed. I gasped, hardly getting a view of the room before the door shut, and we were shrouded in darkness.

Javier positioned me against the wall next to the door. "Bring back any memories?"

"Mmm … it does, but I don't recall it being so dark." I couldn't see a thing, heightening my other senses. The clamor of noise sounding from beneath the door. His warm breath skating across my lips. The hint of smoke, musk, and spice from Javi's cologne added to the intoxicating effect of the wine.

He grasped my hands and held them over my head against the wall in one of his. Out of nowhere, his other hand grazed across one of my nipples, then pinched the hardening peak. Unable to see and anticipate his touch, the sensation was magnified tenfold. Rioting euphoria coiled deep in my belly, a hunger so deep my inner muscles clenched down in a shuddering frenzy.

"Still want the lights on?" he breathed against the skin of my neck, a sharp-edged smile in his voice.

"Shut up and touch me," I purred back at him.

Javi swung me around, chest pressed firm against the closet wall, then tsked by my ear. "Oh, Giada. You've been a very naughty girl."

Thank you so much for reading IMPOSSIBLE ODDS!

The Five Families is a series of interconnected standalones, and the next book in the lineup is *Absolute Silence,* which you can read more about below.

***Absolute Silence* (*The Five Families* #5)**

Camilla thought she'd found a place to explore her darkest fantasies—a private club where her secrets were safe—until Filip De Luca threatened to snatch it all away. He was inescapably alluring, but when you made a deal with the devil, there was always a catch...

Didn't catch the beginning of the series?

Forever Lies (The Five Families #1)

When Alessia gets stuck in an elevator at work, she's trapped with Luca, the hottest man she's ever seen. But she can tell something dark hides beneath his charming facade—especially once he decides he's not letting her go...

Stay in touch!!!

Make sure to join my newsletter and be the first to hear about new releases, sales, and other exciting book news!

Head to www.jillramsower.com or scan the code below.

ABOUT THE AUTHOR

Jill Ramsower is a life-long Texan—born in Houston, raised in Austin, and currently residing in West Texas. She attended Baylor University and subsequently Baylor Law School to obtain her BA and JD degrees. She spent the next fourteen years practicing law and raising her three children until one fateful day, she strayed from the well-trod path she had been walking and sat down to write a book. An addict with a pen, she set to writing like a woman possessed and discovered that telling stories is her passion in life.

SOCIAL MEDIA & WEBSITE

Release Day Alerts, Sneak Peak, and Newsletter
To be the first to know about upcoming releases, please join Jill's Newsletter. (No spam or frequent pointless emails.)
Jill's Newsletter

Official Website: www.jillramsower.com
Jill's Facebook Page: www.facebook.com/jillramsowerauthor
Reader Group: Jill's Ravenous Readers
Follow Jill on Instagram: @jillramsowerauthor
Follow Jill on TikTok: @JillRamsowerauthor

Made in the USA
Las Vegas, NV
20 November 2024

12198448R00166